PASSING

through

PERFECT

A Novel

BETTE LEE CROSBY

PASSING THROUGH PERFECT

Copyright © 2015 by Bette Lee Crosby

Cover Design: damonza.com
Interior Formatting: Author E.M.S.
Editor: Ekta Garg

ISBN # 978-0-9960803-4-7

BENT PINE PUBLISHING
Port Saint Lucie, FL

BENT
PINE
PUBLISHING

Published in the United States of America

To

Joanne Bliven

Because it is she who sees.

PASSING
through
PERFECT

BENJAMIN CHURCH
1958

When the heart of a man gets pulled loose he starts dying. I started dying a year ago, and I'm still working on it. I ain't going all at once; I'm going piece by piece. If you was to see me pushing the plow or chopping wood, you'd figure me a whole person—a heaving, hauling, hard of muscle and stinking of sweat man. But the truth is I ain't been whole since this same day last year.

It ain't my skin and bones what's dying, it's my soul. My body's still walking around doing chores and taking orders from folks like Missus Mayfield, but my soul... that's lying out on Cross Corner Road alongside Delia.

In the year gone by I suffered more misery than God ought to expect a man to bear. Now I come to where I can't take no more. It ain't easy leaving a place where you was born, but I got Isaac to think of and the boy deserves better. I ain't gonna say if this is a good decision or not, but come tomorrow morning Isaac and me is leaving here and we ain't never gonna look back at Alabama.

This is a place of shame and misery. The shame of a man called boy and the misery of losing what you love. 'Course to understand the size of my misery, you'd have to know how it was with me and Delia.

GRINDER'S CORNER, ALABAMA
1946

The war was over, and hundreds of thousands of young men headed home to pick up the pieces of their lives. Benjamin Church was one of them. Many came home missing an eye, an arm, or a leg, but not Benjamin. Although he'd joined up thinking he'd fight Germans, the truth was he'd done little more than unload trucks and work on the motors that kept them running.

In the years he'd been gone Benjamin had sent countless letters home. His mama had written back several times saying things at home were just fine. But after the fall of that third year, he'd received only one letter telling how his mama had gone to be with the Lord. The letter was penned in Reverend Beech's neat, even script, but at the bottom in shaky block letters his daddy had written OTIS CHURCH. They were the only two words Otis could write.

Benjamin climbed down from the bus in Bakerstown, slung his duffle bag over his shoulder, and started walking. It was almost twenty-five miles out to the farm and most of it back road. On the far edge of Madison Street he veered toward Pineville Road and left the town behind.

On the long nights when he'd lain in his bunk thinking of home, Benjamin had remembered raucous rolls of laughter and the smell of pork roasting over a wood fire. He saw girls in flowery dresses and called to mind the sound of their high-pitched giggles. Of course, it had been four years so he expected to see some change: a few new houses maybe, a new store, a cement road. But there was nothing. It was exactly the same as when he left. In a strange way, the sight of sameness felt comfortable. It was the part of home he'd longed for.

The sun was low in the sky when the house came into view. It sat there silent as a graveyard; no motors chugging, no people talking, not even a barnyard chicken squawking. For a brief moment Benjamin wondered if his daddy was gone also, but when he turned into the road the old man came out onto the porch.

Benjamin raised his arm and waved. Otis brought his hand to his face and shielded his eyes from the sun. He leaned forward, trying to identify the stranger.

Dropping his duffle in the road, Benjamin took off running. He was three steps shy of the porch when his daddy finally recognized him.

Otis gasped. "Lord-a-mercy, I hardly knowed it was you."

Benjamin hugged the frail Otis to his chest and laughed. "You saying I put on some weight?"

"Some weight?" Otis echoed. "Why, you done went from boy to man."

It was true. Benjamin had left home a lanky, bone-thin boy and returned a man who was broad of chest and heavily muscled. His face had also changed. It wasn't a change you could point to and say his nose was shorter or his cheeks fuller; it was the look behind his eyes. They were still brown with scattered flecks of gold, but there was a wisdom that hadn't been there before. If you looked only at Benjamin's eyes, you could almost believe him to be an old man.

"I'm sorry about your mama," Otis said.

A look of sadness shadowed Benjamin's face. "I'm sorry too, Daddy. Real sorry."

He said nothing of how for nearly a month his mama's laugh was something he couldn't forget. No matter how hard he tried not to think of her, the thoughts came and he cried. There were nights when he'd fall into his bunk exhausted from the day's work, but the moment he closed his eyes a picture of her came to mind. He'd see her baking a pie, drawing water from the well, or singing in the choir, and knowing she was gone would sting like a hornet nesting inside his brain.

After a short time of talking Benjamin went back, picked up his duffle, and came inside the house. It was the same as the day he'd left. His mama's apron still hung on a peg alongside the wood stove. As he sat at the kitchen table and drank a glass of sweet tea with his daddy, her ghost slid in alongside of them. It was a sadness neither of them wanted to speak of. In time they would talk of it, but not now.

Searching for a less painful topic of conversation, Benjamin asked, "How come the cornfield's not planted?"

"It's planted," Otis answered in the flat dry way he had of speaking.

"Less than half," Benjamin said. "The back lot don't even look plowed."

"It ain't. No sense in plowing what I ain't planting."

Benjamin looked at his daddy. "You're not planting the back lot?"

"Nope." Otis shook his head.

"How come?"

"I run short."

"Short of what?"

"Short of seed money, short of time." Otis gave a heavy sigh. "Short of..."

He let the rest of what he was thinking drift off without being said. Fingering a threadbare spot in his pants for a good half minute he added, "Anyways, Henry's too old to be pulling a plow. That mule done worked way past his years."

"Mister Sylvester ain't gonna be none too happy if you give him half what he's expecting."

"He ain't gonna be happy no way. Long as I been on this earth, I never seen that man smile. Not once." Otis gave his head a worrisome shake. "A body like him's got everything to be glad about, and he ain't glad about nothing. Seems God ought to give second thought to how He's handing out blessings."

Benjamin knew what his daddy said about Sylvester Crane was true. The man owned every square inch of farmland in Grinder's Corner and collected one fourth of every nickel the sharecroppers earned. He also owned the gristmill, so there was no getting around him.

"You remember what happened to Widow Palmer?" Benjamin asked. It was more challenge than question.

"Yeah, I remember," Otis grumbled.

"Well, then."

"I was figuring to give Mister Sylvester most a' what come in. That ought t' satisfy his greedy soul."

"That ain't no answer," Benjamin said. "You give him everything, then what you got to live on?"

"The Bible says the Lord provides."

"Yeah, well, it don't say He's gonna show up and plow that back lot. He's maybe gonna give you sun and rain, but getting those seeds in the ground is up to you."

Although his daddy didn't have anything more to say, the truth of the matter was obvious. It wasn't the seed money or the old mule; without Lila, Otis had lost the will to live. A man who'd reached that point had to be cared for, and Benjamin knew the responsibility now fell on his shoulders. He was their only child; there was no one else.

He'd returned home thinking Grinder's Corner might have changed, that there might be a few new businesses, that perhaps acceptance had blossomed into hope, but looking at Otis he could now see the future looked a lot like the past. He measured the reality of that thought against a lifetime of loving his daddy and against a heart that still ached to hear his mama's voice. His own dreams seemed pitifully small by comparison.

After only a few moments, he decided the love in his heart outweighed whatever plans he had made in his years away from home. Setting aside thoughts of one day being a mechanic, Benjamin knew he would be what he was destined to be: a farmer. It was their way of life. He would follow in the footsteps of his daddy and his granddaddy. In time he would grow to be rooted to the earth as Otis now was.

The next morning Benjamin hitched Henry to a wagon that was older than the mule and headed for town. With the mustering out pay in his pocket and what he'd saved during the past years, he bought enough silver corn seed to plant the back lot and paid fifteen dollars for a 1930 Model A Ford that couldn't cough up enough energy to start.

"That's okay," Benjamin said. "I been taught to fix motors. Sooner or later I'll get her going."

It was later.

He tied the old car to the back of the wagon, and Henry pulled it home.

It was the hottest summer Alabama had seen in more than a decade yet every day, even Sundays, Benjamin was out there working in the field. He worked until a river of sweat rolled down his face and stung his eyes. When that happened he'd stop long enough to wipe his face and gulp down a few swigs of water; then he'd go right back to work. He pushed and Henry pulled the plow until little by little spaced out furrows began to appear. Then walking side by side with his daddy, they dropped in the seeds that would in a few months be a waving field of corn.

Otis's steps were slow and his back hunched even when he wasn't carrying a bag of seed. Benjamin saw this and put less than a third of what he carried in his daddy's bag. He knew that doing it alone he could have finished the job sooner, but sharing the work was a way of giving his daddy reason for living.

Before the end of April the back lot was filled with sprouts of green coming from the ground, and by mid-June those shoots were knee-high.

"It's gonna be a good year," Otis said, but a week later a dry spell started up.

For the first few days, Benjamin and his daddy paid little attention. In the evening they sat on the front porch and waited for the cool breezes that generally followed a rainstorm, but none came. By nightfall the house was so stifling that Benjamin stripped off his clothes and lay naked across the bed. Even lying still as a dead man, beads of sweat rose up on his face and his back stuck to the sheet.

Otis didn't even bother going to bed. He sat in the rocking chair on the porch and creaked back and forth until sometime in the wee hours of morning when his eyes finally fell shut.

After nine days of blistering sun and not a drop of rain, the leaves on the newly-planted corn began to droop.

"Dammit, Daddy," Benjamin said, "when's it gonna rain?"

Sitting on the porch waving a piece of cardboard back and forth in front of his face, Otis shrugged. "Could be today, could be tomorrow. We got no way of knowing."

Benjamin looked up at the sky. It was a hazy blue, the kind of color that gave no indication of either rain or sun. In the distance there was a scattering of clouds but they drifted lazily, moving off towards Tennessee.

"I'm gonna take a look at how them plants is doing," he said, then left Otis sitting on the porch and headed for the back cornfield.

Several stalks had already toppled over. The ground, now dry as dust, wasn't enough to hold on to them. Benjamin walked up one row and down the other. They were all the same, most of the stalks still standing, but another day without water and they too would fall. He straightened a few plants then bent and tried to pack the dirt around them, but grains of sandy earth rolled through his fingers and fell away. Without rain the entire crop would be gone in a day, two at the most.

That afternoon Benjamin began drawing buckets of water from the well and carrying them to the back lot cornfield. He worked throughout the day, stopping only long enough to splash water on his face and drink from the canteen he kept sitting on the porch. After a dozen trips back and forth Otis began helping, but before he'd finished a single run the old man's face turned ashen grey and he began gasping for air.

Benjamin grabbed hold of the bucket Otis was carrying. "You trying to kill your fool self? Go sit down, Daddy, this ain't work you need to be doing."

Otis protested, saying he was perfectly capable of doing a man's work. But after a second trip with a half-full bucket, he plopped down on the porch step.

"It ain't right for a young'un to be doing his daddy's work," he said sorrowfully.

Benjamin laughed. "I ain't a young'un no more. I'm a full-growed man."

"Don't go getting cocky," Otis replied. "You ain't never gonna be too growed for listening to your daddy."

"Yes, sir!" Benjamin smiled and saluted Otis the way he would a senior officer. He eased down beside his daddy and looped a long arm over the old man's shoulder. For several minutes he sat there trying to think of the right thing to say, the thing that would make Otis feel better. The thing that would give back what he was missing.

Unfortunately time is the master of us all; it takes what it will, and often there are no words to ease the emptiness of what is gone. They sat in silence for a long while, and Benjamin thought back to the days when their roles had been reversed. Otis was muscular and strong, capable of packing a day-and-a-half's worth of work into a single day. Benjamin, a boy, trailed behind with a sack of seed not half the weight of his daddy's. He could almost hear his own voice asking for a heavier bag, and Otis saying he was too young for such a load.

His daddy had laughed. "In time. When I'm an old man, you'll have to carry my weight along with your own."

As a boy Benjamin couldn't envision the possibility of such a thing. Back then he'd seen his daddy and mama as two towers of strength, forces so powerful they woke the sun in the morning and pulled the moon into place at night. They'd been the makers of his world; now he struggled to be half what they'd been. Coming to grips with the thought that he could one day be walking in Otis' shoes, Benjamin gave a heartfelt sigh. He stood, went to the well, drew a bucket of icy cold water, and handed a cupful to Otis.

"Daddy," he said nostalgically, "remember when…"

When Otis began to breathe more evenly and his face took on its natural color, Benjamin went back to hauling buckets of water. By nightfall he had watered down the back cornfield and most of the front lot.

That night he did not go to bed but remained on the porch with his daddy. It was the first time they spoke of Lila.

"Your mama was sick for a long time," Otis said, "but she didn't want to tell you."

"Why?"

"She said with you off fighting for your country, you didn't need more worries troubling you."

"I wasn't doing no fighting, Daddy. I was fixing trucks and hauling stuff from one place to another. I told Mama that in my letters."

"I know. She read every one of those letters to me a dozen or more times."

"Then why'd she—"

Otis laughed. "Your mama was your mama. Wouldn't matter none if you was shelling peas, to her it was good as being a general."

For a few moments Otis sat there twisting a scrap of cord he'd picked up in the field; then he turned to Benjamin with a sad smile. "Every Sunday when Reverend Beech asked for prayer requests, your mama stood up and said, 'Please pray for our son, Benjamin, he's a soldier in the United States Army.' Being proud of you gave your mama a whole lot of happiness. Even when she was bad sick, she kept asking the Lord to take care of you."

A look of regret clouded Otis' eyes when he added, "I reckon she should've been praying for herself."

RAIN

T he drought lasted until the first week of August. Then when half of the cornfields in Alabama were burnt to a crisp and the farmers had given up on praying for rain, it came with a vengeance.

The morning dawned with a grey haze hanging over the cornfields and the air heavy with the smell of heat. Benjamin rose from the damp sheet and pulled on a pair of cut-off trousers. "Daddy," he called out to the porch, "any sign of rain out there?"

Otis looked across the dry cracked ground. "Same as yesterday."

Benjamin poured himself a cup of day-old coffee and sliced up a green apple. It was too hot for coffee, too hot for food. Simply breathing was a day's work in itself, and he had yet to carry water to the far field.

Gulping down a few sips of the coffee and leaving most of the apple to turn brown, he walked outside and groaned. "Lord God, ain't this heat ever gonna break?"

"Sooner or later it will," Otis answered. "Sooner or later." He sat there, expressionless as the land.

"I'm hoping it's sooner," Benjamin said and started toward the well.

W hen the first clap of thunder came, Benjamin was in the far field. He'd already made three trips back to the well and dampened the ground with six buckets of water. He set the buckets on the ground and looked up at the sky. It was the dusky grey of early evening. No storm clouds in sight, just a dark, heavy-looking sky.

He raised a fist in the air and screamed, "Rain, dammit, rain!"

A second boom sounded and the sky grew black as night. Benjamin started back toward the house, but before he'd gone halfway a flash of lightning cut across the sky and hit a longleaf pine. The tree, five times taller than Benjamin himself and years older, split in two and crashed to the ground.

That's when he took off running. By the time he reached the house he was soaked through to his underwear and wearing a smile that stretched across the full width of his face.

The dry spell ended with that storm. Throughout the remainder of August and well into October, the rain came most every afternoon; not a deluge, but soft gentle showers that left the field ankle-deep in thick black mud. Once the earth molded itself around the root of the plants, the corn that had days earlier been near stunted grew like weeds. Benjamin walked barefoot through the field checking and then rechecking the plants, the mud squishing between his toes and rising up to cover his feet. He'd come back to the house dragging clumps of mud with every step, but his smile was one he hadn't smiled since the day he returned to Grinder's Corner.

In less than two weeks the corn was ready for picking. Working together Otis and Benjamin harvested the crop, hauled it to market, then cut down the stalks. Otis seemed less weary, the evening breeze cooler, and Benjamin's heart a bit lighter. It was as if the rain had washed away the weariness of summer and brought new life.

The summer corn brought a better than average price, and before they left town Benjamin bought a bushel of sweet potato slips along with the seed and fertilizer he'd need for a field of beets. In the early weeks of September he readied the ground for a second planting, first turning the soil, then leaving it to dry. Once the ground was harrowed, he began to plow, working from first light until he could no longer see his hand before his face. When Henry grew too weary to pull the plow, Benjamin unleashed the mule and pushed the single-blade plow by hand. Before the end of the month he had a field of sweet potatoes planted and the ground ready for a field of beets and a half field of broccoli.

With the ground soft and moist the second plowing was easier and Otis, who was looking a lot less peaked, found the energy to help. He didn't spend long hours pushing the plow as Benjamin did but he'd walk behind, fixing the furrows so they were ready for seed.

The weather stayed warm, and when Benjamin saw sprouts of green coming up the second week of October he began to talk about the possibility of having enough money for a used tractor.

"If we could find one what's broke," he said, "I could get it going."

"That you could," Otis said with a grin. "That you could."

The days were long and the work endless, but the week before Thanksgiving they brought in a second harvest. They filled the wagon with beets and sweet potatoes and hauled it over to Twin Pines, a town that was only half as far as Bakerstown and a place where the color of a man's skin wasn't part of the bargaining. With a good number of summer crops lost to the earlier drought, the price of produce was higher than ever. When Tom Coolidge said he was willing to pay $1.80 a bushel for sweet potatoes, Benjamin could almost see himself riding around on a tractor.

Their next stop was the Supply Depot.

"I'm maybe interested in a tractor," Benjamin said.

Clyde Boone, owner of the shop and a man who was somewhat uppity for a colored, looked at him with a raised eyebrow.

"Them tractors is a thousand dollars; you ain't got that kind of money." The curl in his lip indicated it wasn't a question.

"I was thinking used," Benjamin replied.

"Used is five, maybe six hundred. You got that?"

Benjamin shook his head. "You got one what's broke? Something you're maybe looking to get rid of for a hundred?"

"I got one for a hundred-eighty. It's running but ain't working good."

Benjamin didn't have one hundred and eighty dollars. He had one hundred and thirty-two, and the only reason he had that much was because he'd pocketed most of his mustering out pay and hadn't spent a dime other than buying seed and a few parts for the old car.

"I ain't seeing my way clear for spending that much," Benjamin said. "Can you maybe do better?"

Clyde frowned. "With a little fixing up it's worth four easy. One-eighty's a steal."

"Well, I ain't got one-eighty, so I ain't ready to *steal* it." He turned and started toward the door.

"You planting winter crops?" Clyde called out.

Benjamin shrugged. "Maybe."

It was a known fact that Clyde Boone showed no favor to his own, but neither was he willing to let a loose dollar walk out the door.

"It'd be a lot easier if you had that tractor," he said.

"True enough," Benjamin answered, "but I still ain't got one-eighty."

"How much you got?"

Knowing Clyde would take the pennies off a dead man's eyes, Benjamin hesitated. "Hundred and ten," he finally answered.

"Well, then," Clyde said with a smile, "I reckon we can maybe work something out." He suggested Benjamin give him the hundred and ten now, another forty when he sold the winter crop in early March, and yet another forty when he sold the spring harvest.

Benjamin ran through the numbers in his head. "That's ten dollars more'n you're asking."

"It's a finance charge," Clyde said.

"I ain't buying no fine-nance," Benjamin replied.

They went back and forth for several minutes, then finally agreed Benjamin would pay thirty-five dollars in March and the same amount when the spring harvest was sold.

When they left Twin Pines, Otis was riding in the wagon and Benjamin was following behind in a tractor that was huffing and puffing like a dying man.

On days when the sun was warm and the sky clear, Benjamin would work in the field tending the late crops and readying the other field for an early spring planting. When the wind blew and the temperature dropped to where early morning frost clouded the window, he'd slip on an extra sweater and head for the barn. That's when he'd work on fixing various parts of the tractor. He'd clean them, adjust the belts, and then put it back together again. At the end of the day his palms would be covered with the grease of the engine and his knuckles raw with scrapes, but he'd come in smiling.

The tractor held out long enough for Benjamin to till the front lot and most of the back. When it stopped running altogether, he hitched Henry to the plow and finished turning the back lot. By early December they had planted long rows of parsnips, winter squash, and green onions.

After the seeds were in the ground, Benjamin began rebuilding the tractor from the ground up.

"Come spring," he said, "this thing is gonna be purring like a kitten."

Not as Expected

A week before the final harvest Otis ran short of tobacco and drove into Twin Pines. He used the car Benjamin had repaired and simonized until it shined like a new penny. The minute he stepped out of the car he found himself nose to nose with Denny Walters who'd crossed over from the other side of the street.

"Well, Lordy me," Denny said, laughing. "Look at you, living high on the hog!" He eyed the car and grinned. "Where'd you get a nice car like this?"

"Belongs to my boy, Benjamin," Otis answered. Skinny as he was you could easily see how his chest puffed out with pride. "He's home from the army."

"Already? Seems it ain't been that long."

"More'n four years," Otis answered.

They stood and talked for a while, mostly about crops, weather, and Denny's daughter, Lucille.

"High time she got married," he said. After that he went into the specifics of what a wonderful wife Lucille would make.

"She can whip up cornbread like you ain't never tasted. Ben ought to grab her up 'fore somebody else does," he said.

Otis laughed. "Benjamin's too busy to be thinking of women. Only thing on his mind is farming and making money."

"That ain't good." Denny shook his head ruefully. "Men got natural instincts, and when they ain't got a woman…" He left the rest of that thought unsaid.

A picture of Lila came to mind, and Otis remembered how it was. When she was alive there were hot biscuits and savory stews. On days when the weight of work bent his back, she'd rub his shoulders and ease the pain. And in the dark of night when they were side by side in the bed, she'd press her body close to his and it brought a feeling of completeness. Were it not for Lila, he wouldn't have Benjamin; were it not for Benjamin, Otis would surely have one foot in the grave.

"It's the God's honest truth," he said, sighing. "A man ought to have a woman."

Denny's eyes lit up. "Maybe if Ben was to meet up with Lucille..."

Otis laughed. "Benjamin ain't one to have me meddling in his business."

"I ain't saying we got to meddle, but they got a festival at Brotherhood Hall this Saturday, and if you was to bring Ben and I was to bring Lucille..."

Otis nodded. "Saturday, huh?"

That very evening Otis told his son they'd been working way too hard and needed to do a bit of socializing.

"Now we got everything in the ground, there ain't nothing to do but wait for it to grow," he said.

Although Benjamin had planned to spend Saturday replacing a worn belt on the tractor, he agreed to go to the festival.

"I'm thinking you ought to wear your uniform," Otis said. He claimed it was a prideful thing he wanted to show his friends, but the truth was he had Lucille in mind.

The Brotherhood Hall was a wooden building smack in the center of town; across the street was a dirt lot for parking. By the time Benjamin and Otis arrived, the music and laughter could be heard for ten blocks in any direction. When they walked through the door Denny was waiting. He grabbed hold of Lucille's hand and pulled her closer.

"Ben," he said, "you met my daughter, Lucille?"

"Afraid not. Pleased," he said and gave a nod.

Lucille was plain as oatmeal and shy as a scared turtle. She gave him one quick glance, then ducked back into her shell.

With the music from the jukebox loud and bouncing off of the walls, there wasn't much room for talking.

"Ask Lucille to dance," Otis prodded.

Benjamin did.

As they stepped onto the floor, the Les Brown record ended and the music went from *Sentimental Journey* to *Be-Baba-Leba*. Poor Lucille looked like she was on the verge of fainting.

"I can't jitterbug," she whispered in Benjamin's ear.

"I ain't none too crazy about it myself," he answered. "We'll get us some lemonade and wait for something else."

As they walked off the floor Benjamin got his first glimpse of Delia. She was wearing a red dress, tight around her waist with a skirt that flew up to the middle of her thigh as she jumped around. It was a quick flash of smile with lips scarlet as a ripe cherry, but already Benjamin knew he wanted more.

He guided Lucille over to the refreshment table and ordered two lemonades. As they stood there sipping their drinks he scanned the dance floor in search of the red dress, but by then she was gone.

In time *Be-Baba-Leba* gave way to a soft tempo foxtrot, and they returned to the dance floor. Halfway through the dance Benjamin looked over Lucille's shoulder and saw those red lips smiling; not just smiling but smiling at him. In what was less than a heartbeat, she was gone again.

"There I've said it again," Vaughn Monroe crooned from the jukebox, but Benjamin heard nothing. He stumbled through the remainder of the song, then returned Lucille to her father's side.

"Thank you for the dance, Miss Lucille," he said politely; then off he went in search of the red lips.

Delia stood in the far back and saw Benjamin crossing the floor. When he drew closer she said, "Hi, soldier," and gave a smile.

Benjamin was comfortable talking to most anybody, but when he tried to answer Delia, his tongue got tied in knots. "I ain't exactly...I used to...but...I ain't..."

Delia laughed. "Is this your way of not asking me to dance?"

"No, ma'am," Benjamin stuttered.

"Ma'am?" Delia smiled. "You talking to me or my mama?"

"Why, you, of course…"

"Well, then, call me Delia," she said. "Ma'am sounds like my mama."

As if it were something predestined from the first tick of time, Delia slipped into Benjamin's arms and they moved onto the dance floor. They danced every dance, and before the evening was over she'd agreed to see him again on Tuesday evening.

"We can meet down by the movie," she said. "Six o'clock."

By then Benjamin was in love with Delia and would have agreed to meet her on the moon if that was what she wanted. The promise of seeing her again was enough; he'd asked for nothing more.

On the drive home he told his daddy, "I'm in love."

"Well, I'll be." Otis grinned. "You fooled me good. I could've swore you didn't care a fig for Lucille."

"Not Lucille," Benjamin said. "Delia."

"Delia who?"

Benjamin laughed. "Darned if I know. I got so twisted into knots I done forgot to ask her last name."

"Where's she from?"

"I didn't ask that neither."

Otis chuckled. "Love's more 'n climbing into bed together. Love don't come 'til folks get to liking each other. All you got now is an itch needing to be scratched."

Benjamin knew better, but he also knew when his daddy got a thought in his mind there wasn't any way of arguing it out. Otis hadn't seen the warmth in Delia's eyes; he hadn't heard the ripple of her laugh. Benjamin had. The sweetness of that sound still echoed in his ears, and when he remembered her eyes he could see they were flecked with gold like his mama's.

As they drove the rest of the way in silence, Benjamin thought back on Lila's laughter and when he finally caught hold of a memory and brought it to mind, it had the same lighthearted sound as Delia's laugh.

On Tuesday evening Benjamin was parked in front of the movie theater by five-thirty. He climbed out of the car and stood directly in front of the ticket booth, looking up and down both sides of the street. The minutes ticked by slowly as he waited, and he came to realize how foolish he'd been in not learning Delia's last name. If there was some unforeseen circumstance—a sprained ankle, a flat tire, or an unexpected delay of any sort—it could prevent her from coming and they'd lose track of one another. If that happened he might never find her again. The thought of such a thing sent a shiver of dread down his spine, and he vowed that before the night was over he'd know everything there was to know about her.

By six-ten Benjamin was pacing nervously back and forth in front of the theater. Twice he walked to the end of the street and peered around the corner, but there was no sign of Delia. When she finally came scurrying down Center Street at six-twenty-five, a rivulet of perspiration was rolling down his back.

"I'm sorry to be so late," she said. "Daddy was in one of his preaching moods and supper ran long."

"I was worried," Benjamin said, trying not to show how truly frantic he'd been. "What with not knowing where you live or how to find you."

"Why, I live right here in Twin Pines," she said with a laugh. "My daddy's the pastor at New Unity Church, so I'm easy enough to find."

On Saturday night they'd talked about seeing *The Lost Weekend* but the movie was now of little interest, so they passed it by and went for a ride in Benjamin's shined-up car. There had been little conversation in the noisy ballroom, but once they were alone together Delia bubbled over with things to say. Benjamin listened eagerly and could taste the sweetness of her as surely as he could taste the sweetness in a stalk of sugar cane. When she brought her hand across to touch his arm, he wished the night would never end. Perhaps it was the sound of her laughter, perhaps the warmth that came from her eyes; he couldn't explain the reason, but when her hand touched him he could feel her pulse pounding in his heart.

"You remind me of my mama," he said.

"Your mama?" Delia laughed like it was the funniest thing she'd ever heard. "What kind of sweet talk is that, telling a girl she reminds you of your mama?"

Benjamin glanced across with a shy grin. "I'm meaning it in a nice way. My mama was the prettiest woman I'd ever laid eyes on...until now."

"Go on," Delia said with a giggle. "I bet you say that to all the girls."

"No," Benjamin answered, his voice serious as the day was long. "I ain't never said it to nobody before."

The funny thing was he meant it. Delia had the kind of warmth he remembered from his boyhood days. Although he had known her for just a few short hours he could already picture her standing in the kitchen, stirring a pot of soup or pouring coffee into his blue mug. It wasn't just the warmth of her eyes or the fact that she had a mouth curled into the most kissable smile he'd ever seen. It was because when he looked at Delia he could see the future.

They drove to the edge of town then stopped at a roadside stand, bought two bottles of icy cold cola, and sat in the grass talking. The sky grew dark and filled with stars, but it was the warmth of Delia's eyes that lit a fire in Benjamin's heart.

She was in the middle of telling about how they'd moved from Ohio because her Daddy took on the job of shepherding the flock at New Unity Church when Benjamin blurted out, "I've done decided you're the girl I'm gonna marry!"

Delia laughed. "Marry? A wife ain't like an apple you pick off a tree. A fella's got to court a girl and make her start liking him. Then maybe he can ask if she's willing to marry."

"I know that," Benjamin answered. "And I'm gonna ask proper, when the time's right. But 'til then I thought you ought to know how I'm feeling about you."

Delia smiled and gave a funny little shrug. It was neither an agreement nor disagreement. "I suppose you can feel however you want to feel. But I ain't about to marry somebody I don't know a thing about."

"We got time," he said. "We got plenty a' time to get to know one another." He gave her a knowing wink, then began telling her about the farm in Grinder's Corner.

"Grinder's Corner?" she said. "Where's that?"

"About twelve miles east of here. It's a little town..." Benjamin stopped there because there wasn't much to tell. Grinder's Corner was not really a town; it was nothing more than a wide spot in the road surrounded by a bunch of farms owned by Sylvester Crane. It was a poor comparison to Twin Pines, a town with three restaurants, a movie house, and a Brotherhood Hall that could hold hundreds of partiers.

"Twelve miles ain't all that far," Delia said, "but I still ain't gonna marry you 'til I get to liking you."

Benjamin leaned across and kissed her full on the mouth. It was just as he thought it would be; her lips warm and welcoming, the blush of a ripe peach soft on her skin. They fell back against the grass, and one kiss turned into several. He pressed his cheek to hers and breathed deeply, catching the scent of grass and earth and the fullness of life. When he pressed his lips to hers again, she moved into him like it was something meant to be.

Benjamin lifted his face just high enough to smile down on hers; then he whispered, "You might not know it yet, but you're already liking me."

Delia didn't answer yes or no. She simply tilted her head back and offered her lips again.

It was the only answer Benjamin needed.

BENJAMIN

*F*alling in love is something that sneaks up on you. It don't
come knocking at the door; it storms in, sits down, and takes
hold of your heart. This whole past year I been busy taking
care a' the farm and Daddy and didn't stop to think about how much
I missed the sound of laughter. With just me and Daddy here, we
don't hardly ever laugh. We talk about what work we got to do n'
things like that, but we don't laugh the way we did when Mama was
alive.

Having a woman in your life changes things. It makes hard things
softer, 'specially the inside of your heart. Without a woman you get to
thinking life is nothing but long days a' work and a few dollars saved up
in a tin can.

Delia's changed all that for me. I can't hardly wait from one time 'til
the next to go back n' see her. I gotta admit she caught my eye with that
red dress, but the thing that makes me keep coming back is the sweetness
of her heart.

We only been seeing each other for a short while so this might sound
a bit foolish, but the truth is I can already see us having a flock of babies
and sitting on the porch growing old together. When you find a woman
what makes you feel like that, you gotta hang on to her and that's just
what I'm doing with Delia.

Last night Daddy n' me was sitting on the porch and I got to
wondering if he'd felt the same when he met Mama. When I
asked that question his eyes lit up like Halloween Jack-o-lanterns,

and once he got started talking about Mama I knew the answer was yes.

Falling in love with a girl like Mama or Delia ain't got no explanation, but when it happens all a man can do is let his heart take him where it will.

DELIA'S DADDY

I f it were up to Benjamin he would have gladly driven back and forth every evening to see Delia, but she suggested they make it every other day.

"No sense getting Daddy all riled up over something that might be nothing," she said.

Given the way she responded to his kisses, Benjamin knew the love they felt was something special. He could already see himself as her husband. When he thought of Delia he could feel the warmth of lying close to her on long winter nights, picture Sunday mornings of going to church together, and envision her petticoat hanging beside his shirt on the wash line.

A year ago he might have been hesitant about taking on the responsibility of a wife and family, but not now. The farm was starting to show a profit, and with the fixed-up tractor anything was possible. Given a string of good growing seasons, it was conceivable that he could save enough to flat out buy the land.

Right from the start Benjamin knew Delia was the woman he'd marry, but she insisted it took time for people to fall in love.

"I've got to be sure," she said, "and that ain't something what happens overnight."

He could have easily argued that point based on his own feelings, but he gave her the time she wanted. For nearly two months Benjamin drove the twelve miles to Twin Pines every other day and met Delia in town. They'd see a picture show, go for sodas, or simply walk down the street and across the square. He brought her small presents—a chocolate bar, a bouquet of wildflowers, a pebble formed in the shape of a heart—and he whispered words of love in her ear.

From the moment they met until the moment they parted, some part of their bodies touched one another. Her head nestled against his shoulder, his arm circled her waist, hands held, broad fingers clasping a thin delicate wrist, a thigh pressed so close you could feel the rush of blood pumping through the vein.

Even though Delia snuggled into his arms and pressed her body close to his, the evening always ended the same way. The moment he pulled up in front of her house, she jumped out and bolted toward the front door.

"What's the hurry?" Benjamin would ask, but she turned it off with a shrug.

"I don't want to wake Daddy," she said, but the truth was George Finch was generally sitting in the living room waiting for his daughter to come home.

In late December Benjamin took nine dollars out of his savings can and drove into Bakerstown. He went to the jewelry store and for nearly two hours stood looking at the diamond rings in the display case. He'd hoped he had enough money to buy one for Delia, a small diamond maybe, but a diamond nonetheless. As it turned out even the tiniest diamond, a stone so small you had to squint to see it, cost more than he had in his pocket.

The jeweler, Simon Berg, had been young and in love once also.

"How about a locket?" he suggested and led Benjamin to a side counter. He pulled two small boxes from the case and laid them atop the counter.

Benjamin opened the first box. The locket was an oval with scrolls of filigree circling the edge.

"Six-fifty," the jeweler said. "It's silver plate. Nice, but not as good as sterling."

Benjamin closed the lid to that box and lifted the second one. Inside was a heart-shaped locket that drew his eye right away. In the center of the heart there was second heart, puffed up a bit, just as his was. A heart within a heart. He smiled and without giving voice to his question looked at the jeweler.

Simon grinned. "I figured you'd pick that one. Nine-twenty-five, but it's *sterling*. Any woman would be mighty pleased to get a sterling necklace." His emphasis on the word "sterling" made the locket seem even more special.

Benjamin pulled out the nine one dollar bills, then fumbled through his pockets looking for another quarter. He came up with a dime, two pennies, and a nickel.

"Close enough," the jeweler said. He wrapped the box in bright red paper and tied a green ribbon around it.

When Benjamin left the store he was smiling as he'd never smiled before. He had five days to wait, and already the gift was burning a hole in his hand.

On Christmas Eve he met Delia on Main Street, and they walked hand in hand to the wooded area that was now their special place. They sat on the grassy knoll, and Benjamin whispered words of love that spiraled up from the center of his heart. After she unwrapped the gift he clasped the locket around her neck and kissed her with a depth of emotion that was without question.

"The time has come," he said. "I'm crazy in love with you, Delia. Please say you'll marry me."

Delia no longer needed time to think; she already knew what her answer would be.

"Yes," she whispered; then, putting her lips to his, she let go of all the passion she'd been holding back.

It wasn't planned, but it happened. On that warm December night they made love for the first time. Afterward as he held her so close their heartbeats mingled and sounded as one, Benjamin knew he would never love anyone as he loved Delia.

In early January Delia invited Benjamin to come for Sunday dinner with her family.

"But I'm warning you," she said, "Daddy's gonna be looking you up one side and down the other."

"That's okay," Benjamin replied. "I'll be on my best behavior."

Although he gave off an air of nonchalance, his stomach twisted itself into knots at the thought of having a man-to-man talk with Pastor Finch. "You think maybe I ought to wear my uniform?"

Delia smiled. "Couldn't hurt."

On Sunday afternoon Benjamin arrived at the Finch house a full half-hour early. With long lumbering steps he paced back and forth on the front porch looking down at his feet and wondering whether it was better to go ahead and ring the doorbell or wait until the proper time. Lost in thought, he failed to notice George Finch peering from the window.

When the front door swung open and Delia's daddy said, "What in the blazes are you doing?" Benjamin looked up with a wide-eyed expression. The 'delighted-to-meet-you' speech he'd planned was instantly forgotten.

"I come to call on Delia," he replied.

"Then you should've knocked," Finch said. He swung the door back and motioned Benjamin in. "Have a seat." He pointed to an armchair across from where he sat.

For several minutes they remained there without speaking, Delia's daddy reading his newspaper and Benjamin folding and refolding the hat in his hands. When Benjamin could stand it no longer he said, "I been looking forward to meeting you."

George lifted his eyes from the newspaper and gave Benjamin a hard glare.

"Looking forward to it, were you?" he said, grumbling. "Well, then, you're way ahead of me. I hadn't heard a word about you until yesterday."

Such a statement left Benjamin without words, so he decided to remain silent until Delia came down.

When Finch finished the article he'd been reading he folded the newspaper and set it aside.

"So, I understand you and my daughter have been sneaking around seeing each other."

"Not sneaking around," Benjamin replied. "Delia suggested we meet—"

"It's sneaking around when you don't come calling at the house."

With no argument to come back with, Benjamin said, "I'm sorry, sir, it wasn't my intent—"

"Perhaps not, but appearances are what they are." Finch picked up his newspaper, then laid it back down again. "Delia claims you're a farmer. That true, son?"

"Yes. Me and Daddy have a—"

"Daddy and I," Finch corrected, then he went on to ask why a farmer was wearing an army uniform. The questions came one on top of another, and he didn't allow time for answers. Ever since Delia told him she was in love with Benjamin, a barrage of angry thoughts had been banging against George's head and once let loose they rumbled with an antagonistic roar.

"Delia's mama and I didn't raise her to be the type of girl who goes sneaking around behind her parents back and—"

When Delia walked into the room she heard George's words and angrily stamped her foot. "Stop it, Daddy!"

The sound of Delia's yell brought Mary Finch to the parlor. "George, are you still carrying on about—"

"Yes, Mama, he is," Delia answered. "He's embarrassed Benjamin no end."

Mary gave a sad little shake of her head, then announced dinner was ready.

"Fried chicken will make everyone feel better," she said, looking pointedly at George.

As it turned out their dinner conversation was only marginally better than the earlier one. Delia's daddy kept pounding out questions, and before asking about Benjamin's education he made a point of saying Delia had attended a private school and he'd graduated from Howard University.

About as uncomfortable as he could get, Benjamin had to admit that high school was the best he'd done. "When I signed up for the army, I figured fighting for our country was more important."

His reasoning sounded honorable enough, but the truth was he'd signed up before the war started. The pay was good, and it was easier than working in the fields.

Once George moved past the issue of education, he focused on the negative aspects of being a farmer.

"Grinder's Corner. That's not much of a town, is it?"

"No, sir," Benjamin answered. "It's mostly farms, but nice enough countryside and less than an hour's drive from Twin Pines."

Benjamin had come to the house believing he was hungry, but he barely finished a drumstick and even that was aggravating his stomach. He nervously answered George's questions one after another, and always with a deferential *Yes, sir*, or *No, sir*.

The one time Benjamin found courage enough to talk about how fond he was of Delia, George cut him off before he even got started.

"Do you know my daughter's only sixteen?" he asked. Without giving time for an answer, he added that such an age was too young to be considering anything other than college.

Delia gasped. "Daddy! Mama married you when she was only fifteen!"

"Things were different then," George said and went back to chewing on a piece of chicken.

After dinner they all moved to the front parlor. Delia and Benjamin played several games of checkers, and Mary told stories of how they'd moved from place to place.

"Being settled in one place for all your life sounds lovely," she said. "I'll bet your mama loves living in Grinder's Corner."

It was obvious that no one in the Finch family had ever been to Grinder's Corner; it wasn't a place a person could love.

"Mama passed on two years ago," Benjamin explained and skipped past answering the question.

Benjamin had planned to ask George for his daughter's hand in marriage, but the opportunity never arose. Whenever anything came up that linked him and Delia, George managed to dredge up some sort of unpleasantry.

At ten o'clock Benjamin stood to leave, and Delia stood with him.

"I'll walk you out," she said, hoping they could at least steal a goodnight kiss on the porch.

When George made a move to stand, Mary said firmly, "Sit down, George. I think Delia can handle this by herself."

George fell back into his seat with no argument.

BENJAMIN

*D*elia warned me her daddy was uppity, and she sure enough told the truth. When he got to talking about how he studied at a fine college in Washington, D.C., I knew he was working his way 'round to asking what I done.

I said, Me and Daddy is farmers, *which to my mind ain't nothing to be ashamed of, but he curled up his nose like he was smelling sour milk. Preachers has got their own kind of uppity; it's a holier-than-thou look that would have you believe you sinned even if you ain't done nothing wrong. All preachers ain't that way, but Mister Finch surely is.*

I think it was 'cause I wore that uniform. I figured Delia's daddy would be impressed with knowing I'd been a soldier, but he saw right through me. Mama always said a person shouldn't let on like they're more 'n what they are; I reckon she was right.

When I was on my way out the door Delia whispered she'd meet me by the movie house Tuesday evening. I'm real glad she ain't letting her daddy's dislike come between us. Thanks be to God.

I known Delia for three months, but she's already part of me. I'd sooner lose a leg than lose Delia.

Like it or not, I'm gonna have to figure a way to get on Mister's Finch's good side...leastwise long enough for him to say I can marry his daughter.

AND THE WORD WAS...

After the disastrous dinner, Benjamin made up his mind that he'd do whatever had to be done to get into George Finch's good graces. Whenever he and Delia had a date, he'd call for her at the house and make sure he had something of interest to say to her daddy. He tried football, politics, religion, and any number of random facts pulled from the Farmer's Almanac. But regardless of the subject, Finch took an opposing view. If Benjamin thought Alabama State had a good team, George thought Florida was better. If Benjamin spoke of a popular Democrat, George came up with a Republican who was more intelligent. Determined as Benjamin was to find favor with Delia's daddy, George was more determined to prove a farmer was not good enough for his daughter.

On Sunday mornings Benjamin would drag himself from bed at sunup, shave his face, put on a clean shirt and trousers, and drive all the way to Twin Pines to attend church. When George Finch stepped to the pulpit to deliver his message Benjamin sat in the first row, and when the parishioners began to file out he'd be at the back of the line where there was always a chance to shake Pastor Finch's hand and say what a fine sermon it was.

In the afternoon he and Delia would take a basket lunch and the two blankets Benjamin now carried in his car and head for their favorite spot—that grassy knoll in the woods. They'd spend the afternoon making love, and there was little or no thought of the daddy who stood in the way of a wedding. They had already sworn their lives to one another and were so in love they felt married. On afternoons when there was a chill in the air, they'd lie on one blanket and cover themselves with the other.

It was not at all shocking when Delia said she'd missed her monthly. Twice. By then her breasts were starting to swell, and she had a craving for sour pickles.

"Like it or not," Benjamin said, "your daddy is gonna have to agree to us getting married now."

Delia raised an eyebrow and shook her head doubtfully. "Don't be so sure."

She'd spent sixteen years living under the same roof as George Finch, and not once had she seen him dish out an ounce of forgiveness. What he preached and what he practiced were two different things.

"I think we ought to tell Mama first," Delia said. "If she talks to Daddy maybe he'll be a bit more reasonable."

Benjamin agreed.

That afternoon they returned to the house early. George was napping and Mary was sitting in the kitchen paring apples for a pie. Benjamin and Delia walked into the room holding hands.

"It'll be a while before supper's ready," Mary said.

"Mama," Delia said softly.

It was only a single word, but the sound in her daughter's voice caused Mary to look up and see the tears filling Delia's eyes. Mary stood and came to her daughter.

"What's wrong?"

"I'm sorry," Benjamin said. "Real sorry. We never meant this to happen. We was hoping to—"

Mary's eyes went wide and her voice high-pitched. "What's wrong?"

Delia was the one to answer. "Mama, Benjamin and me are having a baby."

"Lord God, no." Mary grabbed onto the table as if she was ready to faint. "Your daddy is gonna kill you."

"I was hoping maybe you'd talk to him," Delia said.

"This ain't no bastard child," Benjamin added. "Delia and me want to get married. We're gonna be a family and raise the baby up right."

"Your daddy is gonna kill you," Mary repeated.

"Mama!" Delia shouted. "Is what Daddy thinks all you care about?"

"Okay now," Benjamin said. "Let's not start getting on one another. If we talk this through—"

Mary turned to Benjamin. "Talk what through? It's too late for talking. You should have done your talking before you got my daughter pregnant!"

"Don't blame Benjamin," Delia said. "It was both of us, and far as I'm concerned we didn't do anything so God-awful wrong."

For a moment Mary stood there looking like she'd been slapped in the face; then tears began rolling down her face.

"How can you think it's not wrong? The Bible says a woman should only lie down with her husband—"

"Benjamin wants to be my husband!" Delia said angrily. "We'd've been married months ago if Daddy wasn't so pig-headed."

"That's true," Benjamin added. "We made a mistake, but it ain't like we don't love one another."

Mary put her hands to her forehead and began pacing back and forth across the kitchen floor. "Your daddy is gonna kill you," she repeated.

"Mama, saying Daddy is gonna kill me ain't gonna solve nothing. I thought maybe you'd try to help us out."

"Help you out? How in God's name am I supposed to help you out?"

"Talk to Pastor Finch," Benjamin suggested. "Tell him to marry us and give Delia his blessing."

"George won't listen to me any more than he'll—"

Mary stopped mid-sentence because George was standing in the doorway. She looked him square in the eye and said, "Benjamin has something to tell you."

George turned away when Benjamin said he and Delia wanted to be married.

"She's too young and you're not the right man for her," he replied.

It wasn't what Benjamin wanted to do, but he finally had to explain the marriage was a necessity because Delia was expecting a baby. For a moment George stood there looking like a dead man; then he raised his fist and punched Benjamin in the jaw. Benjamin was nearly a foot taller than George and he had arms that could lift the back end of a tractor, but he didn't move a muscle to retaliate. Benjamin stepped back, and George came at him with both fists.

"You'll burn in hell, you piece of trash!" he screamed and kept swinging. Benjamin raised his arms to protect his face, but he never swung back.

All this while Delia and Mary cried and screamed for George to stop. When he finally did he told Benjamin to get out of his house.

"And take this whore with you," he said, waving an angry finger at Delia.

"George, please," Mary pleaded.

But it was no use. George stormed out of the room and said he wanted them gone before supper.

When Delia went to her room to gather her belongings, Mary followed her.

"What you did wasn't right," she said, "but I ain't as unforgiving as your daddy."

Mary slipped her mama's gold wedding ring and twelve one-dollar bills into the palm of Delia's hand. "It ain't much, but it's all I got."

The sky was just turning dusky when they left the house. Benjamin loaded the two pillowcases filled with Delia's things into the backseat of the car, and she slid into the front. She rolled the window down and blew a kiss to her mama standing on the sidewalk.

"I'll try to come visit if I can," Mary said wearily.

"I hope you will, Mama," Delia replied. "I really do hope you will."

Mary stood there and watched the car pull away. "God go with you, child," she said with a sigh. "God go with you."

BENJAMIN

You might think I'm a fool standing there, letting Mister Finch beat on me as he did, but I figured if he got enough revenge he'd go easier on Delia. 'Course that ain't what happened.

I can understand him being mad, but I sure can't understand him saying those awful things to his own daughter. When he called her a whore, it was all I could do not to tear into him. In my head I kept thinking he's Delia's daddy, and when he gets over his mad he'll forgive her. Even when he said to get out of his house and never come back, I figured Delia's mama would step in and put a stop to it but Mister Finch wasn't listening to anybody—not me, not Delia, and not even her mama.

When Delia was packing her belongings in those bags, she was so 'shamed she didn't even look up. She kept her eyes fixed on the floor and grabbed up whatever was within reach. I saw when she took one red shoe and left the other sitting on the shelf, so I got hold of the one she'd left behind and dropped it in the bag.

As we was headed toward the car I started thinking about the baby me and Delia is gonna have, and I swore long as there's breath in my body I ain't never gonna treat our baby mean. No matter if it's a boy or girl, and no matter what good or bad it does.

Me and Delia is gonna be a family what cares about each other, and we ain't never gonna do wrong by our young'uns. That much I can promise you.

AT HOME IN GRINDER'S CORNER

On the drive home it began to rain. At first it was just a light drizzle, but by the time Twin Pines faded into nothingness it was coming down hard. The sound of it washing across the windshield was a welcome relief. In some strange unexplainable way it made the absence of words more bearable. A few times Benjamin gave voice to his thoughts saying he wished it had never come to this, but his words seemed small and insignificant in comparison to Delia's heartbreak.

Hoping to hide her tears, Delia sat with her face turned to the window. Although she and Benjamin would soon be married, their happiness came at a price that was almost unbearable. She could feel bits and pieces of her heart crumbling. The hard truth was that she'd most likely never see her mama or daddy again.

For the whole of her life they'd been there, Daddy picking her up when she fell, Mama bringing her warm soup when she was sick. They helped with her lessons, listened to her prayers, and tucked her in at night. All of that was no more; it was swept away in a parting that was angry beyond belief.

Memories pushed up against one another as she thought back on the days when she was called her daddy's angel, his princess, his little sweetheart. He'd smiled as if she was the sun and he was God in heaven admiring his own work. She tried to push aside the last picture, the one where his angry eyes burned through to her soul. She also tried to deafen her ears to the echo of that bitter word: whore.

As they drove Benjamin saw how the fingers of Delia's left hand rubbed the knuckles of her right. After a few minutes she switched to rubbing the knuckles of her left hand, then just moments later she switched back again. He reached across the seat and covered her hands with his.

"Please don't worry, Delia," he said. "It will be alright." He hesitated a moment then added, "I swear it will."

Benjamin made a silent vow that carried the weight of one sworn with his hand on the Bible. From that day forward he would be everything Delia needed. He would see that she never went hungry, always had a home, and was loved more than any woman on earth.

With the heavy rain and back roads turning muddy, the drive took almost two hours. Grinder's Corner was the sort of place you could pass through and never know you'd been there, so when Benjamin turned into the drive it came as a surprise to Delia.

"This is it?" she asked.

Benjamin nodded. With the dark of night hanging heavy over the land, the only thing to be seen was the lamplight coming from the house. He lifted his arm and pointed across her shoulder.

"Out there's a full field of collards, and the back field..." He motioned out the front windshield, "...that's filled with beets and parsnips."

"Oh my," Delia sighed sounding impressed.

"Yep," he said proudly, "it's gonna be a real good spring harvest."

When he parked the car alongside the house Benjamin leaned across the seat and kissed Delia, not with passion but with the tenderness that had settled in his heart.

"Delia, honey," he said, "you and that baby ain't never gonna want for nothing. I swear."

He climbed from the car, came around to Delia's side, and lifted her into his arms. "I know we ain't official yet, but since this is gonna be your new home I'm figuring to carry you across the threshold."

That night Benjamin settled Delia in his bedroom, and he slept on the sofa. Perhaps it wasn't necessary, but he wanted Otis and everyone in Grinder's Corner to have the respect for Delia that her daddy had taken away.

The next day they drove into Bakerstown and were married by a justice of the peace. It was a simple ceremony with just the two of them and a secretary they'd never before seen serving as witness. Delia wore her pink dress with the lace collar, and when the justice pronounced them man and wife Benjamin slid her grandma's gold wedding band on Delia's finger. It was a bittersweet reminder of the family she'd left behind.

On the far edge of town they stopped at a roadside inn for lunch, then returned home. Benjamin changed into his overalls and headed out to the field.

That afternoon as Delia mixed up the batter for cornbread, she gazed out the kitchen window. For as far as she could see there was nothing but flat land with rows of green coming from the ground. In the distance there were tall pines but no streets, no stores, no lampposts, no people. Being married to Benjamin was something she'd wanted since the first time he'd held her in his arms, but now it seemed that all the happiness she'd envisioned had been replaced by a strange sense of loneliness. She'd imagined a honeymoon, maybe to a city where they'd spend the night in a hotel and dine in a fancy restaurant. She'd never dreamed that on the day of her wedding she'd be left alone in a strange house with chores to do.

Tears swelled in Delia's eyes, and she brushed them back. The words of her father still echoed in her ear: "You've made your bed, now lie in it!"

Otis, who'd been over at Tommy Muller's for the past two days, arrived home just as Delia was pulling a second pan of cornbread from the oven. The first cornbread, blackened to a crisp, had already disappeared into the garbage can.

"Well, now," Otis said with a smile. "Looky what we got here."

Delia wiped her hands on the apron she was wearing and crossed the room. "I'm Delia. Benjamin and me was married this morning."

Otis grinned. "I ain't the least surprised. That boy's crazy in love with you." He reached out and pulled Delia into his arms. "I'm real pleased to have you as part of our family."

Delia smiled. "Thank you, sir, I'm pleased to be here."

"Sir?" Otis let out a rolling belly laugh. "There ain't no 'sir' here, jest call me Daddy Church."

"Daddy Church sounds real good," Delia said.

That evening when they sat down to supper the chicken was fried hard as a rock and the collard greens were swimming in vinegar, but no one complained. Benjamin said it was a fine meal and a real good effort, seeing as this was Delia's first time cooking. There was no mention of a baby and there wouldn't be for several months, not until after Delia's stomach began to swell.

Time is a strange companion. Sometimes it steals from you the things you treasure and other times it acts as your staunchest ally, dulling memories of events and dates. So it was with Delia's pregnancy. When the news that she was expecting a baby finally got out, the townspeople of Grinder's Corner had already lost track of when she and Benjamin were married.

Although Grinder's Corner was little more than a cluster of farms where poor whites and colored sharecroppers scratched a living from the land, it had a general store where people could buy candy bars and a few necessities. It had neither baby clothes nor bolts of fabric.

When Delia was ready to start making baby clothes, Benjamin took the entire seventeen dollars from his savings jar and suggested they go into Bakerstown.

"We'll get you a sewing machine and material enough for a pretty dress," he said.

"I don't need no dresses," Delia laughed, "just material for baby clothes."

"Every woman needs pretty dresses," Benjamin replied with a wide grin.

The department store in Bakerstown was half again as big as the one in Twin Pines, and Benjamin felt a husbandly pride as he took Delia by the arm and ushered her through the door. Their first stop was the fabric department where she selected a bolt of pale yellow flannel and two spools of thread the same color. The next aisle over featured a large display of electric sewing machines. They stood for several minutes looking at the various machines until a sales clerk eventually walked over.

"You need something?" he asked.

"Yes," Delia replied. "We're looking for a foot pedal sewing machine."

"A treadle machine?" he sneered. "We haven't had one of those for more 'n five years. I doubt they make them anymore."

"Oh," Delia said, disappointed. "I thought maybe…"

Before the sales clerk could say anything more, Benjamin tugged Delia toward the door.

"Don't worry," he whispered. "We'll find one."

He'd thought to look in the small appliance store at the far end of the street, but in the front window there was a sign saying "No Coloreds." Passing it by as if it wasn't what he had in mind, he turned and steered her back to where they'd parked the car.

On the way they passed a bakery with another such sign. Delia spied a tray of raspberry-filled cookies in the window and looked at them longingly. She could almost taste the thick jellied raspberry and the crunch of crispy nut topping but said nothing.

They drove to the far side of town, and there in a second-hand store they found the sewing machine.

The white-haired Negro behind the counter pulled out a chair and motioned for Delia to sit down and give the machine a try.

"It's good as new," he promised and handed her a scrap of muslin to stitch.

Delia settled herself in the chair, moved the fabric into place, and began pumping her foot back and forth. After less than a minute she looked up and gave a nod.

"You done made a sale," Benjamin said, "and I reckon you ought to throw in that chair 'cause the missus likes it." He gave Delia a wink and she smiled.

As they drove home a weighty silence hung in the air.

"I don't much like Bakerstown," Delia finally said.

"I ain't none too crazy about it either," Benjamin replied.

In Grinder's Corner the lines of color were blurred. Everyone was poor and everyone prayed the same prayers: that the rain would either come or go away, that the harvest would be good, that there would be food on the table, and that the old folks would live to see another year.

But Bakerstown was different. The lines that divided people were harsh and ugly. There was no ignoring the division, because it was spelled out in fat black letters on signs in shop windows. Swallowing back her dislike of the place was something Delia found hard to accept. Twin Pines was a mostly colored town, but she couldn't remember a single shop with a sign that said "No Whites."

After the trip to Bakerstown a larger loneliness settled over Delia. She missed Twin Pines, missed the shops she knew, and, although she never gave voice to the thought, it was obvious she also missed her mama. When the days grew short she would stand at the window and watch the road that ran by their house. When a car appeared she'd crane her neck and watch. A look of hope would light her face for a brief moment, but once the car passed by their drive that sorrowful look of longing returned.

When Benjamin saw the sadness that lined her face, he took her in his arms and said, "Give it time. It will get better. I promise."

THE DAY OF BIRTH

The twins were born on Thanksgiving Day.

Since it was the first holiday they'd be sharing, Delia wanted it to be special. For four days she'd stood at the kitchen sink peeling vegetables and plucking feathers from the wild turkey Benjamin shot and carried home. When the achiness set in she attributed it to the long hours of work, but when she felt a sharp pain stab in her groin and a rush of water flowed down her legs she knew.

"Benjamin!" she called. "It's time."

He came into the kitchen thinking she was calling them to noonday dinner, but when he saw the way she was slumped in a chair he knew better.

"Daddy," he called, "the baby's coming! Go get Wanda!"

By the time Otis saddled up Henry and rode off, Delia was doubled over with pain. Benjamin helped her to the bedroom, pulled a clean nightgown from the shelf, and plumped the pillow beneath her head as she fell back.

"Thanksgiving is ruined," she sobbed. "After all my hard work—"

"It ain't ruined at all," Benjamin said. "You'll see. When that sweet baby gets here it'll be the happiest day of our life."

Wanda May was said to be the best midwife in all of Alabama, but she was just sitting down to dinner when Otis came for her.

"First babies always come slow," she said and went back to finishing her dinner. With a full plate of turkey and stuffing, then sampling a slice of the pecan pie her daughter baked, it took more than two hours before she arrived at the Church house. Delia had been in hard labor that whole time, and the sheet was soaked through with perspiration.

"Good Lord, child, you is in a bad way." Wanda turned to Otis and gave him an angry glare. "Why didn't you jest say it was a real bad birthing?"

"How you figure I'm gonna know good from bad?" Otis said. "To me they all looks bad."

Wanda began calling out orders for boiling water, clean rags, and fresh towels. She lifted Delia's gown and felt her stomach the way you'd feel a watermelon to judge if it's ripe and ready for eating.

"You got more 'n one baby in there," she said, "and that first one's stuck sideways."

Wanda began kneading Delia's stomach like a roll of dough, and after a long while the baby moved in the direction she was pushing. When that happened Wanda stuck the better part of her hand inside Delia and eased the head into position. Less than five minutes later a squalling boy came into the world.

"Well, ain't you a sight for sore eyes," Wanda said and handed the baby to Benjamin. "Wash him off, but be real gentle."

Wanda turned back to Delia, who was nearly passed out from the pain. "Now let's get that other baby out."

The second baby proved far more challenging and for almost two hours Wanda massaged Delia's stomach, applying hot towels and rolling her from side to side.

"This one's a stubborn little thing," she said and continued working. She moved Delia into a sitting position and propped a pile of pillows behind her back. When there was no movement, Wanda finally pressed her ear to Delia's stomach and listened. She could no longer hear the baby's heartbeat. She poured a bit of chloroform onto a clean towel and pressed it to Delia's nose.

Once Delia was unconscious, Wanda took the pronged instrument from her bag and pulled the baby out. It was a girl, strangled to death by the umbilical cord wrapped around her neck. The tiny girl had turned the blue-black color of a night storm.

That same day Otis cut a long leaf pine from the far edge of the back field, and from it he shaped the boards to make a coffin the size of a breadbox.

On Friday Benjamin wrapped the baby, called Lila, in one of the new blankets and placed her in the box. Although Delia was so weak she could hardly stand, she clung to Benjamin's arm as Otis said a prayer then placed the tiny casket in the ground.

The turkey and pies sat on the sideboard and grew cold. No one ate, nor did they acknowledge that Thanksgiving had come and gone. While they had a son to be thankful for, they had buried a child who had never taken her first breath. It was a bittersweet day that throughout the years would force Delia to remember the girl each time they celebrated the boy's birthday.

They named the boy Isaac and placed him in a cradle Benjamin built. Although the cradle was designed to fit a single baby, it now seemed oversized and strangely empty.

"It's too big," Delia complained, and when Isaac wailed or was given to unexplainable fits of crying she swore it was because he was missing the sister he'd lost.

"How can he not?" she reasoned. "They were side by side for nine months."

When the weather turned cold and she could no longer sit on the front porch to rock the baby, Delia slid into a deep depression. Some days she could see her way clear to thank the Lord for giving them Isaac, and other days she'd curse him for taking their daughter. On the worst of those days, Delia would cry louder than Isaac and swear that losing Lila was a punishment her daddy had asked God to bring down on her.

She moved through the days like a lost shadow, cooking dinner and setting it on the table, then nibbling on nothing more than a spoonful of mashed potatoes or a tiny pile of peas. She was thin to start with, but within the month her bones began to push up against her skin and she grew knobby in places where she'd once been round.

"You've got to eat," Benjamin urged. "Isaac needs food to grow."

With Delia eating less than a sparrow, the milk in her breasts slowed to a dribble and Isaac remained small. He was given to long fits of crying and while she held fast to the thought that it was because he was missing his sister, Benjamin knew it was hunger gnawing at the baby's stomach. On several occasions he'd leave working in the field and go into town to buy candy bars and sweet cakes for Delia. Even though those were the things she'd once craved, she'd nibble a bite or two then set them aside.

"I've no appetite," she'd say and turn to stare out the window.

A week before Christmas Benjamin took money from the jar on the kitchen shelf and bought a milk goat. When he slid the nipple of the baby bottle into Isaac's mouth, the child sucked happily. That night Isaac slept soundly and there was no crying. From that day on the baby was fed with goat's milk, and he began to grow.

In the early spring Otis traded a day's work for a young magnolia tree. He carried it home and planted it on the spot where they'd laid Lila to rest, and for the first time in months the trace of a smile crossed Delia's face.

That evening she hugged Otis' neck and whispered, "Thank you."

When the rain came the tree took root and began to grow. It wasn't expected to blossom in that first year, but in the first week of June tiny white buds appeared on the branches. Within days the buds burst into flowers that were so beautiful they brought tears to Delia's eyes.

"See," Otis said, "this is God's way of telling us He's got Lila in His care."

Such a thought eased Delia's heart, and although her cooking was nowhere near as tasty as her mama's she began forcing herself to eat.

Throughout those early months Delia's moods would go up and down like a yo-yo. One day she'd be laughing at the way Isaac squealed and kicked his feet in the air; then the next day she'd be standing at the window looking for something that was never there.

Benjamin came to know and understand her moods. On the blackest of days when he saw the melancholy draped across her shoulders, he'd find something to cheer her: a flower from the field, a tender embrace, a string of kisses that traveled down the side of her neck. These small kindnesses touched Delia's heart, and while a tear still lingered in her eye she would turn and smile.

DELIA

A chunk of me died when I lost my baby girl. I looked at that sweet innocent baby turned blue as a bottle of ink and I thought, Lord God, how much more of this can I take? First I lost Mama and Daddy, and then you took away one of my precious babies. *It's too much to ask of any woman.*

I believe in my heart my baby girl dying was 'cause Daddy called down the vengeance of the Lord on me. Daddy's a person who don't see no shades of grey, just good and evil. He's got a whole lot of what he calls holiness, but the truth is he can be way meaner than the worst devil in hell.

If I could talk to Daddy I'd tell him Jesus forgives people what's made a mistake; then I'd ask him if he thinks he's better 'n Jesus.

Knowing Daddy, he probably does.

THE BARBEQUE

In early April the weather turned warm, and Delia could once again sit on the porch to rock back and forth with Isaac in her arms. By then he was starting to teethe, and the motion of the chair eased his fretfulness. It was on just such a day that Beulah Withers happened by.

Beulah was on her way back from that wide spot in the road Grinder's Corner called town. "Howdy there," she called when she saw Delia sitting on the porch.

Delia waved back, and that was all it took. Beulah turned and started up the road toward the house.

"The mister done told me Benjamin got hisself a sweet little wife; I'm guessing that's you," she said.

"I ain't gonna swear to sweet, but I'm sure enough Benjamin's wife." Delia gave the lighthearted laugh that hadn't been heard in a number of months. It was picked up by a passing breeze and carried off to the side field.

Benjamin was busy spreading fertilizer, but hearing the laugh caused him to stop and listen. When it sounded again, he started back toward the house. As he came around the side, Beulah tickled Isaac under the chin and Delia laughed the way she did back in Twin Pines. It was a happy sound, free of heartache and sour memories. Benjamin stood and watched for a moment; then without them ever knowing he'd been there he turned and headed back to the field. As he walked a smile spread across his face, and his step became lighter.

He was still smiling that evening when they sat down to supper.

After he'd polished off a full plate of rabbit stew, he pushed the plate back and said, "I'm thinking it's time you got to know our neighbors."

Delia beamed. "I met one today. Name's Beulah."

"Beulah's a fine woman," Otis said. "Her and Tom got six young'uns. The eldest ain't yet in high school."

"Six?" Delia repeated. "However does she manage?"

Before the conversation could settle into the worrisome thought of six children, Benjamin went back to what he'd had in mind.

"I'm thinking a big ole barbeque," he said. "Invite a buncha neighbors and make a cooking fire in the yard."

It was as if a light snapped on inside of Delia. "Really?" she said, her eyes sparkling.

Benjamin nodded. "Really. It's been a good year, and we got spare money."

"Caleb got hogs he's looking to sell," Otis said. "Might be he'd give you a good price on one of 'em."

"Pork barbeque, huh?" Benjamin smiled. "That sounds mighty good."

Late into the evening they remained at the table making plans for the cookout. It was decided that Benjamin would buy one of Caleb's hogs and butcher it. Fresh meat from the hog Benjamin bought from Caleb would be used for the barbeque, and what was left would be cured and stored in the smoke house.

In a voice laced with excitement, Delia asked question after question. What were the names of the people who'd be coming, and did they have children? How many were there? How old were they? Did anyone have babies? What were the women like? As Benjamin described one family or another, she leaned forward with her elbows on the table and her neck stretched out to catch every word.

"There's Digger Perkins," Benjamin said. "Him and Marybeth have a girl what's still in a cradle; she's close enough to Isaac's age."

"What about boys?" Delia asked. "Any boy babies?"

Benjamin rubbed a calloused hand across his whiskers. "Let's see. There's the Wilsons. Virginia's got a boy, but he's about five, maybe six."

Delia wrinkled her nose. "He'll be eight when Isaac's two," she said, disappointed.

Benjamin laughed. "'Course there's the Jacksons; Will and Luella got a newborn what's a boy, but they live on the far end of Cross Corner Road. That's a good five miles."

"Oh, please invite them. Five miles ain't so far. Soon as Isaac starts walking around, he's gonna need a friend to play with."

The second Benjamin nodded yes Delia began asking what Luella was like. Was she young? Did she like to garden? Did they have other children?

For the next two weeks Delia busied herself with preparations for the party. She cleaned every corner of the house and painted the railing around the porch. After planting a row of begonias alongside the front steps, she raked the drive so it would be free of stones and soft enough for toddler-sized bare feet. The whole time she worked she sang or whistled. Twice Benjamin heard her humming a song they'd sung in her daddy's church.

With the cleaning now finished Delia realized that she'd done a dozen different things to assure the grownups had a good time, but she'd made no preparations for all the children who would be coming. Isaac was still a baby and needed nothing more than a soft basket and warm bottle of milk but there were other kids, some just toddlers and some old as fourteen.

"Daddy Church," she asked, "do you think you could build a swing for the kids to play on?"

He grinned. "Yep. Long as you ain't wanting nothing fancy."

Delia was going to say there was no rush since they had another three days until the party, but by then Otis had walked off leaving the bottom half of his coffee sitting on the table. Minutes later she heard him in the yard; he was sawing a piece of wood and whistling *Dixie*.

She had barely finished clearing the table before he was back.

"All done," he said. "Wanna give it a try?"

Gathering Isaac into her arms, Delia followed Otis into the yard and climbed onto the swing. With Isaac in her lap she pushed herself back and forth. He squealed, and she laughed out loud.

"This is wonderful," she said. "The kids are gonna love it!"

As Otis stood there watching, he thought back on the days when Benjamin was the baby in Lila's arms. If he closed his eyes he could see the picture and feel the happiness he'd once felt. It was a sad thing to grow old and an even sadder thing to lose your sense of purpose. Otis lost his after Lila was gone, and with it went whatever happiness he'd known.

The odd thing about happiness is that it doesn't make a big show of leaving. It just slips away silently. You continue moving through the days expecting it to be there, but it isn't. Occasionally a look-alike pretender comes along and you think, *Ah, my happiness is back again*, then you realize it's not. When real happiness finally returns, you're certain of it.

Listening to Isaac's squeals of delight, Otis gave a wide grin and settled into his newfound happiness. This one was no pretender.

The next day he began building a seesaw.

"What's this?" Delia asked.

Otis, not a man given to sentimental gestures, mumbled, "A seesaw."

"Oh, Daddy Church," Delia sighed, "I can't believe you'd go to all this work just for the party."

"It ain't jest for the party," he said and kept hammering.

At that time Otis expected there'd be other babies. That Isaac would have sisters. And brothers. He'd imagine the future and could see the kitchen table surrounded by a circle of chairs. In each one there was a grandchild with a shiny bright smile.

But the future is a thing made of whisper-thin glass. The tiniest crack causes it to shatter and break into pieces. One moment you're holding it in your hand, and seconds later it's gone. Like happiness, it disappears before you realize it.

The day of the party dawned with a bright sun and gentle breeze. Delia declared it to be the finest weather God ever made. All morning she bustled from task to task, carrying Isaac in her right arm and setting out plates with her left.

At noontime the visitors started arriving. They came with cakes and pies and dishes of food. "Welcome to Grinder's Corner," the women said as they oohed and awed over Isaac. As Delia handed out dishes of potato salad and turnip greens, the women passed Isaac from one set of arms to the next. The whole while he gurgled and laughed, his little arms and legs spinning like pinwheels.

Until that day Isaac's only food had been goat's milk and mashed grits, but at the party he sucked the last bit of flavor from an almost bare rib bone and tasted bits of sweet potato pie.

"He's after more 'n milk and grits," Benjamin said, laughing. He poked his finger into a dish of cooked apples, let Isaac taste the sweet sauce, and then laughed again.

In all there were thirty-six people at the barbeque. Twenty-one of them were children, the youngest being Luella Jackson's boy who was just six weeks, and the oldest Beulah's girl, who'd be starting high school next year.

In the late afternoon when the babies slept and children played, the adults gathered in small groups. The women shared recipes and talked of visiting one another; the men spoke of crops and pay. Delia saw Benjamin sitting on the south edge of the grass so she went and sat next to him. She leaned her head on his shoulder. Threading her fingers through his, she lifted his hand to her mouth and kissed it.

"Thank you," she whispered and smiled.

In the days following the party, Delia began visiting back and forth with the women she'd met at the barbeque. Once she walked the full way to Luella Jackson's house carrying Isaac in her arms. Benjamin volunteered to drive her there, but Delia shook her head.

"I like walking," she said. "I like the feel of sun on my shoulders and the smell of growing things."

A few weeks later Beulah came to visit with two of the babies and the teenage girl. They spent a full afternoon sitting on the porch, talking and laughing as they lingered over sweet cakes and lemonade.

That evening sitting across from Benjamin at the supper table, Delia said, "Now that I've come to know Grinder's Corner, it's not so different from Twin Pines after all."

Benjamin smiled.

LETTERS

During that first year Delia wrote countless letters to her mama; some were answered, some were not. She also wrote four letters to her daddy, but each one of those was returned with a heavy-handed scroll saying "Return to Sender." Delia recognized her daddy's handwriting, and after the last one came back she stopped writing.

When Isaac was just a few months old, Delia took a picture of him and sent it to her mama. She told of the clever things he did and how although he had Benjamin's features, he had her own coloring and frame. "He's got eyes exactly like you, Mama," she wrote, then slid the picture inside the envelope and sealed it.

That letter was answered the very next week. Mary claimed the picture was dear to her heart and that she was keeping it hidden inside her underwear drawer.

"I've been wanting to come for a visit," the letter said, "but your daddy won't hear of it. Every night I pray God will make him a more forgiving man, but so far those prayers haven't been answered."

Mary went on to say how much she loved Delia and wished her well.

"What happened, happened," she wrote. "It may not be right, but it sure isn't reason enough to turn your back on your own child. I can't come to see you and Isaac, but that don't stop me from loving you."

There was a five-dollar bill tucked inside the envelope.

Through the years Delia and her mama sent letters back and forth on a regular basis. She sent pictures of Isaac with his first tooth, when he started walking, and then throwing a ball. There were a few pictures where Delia was sitting alongside of Isaac but only one where Isaac was sitting on his daddy's lap.

Mary usually wrote back with gushing comments over the boy. "He's such a handsome lad," she'd write, "he's got his granddaddy's build." She expressed amazement that Isaac was walking at just nine months. "Why, you were full into a year before you'd take a single step."

But when Delia sent the picture of Isaac with his daddy, there was no answer for two months. When the letter finally came, it made no mention of the picture.

They say that given time all wounds will heal, anger will be forgotten, and sins forgiven, but that was not true of Delia's daddy. He never forgave her and forbid Mary to speak her name.

"As far as I'm concerned, she's dead," he said and stuck to it.

Once when George's cousin came from Baltimore for a visit, they were sitting at the supper table and the cousin asked how Delia was doing.

"She's dead," George answered and stuffed a chunk of pork chop in his mouth.

Mary gasped and clutched her hand to her heart as if the death had occurred that very second. "George, don't..." She was going to say more, but the anger in George's eyes and the hard way he chomped down on that piece of pork stopped her.

The cousin, sensing something was amiss, moved on to talking about baseball.

Just as time didn't dull George Finch's anger, it didn't dull the hurt in Delia's heart. When Mary's letters came, she would sit on the porch reading and rereading every word. Each sentence was carefully constructed to say only certain things, but threaded through the words were feelings of fear and anger. After that first time there was never another mention of her daddy.

Delia and Benjamin hoped for more children, but it never happened and by the time Isaac turned three she had given up hoping.

"I can only assume this is another thing Daddy has wished on us," she said.

Setting aside the sadness, she poured her love into Isaac and the life she and Benjamin were building together. She found a new kind of happiness in the small things that filled her days. Winters were long and sometimes harsh, but during those days Delia threaded her sewing machine and stitched patches for a quilt. The week after Isaac's first birthday, she finished the first quilt and began stitching a second.

Keeping busy proved to be a way of forgetting her daddy's words. When the cold of winter left, she planted a garden nearly as wide as the house. She grew the things they ate: sweet potatoes, carrots, cabbage, tomatoes, beans, watermelons, and strawberries. As things ripened she carried them inside and began canning. Everywhere she went Isaac trailed behind her. Shortly after he began to talk, he started to learn the names of things she grew in the garden.

"Dat's coo-cumer," he'd say and point to a tomato.

"No, no," she'd say with a laugh. "That's a tomato." Pointing to the far end of the row, she'd explain, "That's a cucumber."

In the height of growing season Delia worked alongside Benjamin and Otis in the fields. When she went she allowed Isaac to tag along. Whatever she did, he mimicked. When he was only half the size of a full-grown stalk, he could tell the difference between a weed and a young corn sprout.

"Dat a weed," he'd say and start tugging away at a piece of fern or skunk-vine.

Although it took twice as long to work a row, Delia liked having the boy beside her. They would work for three or four hours then she'd bring him back to the house, tired and happy.

After a bowl of warm soup or a peanut butter and jelly sandwich, she and Isaac would sit together on the porch swing, and as they swayed back and forth she'd tell stories. Sometimes it would be a made-up tale of when his daddy was his age, but many times it was her foretelling of the future.

On one particular occasion Delia told Isaac what it would be like when he grew up.

"When you're old enough," she said, "you can go off to college and get a fine education. Then you can be a doctor, or maybe write stories for a newspaper. You might even get to live in New York City."

"Is Noo York got farms?" he asked.

"Afraid not," Delia laughed.

"Me not wanna go dere," Isaac said. "Me gonna be farmer like Daddy."

Delia gave a sad shake of her head. "You don't ever want to be an Alabama farmer. It's a hard life."

"Daddy ain't got no hard life."

"Yes, he does," Delia laughed. "He just don't let it show." She gave the swing a push and said, "In New York City colored folks got it way better than they do in Alabama."

Isaac's world was small. He'd never been outside of Grinder's Corner and didn't understand the meaning of her words.

"Is Daddy colored?" he asked.

She looked down at him and laughed. "Yes, Daddy's colored, I'm colored, you're colored. We're all colored."

"If you ain't colored, what is you?"

"White," Delia answered sadly.

Isaac started school when he was five. On the first day Delia took a picture of him wearing the new checked shirt she'd made, then she walked with him the whole two miles to the First Baptist Church where colored kids went to school.

She went inside expecting to see classrooms like the one she'd sat in, but such was not the case. There was a single room with a cluster of chairs bunched around a long wooden table. The smaller kids gathered at one end and the older ones at the other. Delia's heart fell when she saw the room and plummeted even further when she caught sight of the stack of ragged looking books piled on the window sill.

"Lord God," she murmured. With a heavy heart she kissed Isaac on the cheek and promised to come for him at three o'clock.

On the walk home Delia's eyes overflowed with tears, and they rolled down her cheek. The sound of her daddy saying "You made your bed, now lie in it" still echoed in her ears. How long, she wondered. How long did she have to pay for a single mistake?

Although she was content with her choice, it saddened her to believe that choice had determined the pathway for Isaac's life.

"Please Lord," she prayed, "stay beside my baby."

After seeing the Grinder's Corner school, Delia knew whatever Isaac learned he was going to have to learn at home. From that day forward, every afternoon she'd sit beside him at the table and they'd practice numbers, letters, and words. Before a month had gone by he knew the alphabet and could count to fifty.

In early October Isaac's first-day-of-school picture was developed and Delia wrote to her mama.

"I'm so proud of my little man," she wrote. "I'd give anything in the world if you could see him." She told how Isaac already knew his letters and numbers but said nothing about the makeshift school he attended.

"If you could slip away from Daddy and meet me in town," she suggested, "we could have lunch and you could get to know this fine little grandson of yours." She went on to say Benjamin would drive them to Twin Pines and then do errands while they were having lunch. At the end of the letter she wrote, "Please say yes, Mama." Delia slid the school picture into the envelope and sealed it.

It wasn't unusual for a week or two to go by before a letter was answered, but when it became a whole month Delia started to worry.

"Maybe I shouldn't have asked Mama to come for lunch," she said. "Maybe I should've left well enough alone."

"Inviting your mama to lunch ain't a bad thing," Benjamin said. "Could be she's just been busy. Give it time."

Another week passed and there was still no answer, so Delia sat down and wrote a second letter.

"I'm sorry if my asking you to lunch put you in a bad spot," she wrote. "I'd be willing to just forget about that. Please write me back soon."

The days dragged as Delia watched and waited for an answer. After two weeks she began to believe none was coming. Trying to make amends for whatever wrong she'd done, she started sending a new letter almost every day. In one she begged for forgiveness, in another she promised to never again suggest meeting, and in one she even apologized for her sloppy handwriting. Still there was no response.

Delia's garden became overgrown with weeds and tomatoes waiting to be picked; still she did nothing but pace the floor cursing herself for alienating her mama as well as her daddy. "Why'd I do it?" she'd sob. "Why?"

On the day that marked the second month without a letter, Benjamin came in from the field to find her red-eyed and weepy.

"I should've never suggested Mama sneak away from Daddy," she said. "He must've found out and now he's turned her against me."

"I don't think any such thing—" Benjamin said but before he could finish the sentence, she cut him off with a comment about how he didn't know her daddy.

"Yeah, I do," he replied, but after that he kept quiet.

"Maybe your mama can't write," Otis suggested. "Maybe she's sick or down with a fever."

Delia gasped. "Lord God Almighty, don't even think such a thing."

Although nothing more was said, that evening Benjamin tucked the thought inside his head and a day later, without mention to anyone, he drove into Twin Pines. He went past the Finch house three times before he finally worked up enough courage to park the car and go knock on the door.

The first time he rapped lightly and stood waiting, but when there was no answer he knocked with a heavy hand. Still no answer. He walked around to the back of the house. The curtains were drawn, and there was no sound coming from inside.

"Hello?" he called out.

After he'd been there a good fifteen minutes, a woman came from the house next door. "Are you looking for the Finches?"

"Yes," Benjamin answered. "Missus Finch is my wife's mama."

"Your wife's mama?" the woman said. "And she doesn't know?"

"Know what?"

"Mary passed away this past September and George—"

"Missus Finch is dead?"

The woman nodded. "I'm surprised Pastor Finch didn't let you know."

"He ain't close with family," Benjamin said; then he turned and walked away.

"I'm sorry," the woman called after him. "I'm real sorry."

"Thanks," Benjamin hollered back and kept walking.

For the remainder of that day Benjamin debated what to do. There was no good answer; there were only two different kinds of terrible. It was a painful thing to know your mama died without ever giving you one last hug or holding your baby in her arms. News such as that would break Delia's heart. It would rip loose the thin thread of hope she'd been clinging to. But if he didn't let her know, she'd go on hoping.

Which was worse—to destroy the little bit of hope she had or let her go on wishing for something that would never happen? Long after Delia had gone to bed Benjamin sat on the porch and pondered the thought. It was near dawn when he came to a decision.

There was little conversation during breakfast. Delia hurried Isaac along so he wouldn't be late for school, and Otis claimed he had chores to finish up. Benjamin was silent. He took a few sips of coffee and left the plate of biscuits and gravy untouched.

"You feeling okay?" Delia asked.

He nodded then said he'd feed the chickens while Delia walked Isaac to school.

"Leave it be," she said, "I can do it when I get back."

"You got enough to do," he replied and disappeared out the door.

When Delia returned, Benjamin was sitting at the kitchen table.

"Delia, honey," he said. "Sit down. There's something I got to say."

After years of loving him, she'd come to know Benjamin's thoughts as well as her own. A single glance at the serious expression on his face told her something was wrong.

"Lord have mercy," she moaned and dropped into the chair.

"I know you been worried about your mama not writing," Benjamin said, "but it ain't your fault. Sometimes things happen and it ain't nobody's fault, it's just a thing what happens—"

"For heaven's sake, Benjamin, say what you got to say and be done with it."

"Don't hurry me; what I got to speak ain't easy." He stretched his arm across the table and took her hand in his. "Delia, honey, I'm sorry I got to be the one to tell you this, but the reason your mama didn't answer those letters is 'cause she's gone to be with the Lord."

Delia yanked her hand loose and let out a gasp that could be heard a mile away. "Mama's dead?"

Benjamin nodded and reached for her hand again. "I know it's a real hard thing to hear, but I couldn't let you go on thinking it was your fault."

"Mama's dead?" she repeated.

Benjamin nodded again; then he began to explain how he'd driven to Twin Pines and spoken with the neighbor lady. As he told the story, Delia sat there with tears rolling down her cheeks. When there was nothing more to tell, he remained beside her.

Outside there was the sound of chickens squawking and Otis sawing firewood, but inside there was only the muffled sound of sobs and Delia's heart breaking.

DELIA

You can say a thousand times from Sunday Mama dying ain't my fault, but I know better. Me asking her to sneak around Daddy to come and see Isaac broke her heart. Broke it the same as if I stomped on it with my two bare feet. Mama loved me; I know she did. How can any mama not love her own child? Long as I was happy with just getting letters Mama could be happy for me, but when I started wanting more than she could give, her heart started fighting against itself. Mama's heart wanted to come see her grandson, but her body had to do what Daddy said.

The sorry truth is Mama's never been a strong-willed woman. I ain't laying no blame, 'cause I seen the mean-spirited side of Daddy and it's enough to make anybody fearful. He'd be sweet as pie long as Mama was doing what he wanted, but the minute she went up against him he'd start in saying the Lord would smite her dead for such a thing. It didn't matter what she was doing, Daddy'd come up with a Bible verse claiming it was a sin. Even for a woman staunch as a brick wall, it's impossible to go up against a man who claims he's got the Lord on his side.

Losing your mama leaves a hole in your heart that's never gonna be healed. You got one mama, and once she's gone you ain't never gonna get another one. I want to be forgiving of Daddy, but the truth is it's real hard. I keep arguing inside myself. One minute I'm ready to crawl on my hands and knees asking him for forgiveness, then the next minute I'm hating him all over again 'cause of the heartache he's given Mama and me.

59

The saddest part of all this is that I keep wishing I could talk to Mama one last time. I'd ask her how I'm supposed to get over all this hurt. Knowing Mama, she'd have just the right words for answering.

I know I'm a growed-up woman with a child of my own, but Lord God how I do miss Mama.

REVISITING TWIN PINES

D elia remained on the verge of tears for a full two weeks after she heard the news of her mother's death. She went about her household chores, cooked dinner every night and set it on the table, but would do little more than pick at the food on her plate. One question after another popped into her mind, and she prodded Benjamin for details of her mama's death.

"When did it happen?" she'd ask. "How can you say for sure it's true?"

Benjamin answered the questions with little more than a shrug. "All I know is what the woman next door said, and I done told you that word for word."

Delia would give an understanding nod, but less than an hour later she'd think of another question and start in again.

"Why don't you go with me to Twin Pines," Benjamin finally suggested. "By now your daddy might be willing to let bygones be bygones. After all that's happened..."

He left the rest of his words unsaid. It hardly seemed necessary to remind Delia that her daddy's loss was as great as hers.

Delia shook her head. "No," she said sadly, "it's too late for mending fences with Daddy."

At the time it seemed she turned away from the idea, but the suggestion took root in her mind. Before the week was out she told Benjamin going to Twin Pines was a fine idea.

On the following Saturday Delia rose early and dressed in the flowered dress she usually saved for church. She applied a thin coat of rose-colored lipstick and looked back at the mirror. It was good. There was nothing trashy about her appearance, nothing her daddy could find to pick at or criticize. Before anyone else was up, Delia cooked a pot of grits and set a stew to bubbling. If things went as she hoped, they might be late in returning.

It was almost nine when they finally left. Delia toyed with the thought of bringing Isaac to meet his granddaddy, but the fear of what could possibly happen stopped her. She wanted to believe enough time had passed, enough time for forgiveness to set in and soften her daddy's heart, but George Finch was a hard and unrelenting man. Still, even a stone could be worn away by time so there was always a chance. After all, she was his daughter. His only daughter. Surely that counted for something.

When Benjamin turned onto Cross Corner Road Delia said, "I'm not taking no for an answer." The thought was powerful, but her words were small and wobbly at the edges. "It's not gonna be easy," she added, "but I'll tell Daddy it's what Mama would have wanted."

As Benjamin drove, Delia spoke of her childhood. She searched her memory and pulled out stories that pictured the good side of her daddy: the Christmas Eve he carried her home from church on his shoulders; the morning he made her pancakes; the shiny locket he'd given her on her tenth birthday. She said nothing about the all-too-familiar scowl he wore, the demands he made, or the reason why she'd had to sneak out to meet Benjamin. The truth was if you could open up Delia's box of memories, you'd see she was picking at a skimpy handful of good ones and closing a blind eye to all the others.

When they passed through a narrow section of the road where dense thickets of pines changed daylight to dark, Delia gave a wistful sigh.

"If Daddy can keep an open mind I think he'd come to love Isaac." She sat silent for a moment then added, "I brought a picture to show what a fine boy he is."

"That's a real good idea," Benjamin said, but when he looked across to smile at Delia he saw her turned away. A tear slid from her cheek and dropped into her lap.

As they moved past the thicket Benjamin stretched his arm across the seat and covered her hand with his. "You gotta stop crying, or your daddy ain't gonna see nothing but red swelled-up eyes."

They drove the rest of the way in silence.

When they arrived in Twin Pines, Benjamin parked directly in front of the Finch house. Three weeks earlier he'd parked a few doors down, trying not to be obvious. Now he no longer cared whether George Finch recognized his car; his thoughts were only of Delia.

"Are you sure you don't want me to come with you?" he asked for probably the fifth time.

"I'm sure," she answered. "Even if Daddy's forgiving of me, he for sure ain't gonna allow you to step foot in the house."

Benjamin sighed reluctantly. "Okay. But if he raises a hand…"

Delia got out of the car then leaned back in. "Don't worry," she said, then closed the door and started up the walkway.

The first thing she noticed was that the wicker rocking chair her mama sat in was gone from the front porch. Although it had been just six years, it seemed a lifetime ago. Everything felt strange; different in a way she couldn't put a finger to. She rapped on the door and waited.

After nearly twenty minutes of knocking on the door and tapping at the window, Delia decided her daddy was not at home. She returned to the car and said, "I guess we ought to drive over to the church; Daddy must be there."

It was a short drive to the New Unity Church, and when Delia climbed from the car a second time Benjamin repeated his warning. "Be careful."

She didn't answer but moved toward the building with slow deliberate steps. A few seconds after she knocked at the door it swung open. The man standing there was tall and years younger than her daddy.

"I'm looking for Pastor Finch," Delia said.

"Pastor Finch is no longer here," he answered. "I'm Brother Anders. Is there something I can do for you?"

"No longer here?" Delia echoed. "He's the preacher, how could he not be…"

Brother Anders gave a soft smile. "Pastor Finch left Unity two months back."

"Left?" A look of disbelief took hold of Delia's face. "Where'd he go?"

Anders shrugged. "I'm afraid I don't know. He left before I was assigned to the church."

"You're the pastor?"

"Yes." Anders nodded. "If there's anything I can do—"

Delia gave a sad shake of her head. "There's nothing," she said, then turned and walked away. When she got back into the car a stream of tears rolled down her face. It was several minutes before she could pull herself together enough to tell Benjamin what had transpired.

"It's bad enough to not know what happened to Mama," she said, sobbing, "but now Daddy's gone too."

"Maybe one of his friends can say where he is," Benjamin suggested.

"Daddy didn't have friends."

"What about your mama, she have friends?"

Delia pulled a hankie from her purse, wiped back the flow of tears, then blew her nose and nodded.

That afternoon they visited the woman Delia had for many years called Auntie.

Tilly Jessup was a woman with an ample bosom and a face made for smiling. When she saw Delia standing on her doorstep, she pulled the girl into her arms and squealed. "Land's sakes, girl, where you been?"

Before there was time for an answer, Tilly swung the door wide open and motioned the two of them into the house.

"Come on in here," she said. "Sit yourself down, and I'll fetch us some lemonade."

If Tilly knew the circumstances of Delia's marriage to Benjamin, she never let on. She spoke only of how much she'd missed her and how Mary had eagerly shared the news of Delia's baby boy.

"Isaac ain't exactly a baby no more," Delia said. "He's six years old."

Tilly laughed. "Don't you think I know that? Why, your mama read me every letter you wrote. The very same day she got a letter she'd hurry over and read it to me line by line."

"I sent pictures too," Delia said.

"I seen every one of them," Tilly chuckled. "Your mama sure did brag on that boy."

"Then why didn't she want to meet him?"

"What you talking about?"

"I wrote and asked Mama about bringing Isaac to visit, but she never answered."

Tilly wrinkled her brow. "That don't sound right. Mary never mentioned no letter about you wanting to come visit."

"It was early October, not long after Isaac started school. I sent a picture of him showing off his new lunchbox."

"Ah, well." Tilly sighed. "That was after…" She hesitated a moment then said, "Your mama never got that letter."

Tilly left the chair she'd been sitting in and squeezed herself onto the sofa between Benjamin and Delia.

"Sugar," she said, wrapping her arms around Delia, "your mama passed on in September."

Delia buried her face in Tilly's shoulder and cried.

It was several minutes before Tilly spoke again. "I know you got a lot of sorrows inside your heart, but dying is part of living. Sure as a body's born they're gonna die. It's God's plan."

"But why now?" Delia sobbed. "She never even got to know Isaac."

Tilly pulled Delia closer and rubbed her back with gentle strokes. "Your mama surely did know Isaac. She knew him and loved him. All those pictures you sent was the same as coming for a visit. Why, Mary showed me those pictures a hundred or more times and bragged on that boy like he was the smartest ever born."

"Really?"

"Really," Tilly answered and continued to rub her back.

The dusk of evening was settling in the sky when they finally left. Although Delia had wanted to know the circumstances of her mama's death, it brought little comfort to learn she'd collapsed in the backyard and lay there in the scorching hot sun until that evening when George got hungry and went in search of his wife. He found her behind the honeysuckle bush, but by then she was gone. There was no autopsy and no definitive cause of death. Mary Finch was simply a Negro woman who was dead. It was what it was.

According to Tilly, George left town two days after Mary was laid to rest. He took only his clothes, said goodbye to no one, and left no forwarding address.

The following Sunday morning when the parishioners came for church service the pulpit was empty. Brother John led the congregation in the Lord's Prayer and the singing of three hymns; after that everyone went home. No explanation was ever given for George's sudden disappearance. Some said he went back to Ohio where he supposedly had a sister; others said a man's wife dying as she did was reason enough for leaving town and it made no never-mind where he went.

Brother Anders arrived two weeks later. That's when the parsonage house was cleaned and readied for him. Any personal leftovers were removed and passed on to needy families.

As Benjamin drove by what had once been her family's house, Delia buried her face in her hands and tried not to see. Before they'd reached the corner she spread her fingers and took one last look back.

A light lit the room that was once her bedroom.

DELIA

Sometimes I think I haven't got another tear left inside of me. I cried an ocean over these past six years, and now I've come to a point where I'm dried out. I've got no more tears to give. I tell myself, You done cried over everything there is to cry about, and I get to believing I'm never gonna shed another tear.

The thing is that ain't true. I still got a lot of hurt inside, and it's the kind of hurt that don't go away easy. It ain't your head what causes the crying, it's your heart. Heart hurts is something a body can't do a damn thing about.

When we went back to Twin Pines, I figured for sure Daddy would be big enough to forgive and forget. What good can come of carrying a grudge against your own daughter? As we was driving in I pictured him sitting all alone in that big chair, nobody to cook him supper, nobody to give him a goodnight kiss. I was thinking maybe, just maybe, Daddy would ask us to come and live in that nice house the church gave him. Never in a million years did I think he'd leave without so much as a goodbye.

Daddy's supposed to be a godly man, but the truth is Benjamin's ten times more godly than Daddy. He got a heart filled with love and he got a soul filled with kindness. Even when he's so tired his legs could fall off, he still got strength enough to do a kindness for Daddy Church. It ain't the preaching what makes a man godly, it's the doing.

I thank the good Lord for Benjamin. This ain't an easy life, but one thing I know for sure: he ain't never gonna turn his back on our boy. Knowing that makes up for a whole lot of doing without.

THE SADNESS OF BAKERSTOWN

Once they returned home from Twin Pines Delia became as dry and sorrowful as a dead tree. She seldom gave voice to her thoughts but kept picturing her mama lying dead in the hot sun.

"This Alabama heat is too much for anyone," she'd say. "It's likely Mama died of sunstroke."

In February a cold spell came through, and even though there was a morning frost on the windowpanes Delia still complained about the heat of the sun.

"We ought to think about moving north," she said, then slid into stories of the time when her family had lived in Ohio. "They got nice cool evenings in Ohio and winters where a person can see real snow!"

"Yeah," Benjamin answered, "and they also got a short growing season."

For the past five years Benjamin had made a good living with year-round crops, so Delia couldn't argue the point. Still, that didn't lessen her growing dislike of Alabama.

A few days later she began talking about how the schools were better.

"There's places where coloreds go to school same as whites," she said. "Whites in the morning, coloreds in the afternoon. Same school, same exact seats."

"I find that hard to believe," Benjamin said and turned away.

When Delia persisted, he flat out said that he and Otis had gotten the farm to where it was earning a good living and he wasn't leaving—not for weather, not for schools, and certainly not because Delia now had a suspicion her daddy may have gone back to Ohio.

"He ain't a man worth chasing after," Benjamin said, and that was the end of it.

On the Saturday after Valentine's Day Benjamin and Otis took Isaac with them when they went to work in the north field, but a rainstorm came up and Benjamin told the boy to get back to the house. When Isaac slammed through the door, Delia was sitting on the sofa dabbing tears from her eyes.

"What's the matter, Mama?" he asked.

Startled, she looked up and sniffed the tears to a stop. "It's nothing. I was just crying over old times."

He slid onto the sofa and wriggled his way under her arm. "Why? Is old times bad?"

"Sometimes," Delia answered, "but sometimes it was good. Back in the days when me and Mama could talk and laugh together, it was real good."

"If it was good then why you crying?"

"'Cause with Mama gone and Daddy gone, I feel like an orphan."

"What's an orphan?"

"Somebody who got nobody, no family."

"You got me," Isaac said. "Ain't I family?"

Delia looked down at the earnestness in his six-year-old face and smiled. She hugged him to her chest and laughed out loud. It was the first time in months she'd laughed, and the sound seemed to ricochet off the walls and grow bigger in size.

"Yes, Isaac, you surely are family," she said. "I got you and I got your daddy and Grandpa Church." She squeezed him a bit closer and whispered, "Thank you for reminding me."

By the time Benjamin and Otis came from the fields cold and soaked to the skin, Delia had a tray of hot biscuits sitting on the stove and chicken frying in a pan. She'd also scattered pictures of Isaac throughout every room of the house.

From that day forward whenever the image of her mama came to mind, she'd grab a picture of Isaac and go back to counting her blessings instead of her losses.

The winter of 1953 brought forth a bountiful harvest, and in the spring when they sold a cartload of cabbage and turnips Benjamin claimed they had enough money to replace the car with a pickup truck.

"I hate to let this car go," Delia said. "It reminds me of our good times."

Benjamin smiled. "Yep, them is sweet memories for sure. But we ain't getting rid of them, just the car."

"Thing is," Otis added, "memories can't pull a wagon. Henry's getting on in years and can't haul a full load."

What Otis said was true. The mule was past twenty and slower than ever.

Twin Pines, while it was considerably larger than Grinder's Corner, was still a small town. The automobile dealers were in Bakerstown.

The mention of Bakerstown caused Delia to think about the signs she'd seen in windows.

"I've no need to go," she told Benjamin. "You and Daddy Church pick out whatever you think best."

"I got things to do," Otis said. "Benjamin don't need no old man tagging along. You young folks go and have yourselves some fun."

"Can I come too?" Isaac asked.

Before Delia could say she didn't think that was such a good idea, Benjamin had already answered yes.

With bad roads and a cranky car, the drive to Bakerstown took more than two hours. As they drove Benjamin whistled a happy tune, and Isaac chattered about seeing a real city. Neither of them noticed how Delia fidgeted and twisted in her seat.

"Let's not dally over this," she said. "I got things to do at home."

"Work can wait," Benjamin replied happily. "You're in need of a day out."

"We gonna buy a new truck, Daddy?" Isaac asked.

Benjamin laughed. "I don't think we can afford a brand new one."

"Can we afford a store-bought ice cream?"

"Yep," Benjamin said, chuckling, "ice cream and maybe even a nice dinner for you and your mama."

Delia wanted to say she was not the least bit interested in staying for dinner, but with Isaac excited as he was she hadn't the heart.

There were three automobile dealers in Bakerstown. At the first one Benjamin parked the car on the street, and they walked across to the lot. When they headed toward a green pickup, an older man came from the office.

"You want something?" he asked.

"Yes, sir," Benjamin nodded. "I'm looking to buy a used pickup. Don't matter if it needs work."

"You got cash?" the man asked.

"Some. I'm figuring to trade in the car I got and pay the difference."

The salesman pointed a finger at the car on the street. "That yours?"

"Yes, sir," Benjamin answered.

He scowled. "That thing's more 'n twenty-five years old. I ain't in the junk business."

Benjamin was going to explain the car was in decent running condition, but by then the salesman had turned back toward the office building.

The second dealership was pretty much a repeat of the first, and the third only handled new cars.

"Try Peter's," the salesman said, "they might have something."

Peter's was not a dealership; it was a used car lot on the back side of town about two blocks from where they'd bought the sewing machine. Peter's was willing to take the trade in and had a 1941 Chevrolet pickup that was affordable and in reasonably good shape. They went back and forth on price a few times, then shook hands on the deal.

As the Church family drove crosstown in the new pickup, Isaac reminded Benjamin of his promise. "You gonna get that ice cream now, Daddy?"

"You bet," Benjamin said. "Keep a sharp eye out for the ice cream store."

Delia looked across at Benjamin and mouthed the words *I don't want him seeing those signs.* There was an exclamation point in the glare she gave him.

"Tell you what," Benjamin said to the boy, "I know a real good place just outside of town with barbeque and ice cream. How about we go there?"

Isaac was smiling ear to ear when he answered yes.

As far as Delia was concerned, they couldn't leave Bakerstown fast enough.

The barbeque place was a roadside stand eight miles outside of town. Delia and Isaac sat at the outside table while Benjamin went in for food. He came back with three paper plates piled high with chicken drumsticks in a thick red sauce.

"This is gonna be the best you ever tasted," he said smiling.

As he tore into a piece of chicken, Delia nibbled at bits of coleslaw. It was good to see Benjamin so happy, but she couldn't shake loose the hurt settling into her stomach. Trips to Bakerstown made her feel dirty, the kind of dirty that didn't wash off. The same dirty she'd felt when her daddy called her a whore. In Twin Pines there were only a handful of whites, so the shop windows were without signs saying "No Coloreds." But in Bakerstown the signs were everywhere. They were like one great big giant finger pointing you out as something trashy.

"I hate coming here," she grumbled.

"Why?" Benjamin asked. "Isaac and me likes the food."

"Not here," she said, "Bakerstown." Delia chewed on her lip for a moment and focused her eyes on a crack in the table; then she added, "Bakerstown treats Negros like they're dirt."

Benjamin knew without asking she was thinking back on the sewing machine incident. "Aw, Delia, you gotta stop thinking this way. Those people got their ways, and we got ours."

"I don't see any No Whites signs in Grinder's Corner."

Benjamin gave Delia a hard look. "It ain't good for Isaac to hear that stuff."

"Maybe not," she said, "but if we was living in New York or Ohio, he'd be eating in a fine restaurant instead of a barbeque stand."

"I like barbeque," Isaac said.

Delia forced a weak little laugh. "I can see that."

When there was nothing but a pile of chicken bones left on the table, they climbed into the new pickup and started home. They'd driven for a good twenty minutes when Benjamin finally gave voice to what he'd been thinking.

"In case you ain't heard," he said, "there ain't a whole lot of farms in New York City."

"You don't got to be a farmer," Delia said. "You could be a mechanic. You know how to fix engines, and there's always a need for that."

Benjamin didn't answer, and she said nothing more. It was neither the first nor last time they had this discussion.

There were times—days, weeks and sometimes even months—when the subject never came up, but the thought was always there in the back of Delia's mind. It was like a boil that would fester and pop open, then start festering all over again. When something triggered the thought, she'd dream of being back in Ohio in the small town where her daddy was a respected preacher and no one looked down their nose at her. When Isaac carried home schoolbooks with torn and missing pages she'd remember the schoolhouse she'd attended, one where students had their own desk and books with hardly any wear. When she tired of dreaming of Ohio, she'd switch to New York City and imagine streets lined with stone buildings and rows of fancy shops where she could wander in and out free as a bird.

Once when Benjamin heard Delia telling Isaac about life in other cities, he laughed out loud. "How long you gonna keep filling the boy's head with those fairytales? 'Specially since you know they ain't true."

"Long as it takes," Delia answered. "Long as it takes for him to know every place ain't like Bakerstown." She turned back to Isaac and continued her tale of a toy store that stood five floors high. As he sat there with a wide-eyed expression of wonderment she said, "That's bigger than the bank in Bakerstown."

Isaac gasped. "Really?"

"Not really," Benjamin said. "Your mama's making all this stuff up. She ain't never even been to one of those big cities."

"Maybe not," Delia answered, "but I know others what's been there."

"Who?" Benjamin challenged.

"Mister Paul Robeson, for one."

Benjamin laughed. "I ain't believing that for one second. You ain't never even seen him."

Delia squeezed her brows together and looked up.

"I have so," she said indignantly. "He come through Ohio once, and I saw him singing. I was standing close enough to reach out and touch his shoes."

"Touch his shoes?" Benjamin said. "Why, that ain't knowing somebody."

Delia turned off in a huff. "You're just saying that 'cause you wasn't there. Them shoes had magic. I know 'cause I saw it. They was so sparkly and shiny, you could see your own face if you looked close."

"Aw, nonsense," Benjamin said. "You was just a starry-eyed teenager what don't know magic from boot shine."

Isaac followed the back and forth of the conversation and was squarely in Delia's corner. "I'd like seeing those shiny shoes," he said. "And I'd like seeing all those big toy stores in New York City."

"I thought you was gonna be a farmer like Daddy," Benjamin teased, and then he laughed like it was the funniest thing ever. Doubled over laughing as he was, he didn't see the sadness stretched across Delia's face.

But Otis did.

THE KNOWLEDGE OF WHAT WAS

For two days Otis thought about the conversation he'd overheard. There was a part of him that wanted to help and another part that knew not to meddle in other people's business. He thought about it long and hard, but the question remained: was it meddling if you were trying to help someone you love?

On the third day when Benjamin went to work in the field, Otis stayed behind. While Delia was mixing up cornbread, he came and sat at the kitchen table.

"I got something bothering me," he said, "and I'm hoping you ain't gonna be mad if an old man speaks his mind."

Delia turned with a smile. "Daddy Church, you ain't never said a mean word in all your life. Just say what you got to say."

He sat there for a moment, fidgeting with his fingers and squirming to find a comfortable spot in the seat.

"Well," he finally drawled, "I know a man's got no right listening to other folks' private business, but I couldn't help hearing you and Benjamin talk about Bakerstown."

"Oh." Delia's smile turned edgy, not quite angry but teetering on the verge.

"Now, don't get riled up," Otis said. "I'm thinking you is both part right and part wrong."

"Part wrong?" Delia repeated. "What'd I say part wrong?"

"It ain't so much the words what was wrong, it's what you got no knowledge of."

"Oh?" Delia left the batter half-mixed and sat in the chair across from Otis.

"Benjamin acting as he does is 'cause of things he don't talk about."

"He tells me everything," Delia cut in.

"Benjamin don't tell nobody about when he was in the army. Oh, he might talk about those last two years, but he don't say nothing about the first two."

Delia fixed her eyes on Otis's face and waited for the words to come.

"There was a time when Benjamin was like you. He figured he'd step up and be all God intended, then white folks would see him same as equal. It was a hard lesson when he come to know that ain't how it is."

"What happened?"

"He joined the Army Air Forces. It was a short while before the Japs bombed our boys in Pearl Harbor. He walked all the way to Bakerstown and signed up."

"There's nothing wrong with that," Delia said.

"It wasn't 'cause he joined, it was 'cause he joined thinking he'd get to learn all about airplanes and maybe be a pilot."

"Didn't he?"

"No, ma'am. Them first two years only thing he did was scrub toilets and clean mess halls."

"That doesn't sound right," Delia said. "Benjamin told me he worked on engines."

"He did, but it was cars 'n trucks. Even that didn't happen until after he met Sergeant Callaghan. Ed Callaghan was a white man from Baltimore. One night he come back to the base drunk as a skunk and puked all over the place. Benjamin cleaned up the mess and got Callaghan into his bunk so nobody was ever the wiser. Two days later Callaghan pulled Benjamin out of the colored duty pool and sent him to mechanic training."

Delia eyed Otis suspiciously. "How'd you come to know this?"

"Benjamin used t' send his mama a letter most every day. Him and Lila was like you and Isaac, close as peas in a pod."

"Then he ought to understand why I want Isaac—"

Otis shook his head sadly. "Oh, he knows the love you got for that boy, he just don't want him to grow up expecting too much outta life."

"But if Isaac don't know there's a better life, how can he expect—"

Otis stopped Delia mid-sentence. "See, that's the problem. When somebody's thinking the best will happen and they get the worst, they's sad clear down to their toes. But if they ain't expecting nothing but bad and good comes along, they got cause to celebrate. It can be the very same thing, but if they's happy or sad depends on which side they is seeing it from."

"What you talking about?"

"When Benjamin went off to the army he was thinking he'd maybe get to be a pilot, flying one of those big bomber planes, but the best he ever got was being a mechanic and that made his heart sad. If he'd gone in expecting to clean toilet bowls, he'd' been real happy for the chance to be a mechanic."

"Oh." Delia leaned forward. "But he did get to be a mechanic, and that's something to be proud of."

Otis nodded. "True enough. But it was a big step down from being a pilot, and that's what hurt Benjamin's heart. After that he stopped expecting so much and started being thankful for what he got."

"But Daddy Church, it ain't fair."

"It sure ain't."

"The money we got is the same as white folks' money, so why those stores gotta have signs saying we can't go in?"

"Plenty of them folks in Bakerstown is getting through by the skin of their teeth. They is like a small toad sitting in a small pond. They ain't none too crazy about being a small toad, so looking down their nose at us makes 'em feel like they is a bigger toad"

"That's silly," Delia said. "If we was to go in the store and spend money they'd be richer, and ain't that like being bigger?"

Otis laughed. "That ain't their way of thinking. They is happy being a look-down-your-nose small toad."

Delia sat and talked with Otis for nearly two hours, but when Benjamin came in nothing more was said. From that point on Delia weighed her words as she told stories of what could be. She held off promising Isaac he'd be treated exactly like a white man and focused on saying how there were plenty of Negro doctors, teachers, and even entertainers.

"Being a Negro ain't a bad thing," she told him, "it's just different."

More than once Benjamin overheard her say Isaac shouldn't go through life expecting too much. Hearing such advice gladdened his heart, but he never knew how it came about. Otis said nothing about their conversation, and neither did Delia

As that year rolled into the next, Delia began staying at home whenever Benjamin had to go into Bakerstown. She'd claim she had washing to do, or she'd pull out the quilt she was working on and start stitching another patch. On occasion Isaac went along, but Delia tried to discourage it. He was still a boy, she reasoned; there'd be time enough to discover the ugliness of life.

DELIA

I *t's funny how you think you know a man clear down to his soul,* *when the God's honest truth is you don't know a bean about* *what's inside his head. I always figured Benjamin was an easy sort* *because of how he didn't fight my daddy back and didn't get riled over* *them damn signs. I never dreamed there was a time he was different.*

I can see now, Benjamin's a lot like Daddy Church. They's both proud men. Too proud, maybe, to show their heartache.

Daddy Church don't never talk about missing Benjamin's mama, but he got a little picture sitting alongside his bed and every night I see him whispering stuff to that picture. The thing is he don't look sad when he's talking to the picture; it looks almost like he's saying how much he still loves her. You can bet my daddy didn't do that when Mama died.

Sometimes I feel bad because Isaac don't have the things I had when I was growing up, but when I see all the love Daddy Church has for Benjamin and Benjamin has for Isaac, I know he's way better off. Having a daddy who loves you is a lot more important than having schoolbooks with no ripped pages.

Benjamin is a good daddy and when poor Miss Lila was alive, he was a good son.

He cared enough to send his mama a letter most every day, and there ain't many who can say that. The truth is if I had to choose for Isaac to be more like my daddy or his I'd choose his, even if it means being a farmer.

HARD TIMES

For two years the land Benjamin farmed produced a bountiful harvest in both summer and winter. During the years of plenty they came to believe it would always be that way, and Delia seldom voiced her thoughts of moving north. When she did it was little more than a passing comment.

Otis, now fifty-nine, had developed a limp that caused him to lean heavily on his right leg. On good days he could work two, maybe three hours in the field, but by then he'd have a sharp pain shooting up his leg and crossing into his back. When Benjamin saw his daddy wincing, he'd insist Otis go back to the house.

"I don't like the thought of Delia being alone all the time," he'd say, making the request seem more a favor than pity. When that ploy didn't work he'd find a dozen different reasons why Otis was needed at the house—the screen door needed fixing, the pump was leaky, the smokehouse fire was too low.

That's how it was; Benjamin fabricated excuses and Otis pretended to believe them regardless of how thin or frail they were. It was an arrangement that gave each a measure of pride without one taking from the other.

Most days when Otis limped back to the house, Delia would spot him coming and have a steaming cup of coffee waiting. For hours on end they'd sit side by side on the porch and talk. They never again spoke of Benjamin's days in the army, but they spoke of everything else and Delia came to love Daddy Church in much the same way she loved Benjamin and Isaac. He was family and in a softer, less sandpapery way he filled the empty spot left by her own daddy.

A bitter cold frost hit Alabama in January of 1954, and it lasted until early March. That spring the harvest was small enough to be considered puny. The cabbages grew to the size of a baseball and never got any larger. The turnips survived the frost but brought in barely enough money to buy seed for the summer planting.

"We got nothing to worry about," Benjamin said and assured Delia that the summer harvest would more than make up for what was lost.

At times it seemed like summer had forgotten about Alabama, but when it finally arrived it roared in with a vengeance. In just a handful of days the temperature zoomed from a cool 60 degrees to well over 90, and the sun baked the ground until it was so hot you couldn't walk across the road without having your feet blistered.

Alabamans could generally expect a thunderstorm to pass through in the evening and cool the heat of day, but for the entire month of July there was not a drop of rain. After the first two weeks Benjamin began to draw water from the well and carry it to the fields. He climbed from the bed and started work three hours before dawn. While the sky was still too dark for a man to see where he was walking, Benjamin worked his way through the rows by counting the number of steps he'd taken. When the sun moved high in the sky he stopped carrying buckets of water and sat on the porch, but after an hour or two of rest he was back at it.

When Delia saw Benjamin nearing exhaustion, she and Isaac both began to help. They used anything that would hold water: cleaning buckets, cooking pots, jars even. Otis, whose leg was worse than ever, stayed behind to help draw water from the well and fill the jars. There were any number of times Delia was tempted to tell Benjamin that if they'd move north he could be working as a mechanic and wouldn't have to be carrying buckets of water, but she held her tongue. When a man had that much worry strapped to his back, it seemed cruel to add another brick.

The heat of July moved into August, and still there was no rain. Twice they saw lightning flash across the sky and heard thunder boom with such ferocity it shook the house, but then there was nothing. Benjamin stood on the porch waiting and watching.

"Please, God," he prayed, but still the rain never materialized. It was the kind of summer where rain thundered down on one farm and then bypassed the one next to it.

On a morning in late August, Benjamin lowered the bucket into the well and waited. It was several seconds before he heard the splash. The water table was low. Too low. They could live without a lot of things, but they couldn't live without water. He dipped a tin cup into the bucket of water, took a long drink, and then poured the remainder of the water back into the well. There would be no more watering of crops.

When Delia rose that morning she found Benjamin sitting on the porch step. Seeing the sorrowful way his head was buried in his hands, she asked, "What's wrong?"

"The well's running dry," he said. There was no need for further explanation; anyone who lived in Grinder's Corner knew what a dry well meant.

Once Benjamin could no longer carry water to the fields, he sat on the porch looking to the sky then looking back at the stalks of corn. They were half the size they should have been and leaning over like a man ready to die. Sometimes Benjamin prayed; other times he shouted angry curses at the God who would deny him rain.

In the third week of August it came. Benjamin was inside the house when he first heard the thunder, but by then he'd given up hoping.

"Sounds like we're gonna get a storm," Otis said.

Benjamin grunted. It was neither a confirmation nor denial; it was simply a grunt of annoyance. Too many times he'd been disappointed. Too many times he'd prayed for rain and gotten no answer.

"This one sounds real close," Delia added.

Benjamin remained at the table drinking his coffee.

Moments later the downpour started.

The rain came in huge sheets of water that were too much for the baked-dry ground to absorb. A small portion soaked through, but much of it ran off and created puddles in low-lying areas. Although the downpour did little to restore the crops it replenished the well, for which Benjamin was thankful.

That summer there was no harvest. Benjamin pulled the dead corn stalks from the ground and plowed the fields under. In the years of abundance he'd set aside a bit of money, and he took it from the jar saying he was going to buy seed for the winter planting. When a look of worry settled on Delia's face he assured her things had to get better.

"Money's a bit tight now," he said, "but come next summer we'll be fine."

Delia could no longer hold back. "Rain ain't something you can swear to," she said and once again brought up the thought of moving north.

Benjamin moved toward her, his expression not one of anger but resignation. He wrapped his muscular arms around her and said, "Delia, sugar, I loves you more 'n anything else in this world, but I still ain't gonna leave here. Grinder's Corner may not be much, but it's where I was born and where I'm gonna die."

When he kissed her full on the lips, Delia felt the depth of love he offered and she knew this was where she also would die. Her love for Benjamin outweighed her hatred of Grinder's Corner.

It was the last time she ever mentioned moving.

BAD LUCK YEARS

For the next two years bad luck clung to Grinder's Corner like a devil with razor sharp claws. The weather was hot and dry all summer, and the rain skipped over the struggling farms like they weren't worth wasting water on. Left with few options, a number of farmers gave up trying to scratch a living out of the dry dirt and left town. Some went west, believing Louisiana had to be better; others went north claiming that at least the mountains of Tennessee would be a bit cooler. Tom Burns, a man who'd been friends with Benjamin since they were in grade school, left town with his wife, Sarah, and all five kids but never said a word of goodbye to anyone, so there was no telling where he'd gone.

After Benjamin watched the second field of corn wither and die for lack of water, he was weary of farming. If Delia had picked that moment to ask about moving north he might have packed up and gone, but she never again mentioned it.

When the money he'd set aside ran out, Benjamin drove into Bakerstown and began rapping on the back doors of white folks asking if they had handyman work that needed to be done.

Emma Burnett was the first to say yes. She was certain a raccoon had gotten into her attic and was willing to pay a dollar if Benjamin could chase the critter out and repair any damage that was done. Even though it was poor pay for such a task, Benjamin did it and collected the dollar.

Day after day he continued to knock on doors and ask for work, and in time he became known as a dependable worker. Emma told Susie

Watkins that Benjamin would be a good man to trim the apple trees in her yard. Then Susie, pleased with what he'd done, began to spread the word. Before the end of summer Benjamin had work enough to fill his days.

He left the farm before sunrise and returned after dark, but the money he made was enough to keep food on the table and pay for the things they needed. Each week he set a small amount aside thinking that next year he'd try planting another crop.

With Benjamin gone all day, Delia's days were long and weighted with emptiness. Although she'd sit for hours on end talking with Daddy Church, she grew restless. On a Saturday when Otis remained in bed because his leg was bothering him something fierce, she sat on the porch with a glass of lukewarm coffee and looked across the flat land. Without the fields of corn fluttering in the breeze it was nothing but brown dirt for as far as she could see. Delia pulled out the bottle of red nail polish Benjamin had brought from town and painted her toes, but once that was done there was nothing else to look forward to.

She called out for Isaac who was off playing with a dog that at one time belonged to the Burns family.

"Yeah, Mama," he answered and came from behind the house.

"Ain't you tired of playing with that ole dog?" she laughed.

Isaac tossed a yellow ball across the yard, and the dog went after it. "Well, there ain't nothing else to do."

Delia smiled. "What if we was to go visit Luella Jackson and her boy, Jerome?"

"That'd be real good," he answered, "except Daddy took the car, and we got no way to get there."

"Ain't we got feet?"

"Yeah, but that's a far ways for walking."

"It's far," Delia said. "Too far for Daddy Church maybe, but not too far for you and me."

"Really?"

Delia smiled. "Really."

She darted inside and told Otis they were going down the road to visit neighbors.

"We'll be a while," she said. "You gonna be okay while we're gone?"

Otis nodded. "I'll be jest fine. Go have yourself some fun."

The Jackson house was more than five miles away, but with a fair bit of eagerness and a snappy step they were there before lunchtime. Delia had taken a liking to Luella, and her having a boy Isaac's age made it doubly nice. While the boys played the women sat on the porch sipping sweet tea and trading stories. Like Benjamin, Will Jackson went off to work each day and like Delia, Luella enjoyed having someone to talk to.

When it got close to four o'clock and Delia said she had to be going, Luella begged her to come again.

She did.

It got to be a regular thing. Delia and Isaac would walk the five miles to the Jackson house at least once a week, and on occasion as often as three times. They also began visiting the other neighbors, the ones who'd been guests at the barbeque. Twice they arrived at a house where they'd expected to find the yard filled with youngsters and instead found the place abandoned. At the Barker house the door was unlocked, but inside there was nothing except a three-legged chair and a broken broom.

That day Delia sat on the step of what was once the Barker porch and cried.

"Lord God," she moaned, "have you no mercy?"

The walk home was long and sad. Delia had been fond of Cissy Barker, and it was heartbreaking to think the family could be without a place to call home. She snuggled Isaac close to her and told him how lucky he was to have a daddy like Benjamin.

"Your daddy works real hard so we can stay in our house and have a good place to live," she said, and the funny thing was she meant it. Two years back when things were good, Delia believed the world outside Grinder's Corner offered untold opportunities. Now with work scarce and times hard, she feared the outside world could be worse yet. Any thoughts she'd had of moving were gone.

In the early days Benjamin believed he'd go back to farming, but with long work hours and traveling back and forth to Bakerstown the weeks turned into months and the months became seasons that disappeared in the blink of an eye. In early March he spoke of putting in summer corn, and when that planting season passed he thought of winter cabbages or parsnips. Before long one year became two and everyone settled into the way of life that was, so he sold the tractor.

"It needs work," he reasoned, but the truth was Benjamin had lost the image of the farm he'd once planned.

He could no longer close his eyes and imagine fields of corn stretching out for as far as the eye could see. Now when he closed his eyes he saw fences that needed painting, trees that needed trimming, and gate hinges waiting to be replaced. It seemed an odd coincidence that at a time when Delia no longer argued for leaving the farm, Benjamin no longer cared about staying.

In June of that second summer, on a day when Benjamin had gone off earlier than usual, Otis sat at the kitchen table complaining that the pain in his back had traveled around to his side.

"I don't gotta go to Luella's today," Delia said. "If you're feeling poorly I can stay here and fix you up a nice hot mustard plaster."

Otis shook his head. "Ain't no mustard plaster gonna fix what's ailing me."

"And just what's that?" Delia asked.

"Too many years of living," Otis chuckled. "A man gets to where he done outlived his usefulness, then—"

"Daddy Church, don't you dare talk that way!" Delia said angrily. "You got more usefulness than a man half your age."

He laughed again. "Delia Church, you is one sweet woman."

Although Delia said half a dozen times she'd be happy to stay and care for Otis, he was insistent she go.

"I need me some peace and quiet," he said. "So take that young'un and do your chattering elsewhere."

A short while later she and Isaac left the house and started toward Cross Corner Road. They were almost to the turn off when Delia got a strange feeling in the pit of her stomach.

"We gotta go back home," she said. "Daddy Church ain't looking too good."

"I thought we was gonna visit with Jerome," Isaac said.

"We ain't going nowhere if Daddy Church is sick." Delia whirled on her heel and started back toward the house.

Isaac reluctantly followed. "Granddaddy looked fine to me," he grumbled.

"Yeah, well, you is ten years old and ain't in charge."

When they got back to the house Otis was sound asleep on the sofa. Delia walked over to where he was lying and listened for the sound of his breath. She stood there for a moment then smiled.

"See," Isaac grumped, "you made me miss out on a fine day of playing for no reason."

"It weren't for no reason," Delia said. "It was on account of loving Daddy Church."

DELIA

*I*t don't matter how old or how young you are, everybody needs somebody to watch over them. Me and Benjamin got each other but Daddy Church, all he's got is a faded little picture.

Benjamin's his boy, true enough, but once your boy gets married he got his own family. He's not really your boy no more; he's some woman's husband. That's just how life is. Right now me and Benjamin got Isaac to watch out for, but when Isaac grows up and marries off he ain't gonna have responsibility for watching over us, he's gonna have responsibility for his own family.

Boys outgrow their daddy, but girls is different. Girls don't ever outgrow needing a daddy to watch over them. Daddy Church knows that, and he treats me good as if he was my own true daddy.

When my baby girl died Benjamin was busy watching over me, but Daddy Church went and carved out a coffin for that tiny baby. On the top of that pinewood box he cut a little heart. It was like he put a piece of hisself in there to watch over our baby. I ain't never gonna forget that.

He thinks I can't see when he makes a face from hurting, but I see plenty. I'd like to say, Let me take care of you, Daddy Church, but I can't 'cause he's too proud a man to be accepting pity.

I been praying and asking the Lord to watch over him, but the thing with praying is that you don't always get what you're asking for.

THE END OF A GENERATION

Otis died the second week of September.

The week prior Delia never left the house because she feared he wasn't looking well, but those days passed uneventfully. Otis ate breakfast, then napped on the sofa for most of the day. With Otis sleeping and Isaac off at school, Delia was left to face the long days of emptiness alone. She cleaned everything that need to be cleaned, drank cup after cup of coffee, and sewed several more patches for the quilt she was making, but she missed having someone to talk with.

"Go visiting," Otis said, "and quit fussing over me like I'm a dying man."

"I ain't going nowhere 'til I see you looking chipper."

"Ha," Otis laughed. "You wait for a man of my years to get chipper, and you for sure ain't going nowhere."

Nothing more was said that day, but by Tuesday of the following week Delia could no longer stand the thought of another day filled with the sound of silence. Visiting Luella Jackson was an all-day thing, but if she walked down to Bessie Mae's house she'd be back before Otis woke from his nap.

"Daddy Church," she said, "you mind if I take a jar of my apple jelly down to Bessie Mae?" Before he could answer she added, "Bessie's house ain't but a few minutes down the road."

The truth was it took twenty minutes to walk to Bessie's, but Delia figured she'd step lively and be there in half the time.

When Otis said for her to go and quit worrying about him, she left.

Once she got to Bessie's they settled in and Bessie, who was a talker to begin with, had a truckload of gossip. Delia intended to stay for an hour, two at the most, but as they sat on the porch enjoying ham sandwiches and sweet tea she lost track of the time. It was well into the afternoon when their conversation was interrupted by a gust of wind ripping through the trees.

"Looks like we're gonna get a rainstorm," Bessie said. "We better get inside."

"Unh-unh," Delia said. "I got to get going. Daddy Church is there all by hisself, and he ain't doing so good."

Without staying long enough to finish her tea, Delia lit out. She headed for the road walking as fast as her feet would move. As she was about to turn onto Cross Corner Road, a crack of thunder rolled through the sky and rattled her bones.

"Oh, Lord," she moaned, already regretting that she hadn't left sooner.

Delia rounded the corner and broke into a run, but before she'd gone half a mile the rain started. It came in torrents with a sharp wind slicing through the trees, smacking against her face then circling back and coming at her from behind. It wasn't just a rainstorm, it was a mean storm, the kind where lightning tears across the sky in search of something to destroy.

In Alabama rainstorms happen in a heartbeat. Wind comes from nowhere, and pellets of water materialize from what was moments earlier a clear blue sky. Delia heard the roll of thunder and saw the lightning bolt that slammed into a long leaf pine. It came crashing to the ground. The lightning was close, somewhere not far behind her. She lowered her head and pushed against the wind. Twice she lost her footing and came down hard on her knee. The second time she'd scrambled up with mud covering the front of her dress. As she turned onto the road that ran past their house Delia heard a second tree fall, this one closer than the first.

When she finally reached the house Delia was soaked through to her skin. Without stopping to remove her waterlogged shoes, she pushed open the door and looked for Otis. He was still right there on the sofa where she'd left him.

"Thank you, Jesus," she mumbled, then stepped out of the wet shoes. When she bent to tell him that she'd arrived home safe, Delia saw he was no longer breathing. His skin was still warm, but he was lifeless as the trees that had fallen.

"Wake up, Daddy Church!" she screamed. "Wake up!"

She grabbed his shoulder and shook it as hard as she could. After a few minutes of hollering and pounding on his chest, she pulled Otis' frail body into her arms.

"Don't do this, Daddy Church, please don't do this!" she wailed, then fell to her knees alongside the sofa. She held his hand in hers and cried as she had cried the night her baby girl died.

When Isaac got home two hours later she sat beside Otis, emptied out of tears.

"Your granddaddy died," she said. Her words were raw and riddled with sadness.

"Granddaddy died?" Isaac repeated, and tears began to well in his eyes. He dropped down beside his mama and wrapped a skinny arm around her shoulder.

"I's sorry, Mama," he said. "I's sorry for you 'n for poor Granddaddy too."

"You can be sorry for me all you want," Delia answered, "but don't be sorry for your granddaddy. He's gone to be with the Lord."

Benjamin didn't get home until nine o'clock that evening, and by then Delia had washed Otis head to toe and dressed him in his Sunday shirt and pants. He was lying in his own bed looking peaceful as a sleeping baby.

Two days later Otis was buried in the Negro cemetery on the far edge of Grinder's Corner. He was laid in a pine box that Benjamin himself built. Even though it rained again that day, a crowd of people came. They gathered graveside and spoke of what a fine man Otis Church was.

"This is no time to be grieving," Brother Albert proclaimed. "This is a time for rejoicing, because Brother Otis is resting peacefully in the arms of the Lord."

Despite anything Brother Albert said Delia couldn't muster up even the smallest bit of rejoicing. Otis was gone, and as far as she was concerned that was pure misery.

CLOAK OF SORROW

In the weeks and months that followed, Delia wore her sorrow like a heavy grey cloak wrapped around her shoulders. She gave up visiting friends and moved through the days like a snail without purpose.

Although Benjamin's pain was equal in size he carried it differently; he worked longer hours and heavier jobs. When his back throbbed from lifting stacks of lumber or lying in a cramped crawl space, he could focus on the physical pain and momentarily forget the anguish tearing at his heart.

Five days after Otis was buried, on an evening when Benjamin came home with his hands bloody from working on the barbed wire horse enclosure at the Paley place, he once again brought up the thought of leaving Grinder's Corner.

After Isaac was in bed he told Delia, "If you're still thinking we ought to leave here, I'm willing."

Delia shook her head. "I ain't wanting to leave no more," she said sadly. "This place is all I got left of Daddy Church."

"But," Benjamin stammered, "what about Isaac?"

"Isaac's fine here."

"You said if we go north—"

"I know what I said, Benjamin," she answered, "but I changed my mind."

"You got thoughts about maybe changing it back again?"

"Not right now I ain't," Delia answered. "Not right now."

The sad truth was living in Grinder's Corner settled into a person's soul like a disease handed down from generation to generation. Folks were born here, lived here, then died here, and there were few exceptions. Delia was once a newcomer and as such she'd had a chance for escape, but that time was long gone. When Otis left this earth, Delia willingly picked up his shackles and slipped them onto her own ankles.

"Well, if you do change your mind," Benjamin said, "let me know."

Delia pretended not to hear.

For nearly six months she went through her days acting as if Otis was there resting comfortably in his bed or napping on the sofa. She washed and ironed his clothes, then stacked them on the same shelf he always used. More often than not, she'd absent-mindedly set a fourth place at the dinner table and not bother to correct the mistake. Not once did she leave the house: not to go visiting, not to go into town, not to go to church, and definitely not to accompany Benjamin into Bakerstown.

"You ought to at least go to church," Benjamin told her, but Delia claimed there was no need since God evidently wasn't listening.

"I prayed every day," she said, "and He still let Daddy Church die."

A week before Christmas Benjamin cut down a small pine, carried it home, and stood it in the front room. It sat there without a single decoration until Isaac started making snowflake cutouts to hang from the branches.

Sitting there at the table and working alone, he said, "It don't hardly feel like Christmas."

Delia saw the tears welling in his eyes and felt a sense of shame creep over her.

"You're right, Isaac," she said, "and I'm real sorry about that." She sat beside him, and for the rest of that afternoon they made snowflakes and a string of paper angels.

That night Delia told Benjamin while he was in Bakerstown to buy Isaac a brand new baseball mitt, some comic books, and a bag of candy.

"Brand new?" Benjamin exclaimed. "That's gonna cost near ten dollars!"

"New," Delia repeated. "It's Christmas, and he's our only boy." She went on to say it wasn't as if she was asking for something for herself.

On Christmas morning Delia rose early, and by the time Benjamin and

Isaac came to breakfast she'd set out three places; in the center of the table was a plate piled high with biscuits sweetened with honey and raisins.

That afternoon Isaac opened his gifts and squealed with delight.

"I don't know nobody who ever got a brand new mitt," he said.

Delia saw the joy in his eyes and smiled. She said nothing to either of them but promised herself that she would no longer cast the burden of her sadness onto Isaac and Benjamin, no matter how heavy her heart felt.

She held true to the vow, and whenever one of them was nearby she forced herself to smile and move with a spritely step. But when she was alone Delia would sit in the rocker and creak back and forth, reliving memories just as Otis had done.

In the third week of June she was busy planting a row of tomatoes on the side of the house when she heard someone yoo-hooing from the front yard. After nearly an hour on her knees she was slow getting up, and before she could stand the holler came again.

"Hold your horses," she grumbled, "I'm coming."

When Delia rounded the house she saw Luella standing in the walkway. "Well, if you ain't a sight for sore eyes," she said and hurried over to hug her.

"Where you been?" Luella asked. "Every day I been thinking you is gonna come today, but there ain't been no you for God knows how long."

"Since Daddy Church died I ain't been up for visiting," Delia said.

"Ain't up for visiting?" Luella repeated. "So what you been doing, just feeling sorry for your poor ole self?"

Delia cracked a smile. "I suppose."

Luella raised an eyebrow and gave a disapproving frown. "All this sorrowful you been hauling around, it make you feel better?"

"Unh-unh." Delia shook her head.

"Well, then, maybe you ought to try visiting."

Delia laughed, and it felt good. It was first time she'd laughed in a very long time.

"Get on in here," she said. "Let's sit a spell and catch ourselves up."

As Luella laughingly told stories of the past months, Delia could see the self-imposed loneliness she'd settled into. It stuck to her skin like a hungry leech, draining away every bit of happiness she'd known. Little wonder she was miserable. She missed the friendships she'd made, and in the span of that single afternoon she came to see what Luella said was true: mourning Daddy Church neither brought him back nor made her less sad.

"I'll come visiting real soon," she promised. "When school gets out for the summer, me and Isaac is gonna be there two or three times every week."

"When I sees you standing at the door, I'll believe it," Luella laughed.

BENJAMIN

S ome folks ask why I didn't shed no tears when Daddy died. *Brother Albert claims a man crying 'cause he lost his daddy ain't nothing to be ashamed of.* Let it out, *he said,* and your burden will be lifted. *'Course, it's real easy to dish out such advice when you ain't the one hurting. I'm not arguing against Brother Albert, I'm just saying it's easier said than done.*

I loved Daddy much as I love Delia and Isaac and I'm missing him clear down to the soles of my feet, but bad as my hurting is Delia's is worse. Hers is like an abscess that's festered and ready to pop open. I see her eyes all red and swelled-up and know I got to be strong for her. When she's real weepy I tell her give it a bit of time and sooner or later the hurting will stop. How could I say that if I was sitting there blubbering myself?

Crying is a lot easier than not crying. Crying cleans out the misery in your soul and pulls loose the knife stuck in your heart. I ain't strong enough to not cry, but leastwise I'm holding it on the inside. On the outside, I go day by day and do whatever I gotta do.

Loving Delia don't stop me from hurting, but it gives me strength enough to move past it. I'm being strong for her 'cause she's being strong for Isaac.

It's easier for me 'cause I got work to do. A man don't think about his misery when he's hauling wood or cleaning out a chimney; but poor Delia, every day she's gotta sit there and look at the empty places where Daddy used to be.

That surely ain't an easy thing to do.

A Plan for the Future

I n the year that followed Isaac turned eleven and grew five inches. He was tall enough and strong enough to help out, so Benjamin occasionally took him along when he needed a second pair of hands. It was always something lightweight: painting a fence, repairing a screen door, or trimming branches from an overgrown bush. Although Isaac enjoyed the work, Delia frowned at the idea and more often than not it brought on an argument.

"The boy's gonna grow up thinking that's the kind of work he's *expected* to do," she'd complain.

Benjamin generally laughed it off, saying the work was honest and there was no shame in it. Even though Delia never came back at him arguing otherwise, she never gave up hoping their son would go off to college and become a professional.

Sometimes she'd claim Isaac would make a fine pastor and maybe one day become a bishop. "You ever hear of Bishop William Decker Johnson?" she'd ask, and when Benjamin shook his head no she'd move on to telling all he'd done and how he came to be respected by even white folks.

"Daddy used to claim Bishop Johnson was a credit to mankind," Delia said. Afterward she remembered the kind of person her daddy was and switched over to saying Isaac would make an even better lawyer.

"You heard about William Henry Hastie?" she asked.

Benjamin and Isaac both shook their heads.

"Well, it so happens," Delia said, "Mister Hastie was a real good lawyer, and when everybody saw what a fine job he was doing defending people President Truman made him a United States judge."

"I ain't never heard of no colored judges," Benjamin said skeptically.

"It's true," Delia insisted. "I read a story about him in one of them newspapers you brought home."

"I'd jest as soon be a farmer," Isaac said. "Farmers got a good life, and they grow stuff people can eat."

"You like seeing signs telling how you can't go in this place or that?" Delia asked. "You like going to people's back door on account of you ain't allowed to knock in the front?"

"What's that got to do with—"

"Respect!" Delia cut in. "You ain't never gonna get respect 'less you earns it!"

"I don't care none about—"

"You will," Delia said ruefully. "You will."

That summer Delia visited Luella once or twice every week. She and Isaac would leave the house early in the morning before the sun got too hot and wouldn't return until after the sun had dropped below the tree line. In the early spring the rain had been plentiful, so the pond near Luella's house was deep and right for swimming. In the heat of the day they'd head over to the pond and cool their feet in the water as they watched the boys swing from a rope then let go and splash down. On just such a day the question of college came up.

It was the week before school was to start, and the boys were frolicking in the water when the echo of thunder sounded a warning. Seconds later a bolt of lightning flashed across the sky.

"Jerome," Luella called, "get yourself outta the water, we got to get home."

"Aw, Mama, it ain't nothing but a bit of—"

Before he could finish complaining, Luella yelled, "Out!"

Still laughing and poking at each other, the boys scrambled out of the water and took off running toward the house. Luella and Delia walked behind at a slower pace.

"I think we is wasting our time setting aside college money," Luella laughed. "That fool boy's likely to get hisself killed 'fore he gets to high school."

"You already saving up?" Delia asked.

Luella nodded. "We got six hundred and twenty-two dollars set aside."

"Six hundred?" Delia gasped.

"And twenty-two," Luella added.

"How'd you do it?"

"Not me. Will. He started saving the day Jerome was born, and he ain't never stopped."

"But," Delia stammered, "don't it take all you got for living?"

Luella nodded. "We can't save nothing out of Will's gas station pay, but he got a side business. That money's for saving."

"A side business?"

"Unh-huh. He buys 'n sells used stuff."

"What kinda stuff?"

"Everything. Ice boxes, baby carriages, kerosene lamps. Just whatever people's got a need for."

"Where's he get things like that?" Delia asked, and before there was time for an answer she added, "And how's he find a body what needs it?"

"There ain't but one gas station what serves coloreds, so everybody goes there. Will knows 'em all, what they got and what they need."

Another flash of lightning streaked across the sky and Luella said, "We'd better hurry." After that she yelled for the boys, who were now rolling in the grass, to get moving.

For the remainder of that afternoon Delia had a hard time focusing on the conversation. When Luella was talking about a lemon cake she'd baked, Delia was thinking through the possibilities of a side business. Benjamin did most of his work for white people and while they might occasionally give him some of their castoffs they weren't likely to buy from a colored man, so that wasn't a good business for him.

Working more jobs wasn't much of an idea either since he already left at dawn and didn't get back until dark. Thought after thought passed through Delia's mind, but each idea turned into a dead end.

It was still early in the afternoon when Delia said she had to be going.

"So soon?" Luella asked.

Delia nodded. "I got a lot to do."

What she didn't say was that the thought of Luella having all that money for Jerome's college was poking a jealous finger at her brain. Her desire for Isaac to go to college rocketed from a distant thought to an immediate need.

That night after Isaac was in bed Delia poured two cups of coffee and sat with Benjamin at the table. For several minutes nothing was said, but a thought had been running through her mind ever since she'd left Luella's.

"Benjamin," she finally said, "we got to start planning for Isaac's college."

He looked across with a puzzled expression. "At eleven years old? Don't nobody go to college at eleven."

"But if we don't start saving right now, we won't have the money he needs."

Benjamin rubbed his big hand back and forth across his forehead several times before he looked over at Delia sorrowfully. "How? How we gonna save when we ain't got an extra dime?"

What he said was true, and Delia knew it. There had been good years when the farm made a profit, but the last three years they'd barely scraped by. They'd already gone through what little bit they'd saved, and now they had to pay Sylvester Crane ten dollars just to stay on land that was too poor for farming.

"Maybe you could have a side business," Delia suggested, trying to sound optimistic. "Will Jackson's got one. Luella said they saved up six hundred and twenty-two dollars from him buying and selling used stuff."

"It ain't all used," Benjamin replied. "A lot of that stuff Will sells is stolen. He buys stuff what supposedly fell off a truck, pays a dime on the dollar, then overcharges folks for things they gotta have. That what you're wanting me to do?"

Delia sighed. "I guess not." Her words were weary and thin as a piece of parchment.

Benjamin stretched his arm across the table and covered Delia's hand with his. "Just 'cause we ain't got money don't mean Isaac can't go to college. He's just got to work a whole lot harder."

"Work harder?"

Benjamin nodded. "If Isaac got the best grades in his class when he finishes up high school, it might be a college will leave him go for free."

"Free?"

Benjamin nodded. "When I was in the army, I knew a pilot what did it."

"A white man?"

"Unh-unh." Benjamin shook his head. "Colored fella."

"Get out," Delia said, laughing.

Benjamin went on to explain how a scholarship worked.

"Isaac's smart enough," he said, "but he ain't real dedicated."

"Well, he'll get dedicated!"

After that single conversation, Delia went from seeing Isaac as a boy to thinking of him as a man getting ready for college. Once school started there was no more visiting with Luella and Jerome. As soon as Isaac came in from school, Delia sat him at the kitchen table and made him start studying.

While she was mixing up a corn pudding or peeling a pile of potatoes she'd call out questions like how much is nine times nine or who was America's sixteenth president. After two weeks of studying and any number of wrong answers, Delia told Benjamin to ask around Bakerstown and find some mending or ironing jobs he could bring home for her to do.

That year there was little time for anything other than working. Delia ironed and mended the baskets of clothes Benjamin brought home, and he began taking on more and more jobs. He'd leave the house long before dawn and wouldn't return until well after dark. Some nights he'd come home too tired to eat supper or even peel the sweat-stained clothes from his body.

Isaac's sole responsibility was studying.

As Delia stood at the ironing board pressing wrinkles from the shirt of a white man she'd never met, she continued to call out the questions and little by little Isaac began to get more of the answers right.

"That's good," she'd say, then move on to arithmetic or some other subject. Every session ended with the same statement.

"I want an A on every one of those test papers," Delia would warn.

When the balmy days of April finally rolled around, Isaac complained about not having time enough for playing.

"There'll be plenty of time for playing when you're done with college," Delia said.

"That's years off," Isaac moaned. "You saying I ain't never gonna have no fun 'til then?"

"No, I'm not saying that," Delia answered. "If you was to get straight a's on your next report card, I'd be willing to take you for a day of visiting with Jerome."

"Straight a's?" Isaac repeated, making such a feat sound impossible.

Delia nodded. "I know you ain't thinking it now, but someday you're gonna be mighty glad I pushed you into studying for college." She gave a wistful sigh and said, "I was gonna go to college, but then I met your daddy and got married."

As much as she loved Benjamin Delia couldn't help but wonder: if she'd been a bit more patient and gone to college as her daddy wanted, would she still be living in Grinder's Corner? If she closed her eyes, Delia could envision the pathway of her life. She had come to a fork in the road and taken one pathway without ever knowing what was down the other. Rushing blindly ahead without weighing one side against the other was the way of youth, and she was determined that Isaac would not make such a foolish mistake.

DELIA

When I listen to myself telling Isaac how important it is for him to go to college, I can hear my daddy's voice saying that exact same thing to me. When folks is young, you don't pay no never-mind to stuff like that. Now the weather's turned warm, the only thing Isaac wants to think about is playing.

That's fine 'n dandy if you're not ever leaving Grinder's Corner. But living here's a hard life. It's a lot of making do and doing without. Isaac's way smarter than Jerome, and he don't have to settle for this life. If he puts his brain to work and studies real hard, he can go off to college and maybe be a doctor or preacher. 'Course, looking back on some of the things Daddy did I'm none too respectful of preachers, but for most folks a preacher's just one step down from God.

I've got no problem with doing the sewing 'n mending Benjamin brings home. I figure every extra dollar puts Isaac that much closer to college. White folks pay good money for work they could be doing themselves, and long as I don't have to go into Bakerstown I'm okay with doing it.

Money is money, and the only color it's got is green.

THE LAST PERFECT DAY

On the last day of school Isaac came home glowing like a stoplight.

"I done it," he said and handed Delia the report card with a line of a's stacked one on top of the other.

Delia smiled and hugged her arms around the boy. For a brief moment she could already envision him walking through the front door of Morehouse College.

"I sure am proud of you," she said.

"Good." Isaac grinned. "Now can we go visit Jerome?"

Delia nodded. "Soon as I finish up this mending."

"You said—"

"I know what I said," Delia replied.

Although Delia had suggested that it would take no more than a day or two to finish mending the things Benjamin brought home, it took the better part of three days and on the fourth day it was pouring rain, which meant the visit had to again be postponed.

When Isaac stood on the front porch looking out at the downpour, Delia walked out and stood beside him.

"Woo-wee," she said. "A day like this ain't good for much but maybe reading."

"Don't I get no vacation?" he replied despondently.

"'Course you do," she answered. "Those books I got you ain't for studying, they're for fun reading."

"Yeah, well, I ain't in the mood for fun reading. I'm in the mood for ball playing."

"You say that 'cause you never learned to love reading. When I was a girl I could sit and read for hours. Rainy days I'd be sitting in the chair and—"

Isaac gave an exasperated sigh, turned, and went back into the house.

With first one delay and then the other, it was eight days before they finally got to go for the visit. Benjamin was barely out of the house when Delia pulled on her pink flowered dress and painted her mouth to match. She woke Isaac and told him to hurry up if he wanted to go see Jerome.

They started out early Wednesday morning and arrived at the Jackson place well before ten. Jerome was first to spot Isaac coming down the road. He let out a whoop and holler that brought Luella running from the house.

"Land sakes," she said, hugging Delia to her chest. "Where you been keeping yourself?"

"I mostly been helping Isaac with his lessons," Delia replied, saying nothing about the mending and ironing she'd been doing.

"Well, I sure as the devil missed seeing you," Luella laughed.

Delia smiled. "Me too."

The day was as perfect as any Delia had ever known with the sun warm on her back, the air fragrant with the scent of spring jasmine, and the sound of Isaac's laughter crackling with happiness. Delia creaked back and forth in the rocker and sipped her sweet tea.

"Times like this is good," she said. "I'd soon as not sit here forever."

"Ain't nothing forever." Luella laughed. "Best you can do is be remembering these good times and forgetting hard times. Folks what can't turn their back on hard times got a heavy load to carry."

"Ain't that the God's honest truth," Delia replied.

The sun was setting when Delia first thought of leaving, and still she stayed a bit longer. The day had been like a slice of blueberry pie; the sweetness of it made her hunger for more.

"I just can't get myself moving," she said.

"Y'all's welcome to stay," Luella replied. "It ain't fancy, but we can make do."

Delia shook her head. "I've got to get home. Benjamin'd be worried to death if we was gone." She stood and called out for Isaac. "Time for us to be going."

Isaac crumpled his face into a frown. "I ain't done playing."

"You ain't never gonna be done playing," Delia said, "but we still got to be getting home."

"If you is dead set on going," Luella said, "leave Isaac stay. Come get him tomorrow, and we'll have ourselves another fine day of visiting."

"That sure enough sounds sweet," Delia replied, "but Isaac's got reading to do." She went on to explain how Isaac was going to need a scholarship to go to college.

"Benjamin don't have no side business, and seven dollars is all the savings we got," she said.

When they finally left the tall pines were black silhouettes against a sky that was already turning dusky.

"Y'all come back real soon," Luella called as they disappeared down the road.

Delia turned and waved one last time.

CROSS CORNER ROAD

Sally Garrett didn't leave Luke because he was a terrible husband and a poor provider. She left him because he was a mean drunk. After three or four drinks the hatred in him came to a boil, and he turned uglier than a mean-assed bear.

When Luke came home smelling of whiskey on Tuesday night, Sally knew she was in for it. He started picking at her about being fat and ugly, then moved on to poking her in the stomach and laughing at how the fat wobbled.

"I don't have to put up with this," Sally said and turned toward the bedroom.

That's when Luke whirled her around, grabbed the front of her dress, and ripped it wide open.

"Look at them ugly titties," he laughed. "Them is the ugliest titties I ever did see!"

At that point Sally had taken all the insults she could stand.

"I may be fat and ugly," she said, "but at least I ain't a white trash drunk—"

She was going to say more, but Luke slammed his fist into her face.

By the time he finally passed out, the right side of her face was puffed out like a cantaloupe and she had a black eye and a broken front tooth.

Once Luke was stretched out on the sofa dead to the world, Sally pulled the cardboard suitcase from the back of the closet and packed the things she needed. In the black of night she walked from the back hill cutoff to Cross Corner Road and then all the way into town. It was a twenty-three-mile walk, most of it through Grinder's Corner where the colored families lived, but Sally didn't care. Enough was enough.

When the early morning bus left Bakerstown headed for Baltimore, Maryland, Sally was on it.

Luke didn't open his eyes until nearly noon, and when he did he started yelling for Sally to bring him a cold beer.

"Hey, stupid! You deaf or something?"

Once the room came into focus, he scrabbled off the sofa and went in search of her. That's when he saw the emptied out closet. There was no note, no indication of where she'd gone.

With no other way to vent his anger, Luke kicked the closet door with such fury it came loose from its hinges. When it fell to the floor, he stomped it until the wood split in half. After giving the broken door one last kick, he headed into the kitchen and pulled a lukewarm beer from an icebox that didn't have a sliver of ice left in it.

Luke drained a long swallow and spit it out. "Warm piss," he grumbled. Still red-eyed and smelling of whiskey, he got into his truck and headed for town.

His first stop was the Good Times Tavern where he had three cold beers to clear his head. Then he went looking for Sally.

Ezra Green, the bus station clerk who'd sold Sally her ticket, had seen the black eye and he didn't have to ask questions to know where she'd gotten it. When Luke swaggered into the station hollering about how he was gonna find Sally and teach her nobody shits on Luke Garrett and gets away with it, Ezra said Sally had boarded a bus headed for Albuquerque, New Mexico.

"Damn that woman," Luke replied. Then he staggered out the door, across the street, and back to the Good Times Tavern.

Luke climbed onto a barstool and ordered a boilermaker whiskey to ease the pain of Sally leaving and then he washed it down with a beer chaser to cool the burn in his throat.

"Ungrateful bitch," he told Alvin, the bartender. "Run off after all I done for her."

All afternoon Luke sat there, drinking boilermakers, smoking fat cigars, and cussing Sally for leaving. As soon as he'd downed one glass, he'd order another.

When it began to look as if Luke was going to topple off the stool, Alvin suggested he go home and see if maybe Sally hadn't returned.

"You deaf?" Luke answered. "I done told you she went to Albuquerque."

Alvin had seen a lot of drunks come and go, and the mean ones were the worst. You couldn't argue with them; the best you could do was get them out the door and send them on their way.

"Maybe she changed her mind," he said. "Got off at the next stop and came back home."

"It ain't likely," Luke replied. "She's spiteful through and through."

Alvin tried a dozen different ploys to get him to leave, but Luke just sat there and continued to order boilermakers one after the other. Nearly two times Luke's size, Alvin could have picked Luke up and set him out on the street and he came close to doing it several times, but mean drunks almost always find a way of retaliation. Luke was well known as a trouble-maker, and there was no way of knowing what he'd do. Alvin waited, hoping sooner or later Luke would pass out.

It never happened. Luke just went from being belligerent and mean to being remorseful. He plopped his head down on the bar and moaned so loudly Alvin had to turn the jukebox music to maximum just to drown out the noise of his sobbing.

It was after dark when Luke finally staggered out of the bar and climbed back into his truck.

Leaving Luella's as late as she had, Delia underestimated the amount of time it would take for the five-mile walk home. Nighttime walking was slower, and there were places where the darkness tricked you into thinking the road turned one way or another. When that happened, she and Isaac would walk twenty or thirty yards then find themselves tangled in a briar patch and have to turn back.

She was already regretting her mistake when she heard a crack of thunder in the distance. Delia wasn't afraid of getting wet, but ever since that trek home from Bessie's house she'd been harboring a fear of lightning. If it could take down a huge long leaf pine, she could only imagine what it would do to a person.

"Let's walk faster," she told Isaac.

The rain started minutes later. A storm came roaring in and dumped three or four inches of water on the ground in less than thirty minutes. They were already sloshing through the mud when they heard the sound of a truck coming up behind them.

Delia turned, saw what she thought was Benjamin's truck, and stepped into the road to wave him down. She was waving her right arm in the air when the headlights came at her.

"Mama!" Isaac screamed and moved to reach for her.

Tears and a veil of self-pity were already clouding Luke Garrett's eyes when the downpour started. With the flood of rain washing across his windshield he could see no more than two or three feet in front of him, and to be truthful he wasn't expecting someone to be standing in the middle of a road as lonely as Cross Corner.

He heard the first thump when the boy bounced off the side of his truck. The second thump came when a woman in a flowered dress came flying across the hood of his car. He skidded to a stop, stuck his head out the window, and looked back.

"Damn stupid niggers," he grumbled. "They done busted up my headlight."

He pushed down on the gas pedal and drove off.

THE SEARCH

Wednesday was a long day for Benjamin. He'd started early with cutting back a thicket of blackberry bushes threatening to take over Sadie Walter's backyard. It had taken hours longer than he'd thought, so he was late getting to the Branson house.

Edwin Branson had no tolerance for tardiness, especially from coloreds who were hired to do a job.

"Least you could do is show up on time," he told Benjamin. Then he claimed he was in the middle of dinner, and Benjamin would have to wait at the back door while he finished eating.

"I can't see any reason to let my meal grow cold because of your tardiness," he said.

Standing in the hot sun, Benjamin waited while Edwin Branson finished his dinner then sat back for a second cup of coffee and a bowl of peaches. Nearly an hour passed before he stepped out onto the back porch and showed Benjamin the two pine trees at the far end of his yard that were to be taken down and chopped into firewood.

"Be sure to dig up them stumps and get rid of them," he said.

It was well into the supper hour when Benjamin finished the job, and he still had Claudia Monroe's roof to repair. He was replacing a row of loose shingles when he heard the distant sound of thunder. Claudia also heard the thunder. She stepped outside and called up to Benjamin.

"When you finish that be sure to check inside the attic, because when that storm hits I don't want rain leaking in."

"Yes, ma'am," he answered.

Once the last shingle was nailed into place, Benjamin climbed down from the roof and crawled into the cramped attic. The heat of the day was still trapped in the narrow space and he had barely enough room to move around, pull loose the rotted board that was there, and nail a new one into place. By the time he finished, the rain was coming down in torrents.

"Benjamin," Claudia said, "it's way past suppertime. Do you want me to fix you a sandwich before you start home?"

"I'm mighty grateful for the offer, Miss Claudia," he answered, "but Delia will have supper waiting, so I'd best be getting on home."

"I understand." Claudia smiled and handed him the two dollars she'd promised.

The rain had slowed to a misty drizzle when Benjamin drove down Cross Corner Road and turned off at the road leading to his house. As he pulled into the yard he noticed there was no lamp burning in the front room, which was unusual. He climbed down from the pickup truck, worried that Delia or Isaac was sick in bed, but when he opened the door and called out no one answered.

"Delia?" he called again. Still no answer.

The house was small enough that she would have heard him regardless of where she was; nonetheless Benjamin walked through it room by room, calling out for her. When there was no sign of either her or Isaac, he began to worry. He searched around back in the smokehouse and in the barn. There was nothing. No sign of struggle, no Delia, and no Isaac.

In all the years they'd been married this was the first time she'd not been there when he got home from work. There was usually a stew simmering on the stove or the smell of fresh-baked biscuits. No matter how late he'd worked, there was always a warm greeting and a welcome home hug. Now there was no note, no indication of where she'd gone. It was all wrong. It was not Delia's way of doing things. He tried to remember the women friends she visited: Bessie, Bertha, Mariam, Luella.

Benjamin got back in the truck and drove to the closest house, which was Bessie's.

"I ain't seen Delia in two, maybe three weeks," she said.

He moved on to the next house and the next. By the time he got to

Luella's it was well past midnight, and there was not a single lamp lit in the house. Benjamin pounded on the door.

"Will," he called out, "I got to ask Luella something!"

A sleepy-eyed Will finally opened the door. "What you want?" he grumbled. "Luella's sleeping."

"I got to know if Delia was visiting with her today."

"Go ask Delia," Will said and started to close the door.

Benjamin pushed against it. "Delia's missing. Her and Isaac both."

Will pulled the door back. "Come on in," he said, then went and woke Luella.

Moments later she came rushing in with a bunch of worry lines tugging at her face.

"Delia and Isaac left here before suppertime," she said. "They should've been home hours ago."

"Did she say if she was coming straight home?"

Luella nodded. "Said she had to get supper started."

Benjamin got in the truck, turned it around, and started toward home; this time he crawled along at a snail's pace. As he drove he looked first right then left, his eyes all the time searching. About four miles down Cross Corner he caught sight of something pink alongside the road. He stopped and climbed out.

Even before he reached her, Benjamin saw the flowered print of Delia's favorite dress. Isaac was lying face down a few yards away.

When he kneeled beside her he found Delia's head swollen to twice its normal size and her breath coming in short desperate gasps. Benjamin let out a scream that rattled across the Alabama countryside and woke people in houses as far as five miles away.

"Don't do this, Delia!" he cried. "Please, don't do this!"

He lifted both Delia and Isaac into the bed of the truck then turned and headed back to Bakerstown, flooring the gas pedal the whole way.

The Bakerstown hospital served both colored and white. Coloreds were housed on the ground floor, whites on the second and third. On Wednesday night there was no Negro doctor or nurse on the floor, but Sam Goldsmith had gotten his medical degree at Columbia University in

New York and didn't hold with the segregationist ways of Alabama. He ordered both Delia and Isaac into examination rooms.

Delia was gone before Doctor Goldsmith finished his examination. She'd suffered two cervical fractures and internal bleeding. There was no hope of saving her.

He turned to Isaac, whose eyelids had fluttered open.

"Can you hear me, son?" the doctor asked.

No answer.

"Do you know where you are?"

Still no answer.

"Can you tell me what happened?"

Isaac closed his eyes.

"Get this kid to X-ray," Goldsmith ordered. "I want the head, neck, and that right femur." He then turned to the assisting nurse and said, "Call upstairs and have them get an OR ready."

"Upstairs?" she replied wide-eyed. "Don't you think we should wait and—"

"Upstairs," he repeated, his tone severe and unapologetic.

For almost four hours Benjamin stood staring out the window of the colored waiting room. The rain drizzled against the pane, but he could see nothing of the outside world. The only thing he saw was his own reflection: a man wide and tall with tears streaming down his face and skin as black as the night.

"Why, God?" he moaned. "Why?"

BENJAMIN

Standing there looking at myself in that hospital window, I see a dead man. If God takes my Delia and our baby Isaac, then He might just as well take me too. Without the two of them, I got no reason to be living.

They's my life. Them two is my reason enough for getting up in the morning. I can't think what a day would be like without seeing Delia standing at the stove with the coffee pot already bubbling or coming home in the evening and not hearing her tell Isaac them fanciful tales of hers.

If ever there was two people what deserve to live it's Delia 'n Isaac. Isaac, he's just a baby, he ain't even had time to sin. And Delia ain't never done one wrong thing in her life. It was me what pushed her into loving before we was married. I been down on my knees asking God to punish me instead of her.

Please, God, I say, let Delia 'n Isaac live; then you can do what you will with me. Hell with all its fire 'n brimstone can't be no worse than this

And Then Sorrow

I t was near dawn when Doctor Goldsmith came to Benjamin in the waiting room.

"I'm sorry," he said. "I did what I could, but your wife's injuries were too severe."

You could almost hear the crack of Benjamin's heart breaking. "What about Isaac? Is he okay?"

"He will be," Goldsmith answered. "He suffered a pretty bad concussion and a broken leg, so I'm afraid he'll be walking on crutches for a while."

Benjamin bowed his head. "Thank you, sir. I know you tried to save my Delia, and I'm mighty grateful for that."

"Would you like to say goodbye to her?" Goldsmith asked. His voice was soft and respectful, not what Benjamin would have expected.

"Yes, sir, I would," he answered.

Doctor Goldsmith had a nurse take him back to the room where they'd left Delia. She was lying on a table with a clean white sheet covering her body. Only her swollen head was visible.

"Lord God, baby," Benjamin moaned. "Who did this awful thing to you?"

Benjamin reached beneath the sheet and lifted her hand into his. It was cold and heavy, the fingers stiff and curled inward. He stood there for a long time, tears rolling down his face as he swore to Delia that he would never stop loving her and he would care for their son as long as there was breath in his body. Moments before he left the room, he bent and kissed her mouth. It too was cold and hard, nothing like the lips he had kissed every day for more than a decade. When the agony of such a loss became too great to bear, Benjamin closed his eyes and stumbled from the room. He walked with a shuffling step and his back hunched. Painful as the grief of this night was, Benjamin knew the worst was yet to come.

Isaac was still in the hospital the next day when they buried Delia, and Benjamin was thankful for that. He had no wish to share such sorrow with the boy. Isaac would have time enough to grieve. He'd have a lifetime to remember the horror of that night; there was no need to pile this misery onto the load he'd be carrying.

Luella came and stood beside Benjamin as a number of people stepped forward to say prayers and speak of what a wonderful woman Delia was.

"I ain't never knowed a more kindly woman," Bessie said. "The Lord is surely settin' a place for her at His table."

There was a chorus of halleluiahs and amens; then Luella stepped forward.

"There's not one here who Delia ain't helped out some time or another," she said. "Now we got to repay them kindnesses! We got to see Benjamin and Isaac is taken care of."

Another chorus of halleluiahs and amens echoed.

Benjamin was the last to speak. His voice trembled, and several times he had to stop because the lump in his throat was in the way of words. After saying how blessed he'd been to have Delia as his wife, he thanked the Lord for saving Isaac. He tilted his face to the heavens and said, "Lord Jesus, I know the Bible says vengeance is thine, but I got to lend a hand here. You got my Delia safe in your arms, but that bastard what did this to her is still walking the earth and he's gotta pay."

"Brother Benjamin," Pastor John said, "it ain't our place to right the wrongs of this world." He was going to recite a passage from the Book of Isaiah, but by then Benjamin had turned and walked away.

Luella ran after him and grabbed onto his arm. "Benjamin," she pleaded, "you got to let the law take care a' this. Isaac needs family, and he ain't got nobody but you. If you get your fool self killed—"

"I ain't gonna get killed," Benjamin answered and shook loose his arm.

Later that afternoon Benjamin returned to the hospital. At first it appeared Isaac was sleeping, but when he entered the room the boy opened his eyes.

"Hey, Daddy."

In three long strides Benjamin crossed the room, then leaned over and kissed his son on the forehead. "How you feeling?"

"I ain't too good," Isaac answered. "My leg ain't moving."

Benjamin nodded. "I know. It's broken, but the doctor says you'll be good as new in time."

"Is Mama gonna be good as new too?" Isaac asked.

Benjamin gave a sad shake of his head, then bent and pulled the boy into his arms. For a few moments he held him close, not speaking the words aloud but praying for strength.

"Isaac," he finally said, "I know how much you love your mama, and she's got the same love for you. Me and your mama, we'd never do anything to cause you hurt but sometimes things happen and we got no say in—"

Isaac pulled back a bit and looked up at Benjamin. "What you talking about, Daddy?"

"Your mama was hurt way worse than you, Isaac. The car that hit her messed up her insides something awful—"

"It weren't no car, it was a truck," Isaac said. "It was a damn truck what hurt Mama. Ask Mama, she'll tell you. She seen it better 'n me."

"I can't ask your mama, Isaac, she's gone to rest."

Isaac yanked himself loose and looked square into his daddy's face. "What you mean, rest?"

"Your mama's gone to be with the Lord." Benjamin answered. "She fought real hard trying stay alive but—"

"Mama's dead?"

Benjamin gave a solemn nod. "I know it's a real hard thing to hear, Isaac—"

A red hot anger flared in the boy's eyes. "You're lying! Mama ain't dead. You're just saying that to scare me!"

Benjamin moved forward and again pulled the boy close.

"I wish I was lying," he said sorrowfully. "They tried to save your mama, but she was too bad hurt."

Isaac broke away again. "Ain't nobody tried to save Mama."

"Isaac, I know your heart's hurting, but Doctor Goldsmith is a good man. He's the one who fixed your leg, and he really did try—"

"I ain't talking about no doctor."

"Who you talking about?"

"The man what hit us. It weren't no accident."

"It had to be an accident," Benjamin reasoned. "Nobody'd do something like that on purpose."

"He did," Isaac sobbed. "You wasn't there, Daddy, you don't know."

Benjamin held the boy in his arms until the worst of his crying slowed.

"You're right, Isaac," he said. "I wasn't there, but you was. You can tell me what happened."

Seemingly glad for the opportunity to tell his side of the story, Isaac sniffed back his tears and said, "Mama and me was coming home from visiting Miss Luella 'n Jerome, and we was walking on Cross Corner Road. We was trying to hurry 'cause it already got dark."

He stopped for a moment, and the fearful look in his eyes made Benjamin think he was reliving the moment.

"It's okay," Benjamin said, "take your time and just tell me what you can remember."

"I remembers it all, Daddy. I ain't got no doubts. We was listening for the motor sound, then the truck come 'round the bend and ran smack into me 'n Mama. He did it 'cause we was colored."

"Nobody does a thing like because—"

"He did so!" Isaac shouted. "He said it!"

"What'd he say?"

"He said we was damn niggers, then drove off."

For a long while Benjamin held Isaac in his arms, the boy sobbing softy as a calloused hand rubbed his back.

"It's okay to cry," Benjamin whispered. "Crying's good for the soul. It lets the misery out instead of keeping it bottled up inside."

No child's tears can last forever. Eventually weariness sets in, and their young soul runs dry. When that finally happened Benjamin asked Isaac if he knew the man driving the truck that hit them.

"I ain't never before seen him," Isaac said, "but I know he got a face with hair."

"Do you know what kind of truck he had?"

Isaac nodded. "Blue like yours. Mama thought you was coming home, that's why she stepped in the road and started waving."

"Was it old like mine?"

Isaac shrugged. "I can't say for certain 'cause it was dark 'n he was going fast."

"Anything else you can remember about the truck?"

Isaac thought a minute then said, "Yeah. It had a black tire on the front and a tire with a white middle on the back."

"A whitewall tire?" Benjamin asked. "One with a white circle all the way around?"

Isaac nodded then began sobbing again. "I 'specially remember the back tire, 'cause I seen it when he drove off."

Benjamin stayed beside Isaac until late in the evening, but all the while he was sitting there he was picturing the trucks he'd seen around Bakerstown. He couldn't remember a blue pickup with a whitewall tire, but he'd find it. In time he would find it, no matter how long it took.

Moving On

The morning after Delia was laid to rest, Benjamin drove into Bakerstown and went directly to Sheriff Haledon's office. A round-faced deputy sat at the front desk.

"I got to report a crime," Benjamin said.

Without glancing away from the paper he'd been reading Deputy Moran asked, "What kind of crime?"

"Murder," Benjamin answered.

"Murder?" The deputy looked at Benjamin with a raised eyebrow. "Is this some nigger fighting nigger thing?"

"No, sir," Benjamin said. "A man run down my wife and boy when they was walking on Cross Corner Road."

"If you ask me, that sounds more like an accident."

"It weren't no accident. My boy seen it and he said—"

"Boy? How old is this kid?"

"Eleven, but he got a good eye and he saw—"

"Eleven?" The deputy laughed. "You want me to start investigating a murder because of what a kid says?"

"It's your job!" Benjamin said angrily.

"Don't get uppity with me, boy!"

The sound of shouts brought Sheriff Haledon from his office. "What's going on here?"

"I got a wise-ass nigger trying to tell me how to do my job," the deputy answered.

"Sir, that ain't the way it is," Benjamin said. "I come here to report somebody murdered my wife and near-killed my boy."

The sheriff recognized Benjamin. He'd done work for Missus Haledon, and he'd done a good job. He painted their back fence and repaired a broken window in the storage shed. He was blacker than most but known for being polite, unlike the smart-mouthed coloreds who lived on the far side of Bakerstown.

"I'm real sorry to hear about your missus," the sheriff said. "Come sit in my office, and I'll hear what you got to say."

As they walked away the sheriff turned and shot an angry glance back at the deputy.

Once the sheriff was willing to listen, Benjamin explained what Isaac said.

"The driver was a white man with hair on his face; a beard or maybe a heavy mustache."

"I ain't being negative," the sheriff replied, "but that description fits half the men in Clarkson County."

"He was driving a blue truck," Benjamin added.

"That ain't much neither; you yourself drive a blue truck. There's likely hundreds of them right here in Bakerstown."

"This truck had a whitewall tire on the back wheel. There ain't many like that."

"Probably not," the sheriff conceded, "but I can't offhand say I seen a truck like that around Bakerstown. Could've been somebody passing through."

"Cross Corner Road don't go nowhere. Ain't no reason for a passerby to be driving that road."

"True enough." The sheriff pulled a single-sheet form from his desk and scratched out a line or two. "I'm gonna look into this, Benjamin. You just sit tight and leave this to me. If the responsible party is here in Bakerstown, I'll find him."

Benjamin stood. "Thank you, sir. I'm mighty grateful."

The sheriff nodded. "Don't you worry, Benjamin. Just go on back to work and take good care of your boy."

As soon as Benjamin was out the door, Sheriff Haledon slid the paper under a huge stack of others.

"Damn shame a thing like this has to happen," he said, and that was the end of it. Haledon was originally from Wisconsin and had no problem with the coloreds, but he also wasn't ready to butt heads with Mayor Wilkes who was fifth-generation Alabaman.

A week later Isaac was released from the hospital with a plaster cast on his leg. Benjamin checked him out and left owing the hospital one hundred and eighty-seven dollars. Since his daddy had gone back to work by then, Isaac was brought home to stay with Luella.

Thus began a new chapter of Benjamin's life. With Doctor Goldsmith's help, he'd struck a deal with the hospital. In exchange for wiping clean his debt, he would clean the colored ward every night for one hundred and eighty-seven days. He'd mop the floors, empty bedpans, carry trash to the Dumpster, and do whatever else needed doing. It had the sound of a hard bargain, but Benjamin was thankful to get it.

Every morning he rose early, drove into Bakerstown, and continued the handyman work he'd done for the past two years. In a single day he might paint the porch of a house, cut back a row of unruly oaks, and clear the soot from a chimney, but at the end of the day he'd head over to the hospital. Some nights he was too tired to drive home, and he'd pull the truck around to the back lot of the hospital and lie down across the seat. In the morning he'd be stiff and bent, but still he'd push on to the next job.

When the pain would settle into his back and shoulders it was a welcome relief, because it pulled him away from the more painful thoughts of Delia that troubled his heart.

Regardless of what job he was doing, every hour of every day Benjamin had his eyes open watching for the blue truck. Sooner or later either he or Sheriff Haledon would find it, of that he was almost certain. Day after day he returned to the sheriff's office and asked if they'd found the owner of the truck yet. The sheriff would generally give a helpless shrug and say, "Not yet, but we're still looking."

On days when Benjamin encountered Deputy Moran, his answer would be a hard-edged "Nope" and nothing more.

Weeks passed and Benjamin settled into this grueling new routine. He worked until his arms ached and the muscles in his thighs quivered when he stooped to lift a load of bricks or lumber. He took to carrying a blanket and pillow in the truck; then when he left the hospital too exhausted to even raise an eyebrow he'd make a bed in the flat bed of the truck and sleep like a dead man. It was never for long, because at the first break of day his eyes would open and he'd drive home to feed the chickens and the dog. He'd throw some water on Delia's vegetable garden, then turn around, drive back to town, and start whatever job he had for that day.

From the money he collected he held back enough to pay Sylvester Crane's monthly land fee, buy a bit of fatback, a jar of molasses, and some ready-made biscuits. He bought nothing for himself and saved every extra penny, hoping one day he'd have enough for Isaac to go off to college. With Delia gone Benjamin took her wish for Isaac and made it his own; it was his way of hanging on to a small piece of their life together.

Sunday was the only day Benjamin set aside and did no work other than the hospital cleaning. Sunday was a day reserved for Isaac.

Saturday night when he finished his work at the hospital, Benjamin most always drove home. He'd sleep for a few hours, then rise, scrub the grime from his skin, pull on a clean shirt, and head over to Luella's to spend the day with his boy.

After the third week, Isaac started asking to come home.

"There ain't nobody home to see to you," Benjamin said. "I thought you liked being here 'n having Jerome to play with."

"Yeah, well, now I'm sick a' being here," Isaac answered.

At first Isaac welcomed the thought of staying at Luella's house. But when Jerome lost interest in a playmate who barely hobbled along, they started to squabble. Two days ago the weather turned blazing hot, and Jerome went off to the pond. They hadn't spoken since.

"Jerome's got no interest in playing with me," Isaac complained. "And there ain't nothing else to do here."

"With me working all the time, there ain't nothing much to do at home neither," Benjamin replied.

"Yeah, there is," Isaac said. "Mama got me some books for fun reading."

Benjamin had already counted up the millions of reasons he had for missing Delia; this was one he'd forgotten to add to the list.

"Your mama did that, did she?"

"Yes, sir. She said they was for fun reading, 'n I'd get smarter if I done it."

Benjamin gave an apprehensive smile. "There's nobody at the house; don't you think it'd be better if I bring those books over here?"

"Unh-unh. I figure it's better if I come home."

After a fair bit of back and forth on the subject Benjamin agreed that on Sunday, a week from the day, he'd come to take Isaac home.

"I got a few arrangements to make," he said, "so you got to wait a week."

That week Benjamin took every job he could get. The day he did the patchwork on Hiram Lettinger's roof, it was near dark when he finished. He was late getting to the hospital and didn't finish cleaning until a few minutes before the sun broke free of the horizon.

That night he didn't sleep at all. Still he pushed through the next day and the day after. This was the last week he'd be working these hours, so he had to make the most of them.

He'd already spoken to Mamie Beasley who was in charge of the colored wing of the Bakerstown Hospital, and she'd given an okay for him to come in at four o'clock each morning to do the cleaning.

"Just make sure you're done by nine," she'd warned, and Benjamin happily agreed.

When the end of the week rolled around, Benjamin took his earnings and stocked up on things he wasn't used to buying. He got five cans of soup, sliced bread, peanut butter, and a can of Spam. It wasn't the same as the hearty stews Delia made, but at least the boy wouldn't go hungry. He also bought Isaac three comic books. He reasoned that although it was a good thing to have an eye to the future, there were times when a man had to be living for the day. This was one of those times.

On Friday morning he went by Bessie's house and asked if she could look in on Isaac every so often.

"'Course I will," she nodded. Although she said nothing else, judging by the look of Benjamin's clothes she figured he could also use some help with the laundry and cleaning. That afternoon she hitched the small wagon to the mule and visited five of Delia's friends.

"It's time we step up to help," she said, and no one disagreed.

Viola said she'd be willing to take care of the laundry. Bertha agreed to do the cleaning, and Rosalie said she'd have her strapping sixteen-year-old son come over and chop firewood for the stove.

"Boy's lazy as a log," she added, "but when I tells him to do something, he knows he got to get it done."

Friendship wasn't a thing that needed to be repaid, but when Bessie Mae returned home she could almost see Delia smiling down from heaven.

BENJAMIN

heriff Haledon is a good man. He's fair, and I'm trusting he'll find the truck that killed Delia. Yes, Isaac's just a boy, but he knows to tell the truth. I don't for one minute think he's lying about what happened. It's a fact that Deputy Moran got a sharp tongue 'n don't care much for colored folks, but the law is the law. The law's got to do with right 'n wrong, it's got nothing to do with colored or white.

It ain't gonna be easy having Isaac living home, but I'm still looking forward to it. I've been staying away most of the time because all this quiet keeps reminding me of how much I lost. Now that Isaac's gonna be here I can't be thinking of how much I lost, I gotta be thinking of how much I still got. I'm Isaac's daddy, and I got to look after him.

A man don't like to say he's got weaknesses, but if I was to be honest with myself I'd admit I need that boy as much as he needs me. He's all I got left in this world and as long as I got him, I still got a piece of Delia.

THE BLUE TRUCK

Benjamin worked late Saturday; then he went to the hospital and did the Sunday morning cleaning. He napped for two hours in the back of the truck, then stopped in at Will's gas station and washed his face. Afterward he headed out to Luella's. It was early, but Isaac was ready and waiting.

"This young'un's been counting off the days 'til you come," Luella laughed. "I'd say he's a mite anxious to get back home."

Benjamin smiled. "I been kinda anxious myself."

Luella handed him a plate. "Here's a bit of ham and blueberry pie for y'all," she said. "And if you get to needing something else, just come on back."

"We're gonna do just fine." Benjamin gave Isaac a wink as he lifted him into the bed of the truck. He'd padded it with rags and blankets so it was soft enough for a baby.

On the trip home Benjamin drove slowly and tried to avoid the deep ruts that would cause the truck to bounce its cargo. Being cautious, he swung into a wide turn as he left Cross Corner Road and started down the lane that led to the house.

As soon as Benjamin switched the motor off he caught the smell of stew simmering, and when he opened the front door it came at him full force. It was an aroma so familiar he could almost believe Delia was there.

For nearly a month he'd been coming and going without stopping to look around the house. He'd worn the same shirt for days on end, and when it got too crusted with dirt to wear again he'd tossed it onto the pile on the bedroom floor. He'd left coffee cups on the table and not once swept the floor, but now everything was clean. On the table there was a note saying "Welcome Home." It was signed by all of Delia's friends.

That night when Benjamin and Isaac sat down to a supper of opossum stew and blueberry pie, the two empty chairs loomed larger than life.

"It's just you and me now," Benjamin said sadly.

In a move that was far beyond his eleven years, Isaac stretched his arm across the table and touched his hand to Benjamin's.

"It's gonna be okay, Daddy," he said. "I miss Mama too, but leastwise we can be missing her together."

Benjamin heard Delia's words in their son's voice, and a lump came into his throat. Isaac was the last remaining piece of Delia.

As they were clearing the supper dishes from the table, Benjamin came to the boy and hugged him to his chest.

"I love you, Isaac," he said. "I love you same as I loved your mama."

Once Isaac was home, Benjamin changed the way he was living. While the boy was still fast asleep, he would set out a breakfast then leave to clean the hospital. Afterward he'd do a job or two, but in the late afternoon Benjamin would quit working and start home. He made money enough for food, kerosene, and the few other things they needed and still had time to spend with Isaac.

That summer Benjamin came to know the soul of Isaac as he'd known the soul of Delia. On warm nights when the sky was still light, he'd hitch the mule to the small wagon and they'd go off together. Sometimes they fished and sometimes they went in search of a rabbit or squirrel they could hand over to Bessie for cooking. But there were many nights when they simply sat on the porch and talked.

In the first months of winter when darkness came early, Benjamin began to worry about the boy coming home alone. By then Isaac's cast was off and he was walking back and forth to the schoolhouse. It was a good two miles but the last mile was along Cross Corner Road, which caused Benjamin's concern.

It was a Tuesday in early November and he was in the middle of tar-papering the roof of Sam Preston's shed when a queasiness started rolling through Benjamin's stomach. It wasn't what he'd eaten nor was it something you point a finger to and say this or that is the problem. It was what Delia had called a premonition.

In Alabama the worst storms occurred in the heat of summer. Lightning, thunder, tornados. They came when the ground was blistering and ready to explode. November rain was soft, showery, refreshing almost. Benjamin looked up at the sky and saw the angry dark clouds pushing against one another. He stopped hammering and listened. In the distance he heard the rumble of thunder, and that's when he scrambled down from the roof. He knocked on the back door and told Sam, "I'll be back tomorrow to finish up," then climbed into his truck and headed for home.

Benjamin circled around the back road and past the First Baptist Church; then he turned onto Cross Corner Road to follow the path Isaac would take. He was looking for the boy to be walking along the roadside so he drove slower than usual. During the past three months he'd grown accustomed to checking the tires of every blue truck he saw, but on this day he had greater concerns. He was worrying over Isaac and not focused on the truck that came rumbling toward him. If it hadn't crowded him onto the shoulder of the road he might never have noticed the rear wheel, but as the truck flew by Benjamin glanced across and saw the whitewall tire.

Making a quick three-point turn, he followed the truck back into Bakerstown. Just as Isaac said, the driver was a bearded man. The truck turned down Beaver Street and then pulled into the parking lot of the billiard parlor. The driver climbed out of the truck and disappeared through the door.

Benjamin parked a short way down the street and sat watching the truck. He thought about Isaac and prayed he'd gotten home safely. What to do, he asked himself. If he left to get Sheriff Haledon, the man might leave; then he'd have nothing. And if the sheriff wasn't around Benjamin knew the deputy wouldn't take action.

There was no way for Benjamin to follow him inside. On the front door of the billiard parlor there was a sign saying "No Coloreds," so he'd be stopped before he crossed the threshold. The only thing he could do was wait. Wait and follow the bearded man back to wherever he lived.

Benjamin climbed out and walked across to where the blue truck was parked. The left headlight was smashed, the hood and front fender dented. He touched his hand to the indentation and knew for certain this was the truck that had killed Delia.

There was no shotgun in Benjamin's truck nor was there a knife. He had a toolbox. A box filled with hammers, screwdrivers, and a sledge, any one of which could be used to kill a man. Isaac's words echoed in his ear. *It weren't no accident. Damn niggers.* This man was someone who deserved to die.

Had Benjamin found him in the week following Delia's death, he would have done it without pausing to consider the consequences. But in the last three months things had changed. Benjamin had always loved Isaac, but Delia had been the one close to the boy. She'd been the one to soothe his hurts and help him build dreams. With Delia gone, he was all Isaac had left.

Benjamin thought back on the sheriff's words: sit tight and leave this to me. And he waited.

It was close to midnight when Luke Garrett stumbled out of the billiard parlor and headed for home. Benjamin switched the ignition on and followed. He stayed a fair distance behind and drove with his lights off. Just outside of town, Luke veered off the main street and headed for Cross Corner Road. Benjamin stayed with him.

When they passed the narrow drive that led to the house, Benjamin saw a lamplight in the window. Isaac had gotten home safely. He knew the boy would be fearful about him not coming home, and after all that had happened that thought tore at his heart. This would be the only time, he promised himself. He had no choice but to follow the bearded man so he could report back to Sheriff Haledon, but that would be the end of it. The law would take it from there. He would never again leave Isaac alone to worry.

About four miles past the house the blue truck turned down a side road with no name, a stretch of dirt that ran past a field of burned-out farmland; the truck stopped alongside a small house. Benjamin pulled his truck behind a thicket on the shoulder of Cross Corner Road, got out, and walked up the dirt road. The night sky was thick with clouds, and dark as it was he had to feel each step carefully. He couldn't afford to stumble and fall. In the stillness of this night even the slightest noise would be a giveaway.

Once he was closer to the house, Benjamin stopped and listened.

No dog. Good. He crouched low and slowly moved across the yard.

The house was dark and when he peered through the side window Benjamin saw nothing. It was several minutes before a lamp flared and a yellowish glow lit the room. Pressing himself flat against the building to avoid detection, he watched as the man opened a cupboard and pulled out a whiskey bottle. He took a long drink from the bottle, then moved off to a room somewhere in the back of the house.

This was where he lived, Benjamin was certain of it. Tomorrow morning he would share his finding with Sheriff Haledon and justice would be done.

Still staying in the shadows, Benjamin moved away from the house and back down the road to where he'd hidden his own truck.

The Whitewall

The lamp was still lit when Benjamin arrived home, and the moment he walked in Isaac came running to him. It was obvious the boy had been crying. Benjamin pulled him close and asked, "What you crying about?"

"I ain't crying," Isaac answered indignantly. He hesitated a moment then added, "I just been worrying."

Benjamin squeezed him a bit closer. "You got no need of worrying. I'm your daddy, and I'm gonna take care of you."

"But what if that man what runned down Mama runned you down too?"

"That ain't never gonna happen 'cause I found who done it. It was just as you said, Isaac. One big ole whitewall tire on the back end of that truck."

"Did you fight him?"

Benjamin chuckled. "Fighting ain't no way of settling things. I'm gonna tell the sheriff and let the law handle it."

"The law ain't gonna arrest no white man!"

"It sure enough will," Benjamin replied. "Sheriff Haledon done said."

Isaac shook his head doubtfully. "I ain't so sure."

The next morning Benjamin was scheduled to finish tar-papering Sam Preston's shed, but instead of going there he went directly to the sheriff's office. Deputy Moran sat at the front desk. He looked up and gave an exasperated groan. "What now?"

"I come to see Sheriff Haledon," Benjamin answered.

"He ain't here." Moran went back to the paper he'd been reading.

Benjamin didn't move. He stood there with his head slightly bowed and a weathered straw hat held loosely in his right hand.

"I said he ain't here," the deputy repeated.

"You know when he's coming back?"

The deputy didn't bother to look up. "Not 'til next week."

This was something Benjamin hadn't expected. He stood there wondering if it was better to wait or go ahead and tell Moran what he knew. It was a risk either way. Moran had a mean streak a mile wide, but waiting meant there was a chance the bearded man would leave town. As far as Benjamin could tell no one else lived there, and if so the man was a loner. No ties. The house didn't have the look of a place someone cared about, so he could be a squatter. Squatters came and went like the wind. They picked up and moved on whenever they had a mind to.

With the responsibility of caring for Isaac and working Benjamin couldn't keep a sharp eye on the man, so he had to trust Moran. Unpleasant as he could be the law was the law, and he was obligated to do the same as Sheriff Haledon.

"I can see you're real busy," Benjamin said, "but, sir, I got to report I found the man what killed my Delia."

Moran looked up. "You did, huh?"

"Yes, sir," Benjamin replied. "I ain't got knowledge of his name, but I can say where he lives."

"And exactly what do you want me to do about this no-name man you think killed your wife?"

"It ain't what I think, sir, it's what I know for sure. He's just as my boy said."

"Oh." Moran cocked his mouth to one side. "And I'm supposed to take it as gospel 'cause a kid thinks he saw something?"

"The night they was hit, Isaac saw that blue truck with one whitewall tire on the back. That ain't something a kid can make up."

"There could be a dozen trucks fit that description. You got a license plate number or any *real* evidence?"

Benjamin shook his head. "It was dark, but Isaac saw the man driving had a beard."

Moran laughed out loud. "Beard, huh? Half the men in town got beards!"

"Maybe so," Benjamin said, "but this here's the only one driving a blue pickup with a whitewall tire on the back wheel."

"That still don't prove—"

"Sheriff Haledon said if I seen this guy, I was to let him know and the law would take care of it."

"Okay, okay." With an annoyed yank Moran pulled a notepad from his desk. "What's the address?"

"It ain't a town address," he said. "It's a dirt road what runs off Cross Corner. About four miles past my place. It's the only turnoff on the right."

"That's Luke Garrett's place." Moran shook his head dubiously. "That man come home from the war half-crippled, it ain't likely he—"

"Excuse me for speaking, sir, but my boy saw what he saw and he got no reason to lie, 'specially about a man what served his country."

"Yeah, yeah," Moran grumbled. He scribbled a few lines on the notepad then said he'd look into it. The truth was if he wasn't certain Benjamin would keep coming back until he got to Sheriff Haledon Moran would have tossed the note in the trashcan, but jobs like this were not easy to come by so he'd take a leisurely ride out there and that would be the end of that.

As Benjamin disappeared out the door, Moran pushed the notepad aside and grumbled, "Niggers gonna take over this town if we ain't careful."

Moran waited until after lunch to drive out to Luke Garrett's place. He'd seen Luke in town and pretty much knew that's who Benjamin was talking about. As soon as he turned down the dirt road he saw the blue pickup sitting in the front yard. Sure enough, it had a whitewall tire on the rear wheel.

"Aw, shit," Moran mumbled as he climbed out of his sheriff's department car.

Luke Garrett was still asleep when he heard the banging. Scrambling out of bed, he pulled on a pair of jeans and flung open the door. "What the hell...?"

"That your truck out front?" Moran asked.

"Yeah," Luke nodded. "But it got license plates."

"It's also got a whitewall tire on the rear wheel," Moran said. "You know what that means, asshole?"

"I come by that tire honest," Luke replied. "You got no gripe with me."

"I ain't here 'cause of you stealing no tire; I'm here 'cause somebody driving a blue truck with a whitewall tire run down a nigger woman and her kid."

"That's it?" Luke smacked his hand against his head. "You're hassling me 'cause of bumping a nigger woman?"

"She's dead."

"I'm real sorry about that," Luke said sarcastically, "but it ain't my fault. She was standing out in the middle of the road. How's anybody supposed to see a nigger woman at nighttime?"

"Whether you seen her or didn't seen her ain't the issue," Moran replied. "Her kid saw you, and he also saw that damn whitewall you got."

"Jesus!" Luke dropped into a chair and cradled his head in his hands. "That was the day my Sally left." He looked up at Moran. "You ever have a woman leave you?"

The deputy gave a halfhearted shrug.

"Man, let me tell you, it tears up your insides. You ain't got mind enough to know if you're dead or alive."

Moran's expression softened slightly. He'd never had a wife leave him, but his mama had walked off when he was five years old. He could still remember the way his daddy sat at the table and cried night after night. Before six months had gone by, he'd put a gun to his head and pulled the trigger.

Luke noticed the change and slid into the opportunity quick as an eel.

"When Sally left I was near crazy. All I could think about was having a few drinks to get me through that day." Putting a pitiful moan in his voice he added, "I loved Sally with all my heart, but she left me 'cause of this bum leg and run off with a man half my age."

"Whew." Moran gave a sad shake of his head and lowered himself into the chair opposite Luke. "A woman like that ain't worth crying over."

Luke went on and on about how he'd given Sally all he could afford, pampered her like a princess, and didn't deserve the treatment he'd gotten.

Moran continued to bob his head in agreement; of course, he hadn't seen Sally's black eye and the missing front tooth.

"Now this." Luke sighed. "A nigger woman's gonna do me in. It's more than a man can stand."

"Well, maybe if you was to get rid of that tire…"

The start of a smile curled the edge of Luke's mouth.

"And shave the beard…"

When Deputy Moran sat at his desk and wrote out the report, he stated that after a thorough investigation he'd found the only similarity between Luke Garrett and the boy's description was that both drove a blue pickup truck. While the truck had a slight bit of damage on one side there was no whitewall tire, he said, and the man in question was clean-shaven.

He left a copy of the report on Sheriff Haledon's desk, then locked the office and headed for home.

A FALSE TRUTH

When Benjamin left the sheriff's office he wanted to believe Deputy Moran would do something, but one small spot in the back of his brain argued otherwise.

Twice he waited until Isaac was sound asleep, then slipped out of the house and drove back to Luke Garrett's place. He parked his car behind the same thicket, walked up the dirt road, and peered through the window.

On the first night the house was dark and there was no movement inside. There was also no truck parked outside, so that didn't prove anything one way or the other. On the second night the truck was parked to the side of the house, and there was lamplight coming from what Benjamin thought was the kitchen. He crept closer and pulled himself up alongside the window. Careful not to move quickly or make a noise, he leaned forward and looked in.

A man sat in a straight-backed chair with a bottle of whisky and a glass on the table in front of him. At first Benjamin believed it to be someone else, but the longer he watched the more it began to look like Luke Garrett. When the figure stood and limped from the room, Benjamin was certain. It was Garrett, but his beard was gone.

A crack of thunder sounded in the distance but still Benjamin stood there staring at the empty chair, knowing what he'd seen but not quite believing it. When the rain began he backed away and started down the dirt road. He got halfway to his own truck when he thought of something and turned back.

This time he didn't bother with looking in the window; it was the truck he was interested in. He walked the full way around it, but all four tires were black. Benjamin bent and scraped his fingernails against the back tire hoping it was just a thin layer of paint covering the white. It wasn't. A whitewall tire was worth maybe five dollars. A man like Garrett wouldn't just get rid of it; it had to be somewhere close by.

Moving to the back of the house and then circling around to the far side, Benjamin searched in back of the woodpile, behind the overflowing garbage cans, under chunks of rusting metal, and even in the wooded areas surrounding the house. Nothing. The whitewall was gone.

Luke Garrett knew. He knew that Isaac had pointed a finger at him and described both man and truck. He knew and he'd covered his tracks. There was no longer a bearded man nor was there a blue truck with a whitewall tire. Now there was only a colored boy's word against that of a white man. Benjamin turned and started back down the dirt road. He no longer cared about being silent. What more could Luke Garrett do to him?

The rain grew heavy and beads of water mingled with Benjamin's tears. As he climbed back into his truck he felt the weight of injustice come down on him like the mudslide of a mountain. It was the kind of thing no man survived; once you were covered you no longer had a desire to live.

With rain flooding the windshield of his truck and tears flooding his eyes, Benjamin drove home. He did not go to bed that night. He sat on the porch with water cascading down his back and tears falling from his face. Never in all his life had Benjamin wanted to kill a man—not in the army, not ever—but tonight he wanted to kill Luke Garrett. Sitting there on the porch, he could close his eyes and imagine putting a rifle to the beardless face and pulling the trigger. When the image became so real he could feel the butt of the rifle slam against his shoulder, Benjamin dropped his head into his hands and sobbed. "Lord God, forgive me."

Before the pale pink crest of morning came onto the horizon Benjamin knew what he had to do. His love for Isaac was greater than the hatred he felt.

For the next four days Isaac was never beyond Benjamin's sight. When Benjamin trimmed Hazel Fromm's oak, Isaac picked up the loose clippings and stacked them to the side. When Benjamin painted Herbert Megan's garage, he did the top half and Isaac did the bottom. It was the same whether Benjamin was hanging a new shutter, fixing a screen door, or patching a water pipe.

Although he'd said nothing about it, Benjamin had grown fearful that Luke Garrett would go to an even greater extent to protect himself. He'd gotten rid of the beard and the whitewall tire. Would he also try to get rid of Isaac? Sheriff Haledon would be back in the office on Monday; until then Benjamin would not let Isaac out of his sight.

On Monday morning when Benjamin walked into the sheriff's office Isaac was with him. Deputy Moran was at the front desk.

"What now?"

"I come to see the sheriff," Benjamin replied.

"He's busy."

"I ain't in no rush," Benjamin said. "I can just wait."

"Not in here you can't," Moran said angrily. "You wanna wait, get your ass out on the street to do it!"

"Yes, sir." Benjamin nodded. He took Isaac by the hand and stepped outside.

When Moran looked up the two of them were walking back and forth directly in front of the sheriff's office storefront window. He bounced up out of his seat and flung the door open.

"What the hell do you think you're doing?" he shouted.

"We're waiting outside like you said," Benjamin answered.

Moran, a third cousin of Mayor Wilkes and with much the same attitude, turned red in the face. "Don't you sass me, boy! Get the hell outta here and—"

He was interrupted by the booming voice of Sheriff Haledon. "What's going on here?"

"This damn nigger thinks he's got the right to—"

"Okay, Moran, that's enough," the sheriff said. "Let's take this inside." He held the office door open and Moran stormed through, followed by Benjamin and Isaac.

Once inside the sheriff closed the door and turned to the threesome. "Okay, now, what happened?"

Moran jumped on it. "I told this nigger you was busy, and he started giving me a bunch a' nigger sass. Him and the kid got out in front of the office and started parading back 'n forth like they was picketing the place. All I did was tell them to move on."

The sheriff turned to Benjamin. "What's your side of the story?"

"I begs your pardon, sir, but I ain't seeing it like Deputy Moran. Me and Isaac come to speak with you and when we got told you was busy, we figured to wait." He looked down at Isaac and said, "Ain't that right, Isaac?"

The boy nodded.

"We was gonna wait here, but Mister Moran told us to do our waiting outside."

Sheriff Haledon turned to Moran. "Is that right?"

"Yeah, I told them to wait outside, but I didn't say nothing about parading back and forth like a bunch a' picketers!"

"We was just stretching our legs," Benjamin said defensively.

"You weren't banging on the window or creating a disturbance of any sort?"

"No, sir," Benjamin answered. "We was just walking."

"Seems to me," the sheriff said, "this is a whole lot of commotion about a little bit of nothing." He turned to Benjamin, "If all you want to do is talk, let's go in my office and talk."

"Well, I'll be damned," Moran grumbled. "If this don't beat all, now we gotta kowtow to a bunch a' ignorant niggers!"

Sheriff Haledon ushered Benjamin and Isaac into his office, and as he turned back to close the door he gave Moran a warning glare.

Benjamin and Isaac stood, but when Sheriff Haledon sat he motioned for them to take a seat in the chairs facing his desk. "I'm assuming you want to talk to me about this Luke Garrett thing," he said. "But I've already read Deputy Moran's report, and I don't see that there's much more we can do."

"I ain't trying to be disrespectful," Benjamin said, "but Deputy Moran ain't saying the whole story." He told how he'd seen the whitewall tire when the truck passed him on Cross Corner Road, then followed Luke Garrett home and peered through the window to see the bearded man.

"And that's the God's honest truth," Benjamin swore.

"Well, Deputy Moran's report says Luke Garrett's truck has four black tires, and the man doesn't have facial hair of any sort."

"I gotta believe somebody warned him."

"Benjamin, I'm hoping you aren't saying Deputy Moran would do a thing like that. I know he has no love of colored folks, but he's a sworn officer of the law."

The sheriff's words landed with a thud. They had the sound of finality, something impossible to argue against.

"I ain't blaming Mister Moran," Benjamin said, "but somebody surely did—"

"Who?" the sheriff replied. "Who else knew? Did you mention this to anyone other than Deputy Moran?"

"Unh-unh." Benjamin shook his head.

"Then it's just your word against his."

"It ain't just my word," Benjamin pleaded. "A man what's got a beard, then don't got a beard. Somebody's got to seen—"

The sheriff shook his head. "It's not gonna happen, Benjamin. Luke Garrett's trashy as they come, but he's a white man with friends. He'll lie, and they'll swear to it."

"But if somebody seen—"

"Even if they did," the sheriff said, "there's no way to prove when Luke shaved it off. It could have been last week, it could have been a month ago."

Benjamin just sat there, the muscles of his face hard as cement.

"I seen the man what run us down," Isaac volunteered.

"I know," the sheriff nodded, "but it was dark at night, and your description was only that the truck had a whitewall tire and the driver was bearded. Did you see anything else that might help us?"

Isaac looked down at his feet and shook his head sorrowfully.

For nearly a minute the room was silent; then the sheriff spoke.

"I hope you can see the problem I've got here, Benjamin. I'm not saying which is right or wrong, but in the best interest of all concerned I've got to accept Deputy Moran's word. If I was to charge Moran with covering up a crime based on nothing but your word, there'd be an uprising in Bakerstown such as we've never seen."

Benjamin listened, expressionless and stoic.

"But it ain't right," Isaac said. "He run down my mama."

The sheriff gave a sad nod. "Maybe he did and maybe he didn't.

Unless we can prove something…" He let his voice trail off; the thought was something no one wanted to hear.

Benjamin stood to leave, but Sheriff Haledon rose from his chair and came around the desk. He put his hand on Benjamin's shoulder. "What's done is done," he said. "Nothing you do is gonna bring Delia back. Maybe this isn't fair, but it's the way life is. The best thing for you to do now is take care of your boy."

Still somewhat expressionless, Benjamin turned and looked into the sheriff's face; the expression he saw was sincere and honest.

"Thank you, sir," he said, then reached for the door.

Although Benjamin never heard it, Sheriff Haledon said, "I wish you well, Benjamin, God knows I do."

When Benjamin left the sheriff's office he walked with long angry strides, and Isaac had to hustle to keep up with him. Without exchanging a word, they climbed into the truck and headed toward the edge of town.

"Ain't we going to work today?" Isaac asked.

"Not today," Benjamin answered.

Isaac saw the tear sliding down his daddy's cheek. "Don't cry, Daddy," he said. "If that sheriff ain't gonna get Mister Luke, you and me can. We can run him down jest like he run Mama down."

Benjamin turned to the boy with the saddest smile imaginable. "No, Isaac, we can't." He reached over and pulled the boy a bit closer. "Don't worry. We're gonna be okay."

Neither of them spoke for the remainder of the ride home. Benjamin searched for words, but none of them were right. There simply were no words to cover up his shame and anger.

That afternoon they went fishing. It was the first time Isaac could ever remember his daddy going fishing on a workday afternoon. They walked two miles to where the creek was wide, then sat on the mossy bank and dropped their lines in. For a long while they spoke of things that had no emotional weight tugging at them: fishing, school, green frogs, and growing things. Benjamin was comfortable talking about those. He spoke to Isaac the way Delia had, asking questions that made the child laugh and give stretched out answers that more often than not jumped off to another subject.

The sun was low in the sky when Benjamin finally said, "Isaac, what you think about us going to New York?"

"You mean like for a visit?"

"Unh-unh. I'm thinking maybe to live."

Isaac looked up with a wide smile. "Mama said in New York there's a toy store six houses high and—"

Benjamin laughed. "I ain't going 'cause of no toy store," he said. "But it's a place what's got schools close by and libraries with hundreds of good books like them your mama gave you."

"You told Mama you can't go to New York 'cause there ain't no farms," Isaac said cautiously.

"There ain't. But there's plenty a' other jobs. Jobs what pays the rent and leaves money left over."

Isaac had a dozen other questions, and one by one Benjamin answered them. They would have to leave the dog behind; he couldn't say exactly where they would live and what kind of work he would do; and, yes, he would miss the friends they had, but they'd make new friends and build a better life. In the time they talked it seemed to Benjamin that Isaac grew older, more responsible about his concerns. Perhaps too responsible for an eleven-year-old boy.

That night they fried the catfish they'd caught, and Isaac picked the last two tomatoes from Delia's garden. When they sat at the table Benjamin asked the Lord to bless the food and the journey they were about to undertake. He held back the sorrow swelling beneath his words, lest the boy be frightened.

After dinner they spoke of what they would take and what they would leave behind. Isaac chose the books Delia had given him and a yellow ball. Benjamin said they'd need their clothes and food to eat on the road. The remainder of their things they would leave behind, just as the Barker family had left their three-legged chair.

Once Isaac was sleeping, Benjamin went out and walked through the fields he'd loved. There were no longer rows of corn or anything that resembled a crop. The ground was covered with a tangle of ferns and kudzu. He tried to convince himself that he wasn't leaving anything of worth, but his heart argued differently. This was where he'd grown up; this was where his mama and daddy died, where their baby girl had been laid to rest. This was a place filled with memories. He tried to collect them as something he could carry with him, but the image of Delia lying out on Cross Corner Road was too overpowering. Some things were best left behind.

BENJAMIN

*L*ast night after Isaac went to sleep I sat on the front porch 'n cried like a baby. All day I been holding back because of Isaac, but sitting there by myself I couldn't hold it no more.

Never in all my years have I felt so low. I been shamed in front of my boy 'n told my word ain't worth speaking. I've got to wonder what kind of God lets a man be born to a life where he got no chance of fairness. I ain't lied or stealed. I ain't never caused nobody harm and I ain't asked for one thing more than I'm deserving of, but none of that counts. I got nigger skin 'n that's that.

I been accepting of we got our place and white folks got theirs, but God's law against killing ought to be the same for both. I trusted it was so, but it ain't in Alabama. Even when the truth is staring a white man in the face, he looks past and don't see nothing but the color of skin.

Somebody in Bakerstown knows the truth of Luke Garrett, but nobody's willing to ask. Not even Sheriff Haledon. I figured him for a fair man, but even he ain't willing to go up against the hate this town's got.

When a man comes to where he can't lift up his head no more, it's time to move on. Delia spoke the truth. If I don't take Isaac away from here, he's gonna one day be sitting right where I'm sitting. I can't let that happen. He deserves better.

Feeling beat down and shamed is punishment I deserve for not minding Delia's words, and knowing that's a misery I've got to live with.

LEAVING ALABAMA

The next morning, with Isaac by his side, Benjamin began to prepare for the trip. He drove into Bakerstown and left Isaac waiting in the truck as he went and knocked on the back doors of the people he'd been working for. He offered an apology and explained they were leaving town and he wouldn't be coming back to work.

Abigail Mayfield, upset because she'd planned on having him trim the bushes next week, said he ought to have given folks more notice and since he hadn't she was in no way obligated to pay him for the day's work he'd already done. Herman Kraus, however, wished them well and handed Benjamin five dollars to help out with the trip. A number of others did likewise. There was two dollars from both Tom Porter and Amanda Gray, and a day's pay or a single dollar from a dozen others. In all Benjamin collected twenty-four dollars before he headed to the hospital.

"I know I got four days' work yet to do," he told Mamie Beasley, "but Isaac and me got to leave town. I can pay the four dollars if that'll square things."

Mamie gave that great big laugh of hers. "Benjamin, you has more than paid your debt. You ain't owing a dime."

"I ain't expecting charity—"

"And I ain't giving none," Mamie cut in. "They been paying you way less than what ought to be, so we's fine with what you already done."

She told him to wait then disappeared into the lounge area. When she returned she pressed ten one-dollar bills in Benjamin's hand.

"The ladies in the back is sending you this going-off present," she said and gave another big chuckle.

That evening they took the dog and chickens to Bessie Mae's house and said their goodbyes.

"I ain't blaming you for going," Bessie said, "but I sure is gonna miss you." She hugged Isaac to her chest and whispered in his ear, "You take good care a' your daddy, 'cause you is all he got."

"I's gonna," Isaac promised.

That night Benjamin tried going to bed, but sleep never came. He tossed and turned for nearly two hours, then climbed from the bed and sat on the porch. As he creaked back and forth in the rocker where Delia once sat, the memories came at him. He closed his eyes and pictured the yard filled with happy and laughing friends, a young Delia carrying Isaac in her arms.

In that long stretch of night he wondered if he was doing the right thing in leaving so much behind. Even with its faults and prejudices Grinder's Corner was a place he knew, a place where he had friends and people who'd watch over Isaac. The world beyond Grinder's Corner was a blank, a thick patch of gray fog where the only way you knew what was waiting for you was to move into it; then it was too late.

In the end it was Delia's voice that convinced him. He could still hear her telling Isaac, "There's something better out there, a place where you can grow and be anything you want to be."

They started early in the morning. There was not much to take: a canvas bag once used for carrying home groceries now filled with clothes, a box of food and threadbare towels, a few pans, some chipped dishes, the rocking chair, and Benjamin's tool box. When there was no more room in the truck bed, the remainder of their things were left behind.

As he pulled away from the house the sun was just lighting the sky, and Benjamin turned back for one last look. He'd expected to see his memories, the good ones; instead there was only a sorry-looking house with a dirt yard. It was then he knew he'd made the right decision. No matter what the future held, it had to be better than this.

The first day of driving was slow going. Whenever Benjamin pressed his foot to the accelerator and tried to move past forty miles per hour the Chevy pickup, now seventeen years old, burped steam. He'd left Bakerstown and traveled northeast thinking he could pick up the highway, but thirty minutes after he turned onto the road the truck overheated and they had to pull to the shoulder and wait for it to cool. Once that happened, he gave up thinking about a highway and stuck to the side roads.

They traveled across the state of Georgia, stopping three times: once for gas and twice to let the engine cool down. When Benjamin pulled open the hood and poured water in the radiator, it sizzled like a steam locomotive.

It was near dark when they reached Leesville, South Carolina. They'd been on the road for twelve hours and had gone just under three hundred miles.

"I was thinking we'd be further along," Benjamin sighed as he turned off the two-lane roadway and onto a smaller road.

He drove until he came to the Oconee River; that's where they camped. Isaac caught two small crappie in the river, and Benjamin cooked them over an open campfire. They sat by the fire talking late into the night, and from time to time Benjamin heard Delia's words tiptoeing through the conversation. It was a good omen, something that told him she hadn't been left behind but was right there traveling with them.

When Isaac grew tired he climbed onto the seat of the truck and fell asleep. Benjamin moved the rocker aside and stretched out in the bed of the truck, his head resting on a bag of clothes. Even though there was no roof over their head, they slept soundly. The river seemed to have washed some of the shame from Benjamin's skin.

The second day started with a breakfast of apples and bread; then Benjamin got back on the road and headed northeast. It was early afternoon when they crossed the border, and Benjamin turned to Isaac.

"We is now in North Carolina," he said.

Isaac grinned. "I likes North Car-oh-lin-ah."

"You don't know nothing about it," Benjamin laughed.

"Don't matter," Isaac replied. "I likes the sound a' it—North Car-oh-lin-ah." He repeated the name over and over again, each time stretching the words out a bit longer. "Why don't we jest stop and live in North Car-oh-lin-ah?"

"It's north, but it ain't far enough north," Benjamin said and kept driving.

At the end of the day when the truck was spitting steam and they were both road weary, Benjamin pulled off the road in Hollister.

"This still North Car-oh-lin-ah?" Isaac asked.

Benjamin nodded. "I'd hoped we be further along," he said again.

Not far from where they'd left the road he found an area called Lightwood Knot Creek, and they made camp there. By the time they parked the truck it was late and too dark for fishing, so they ate bread and the pieces of smoked pork Bessie Mae had given them.

With the cost of gasoline, two loaves of bread, and the bottle of soda pop Isaac wanted, Benjamin was now down to thirteen dollars. That was money enough to get them to Maryland, maybe even Pennsylvania. Once they got that far, then he'd figure out what to do.

ON THE THIRD DAY

The rain started about an hour before dawn. At first it was just a drizzle, but before the light of day settled in the sky it turned to a downpour. Benjamin had spent much of the night worrying about money and hadn't slept well; now he was both weary and wet. He climbed into the cab of the truck and sat alongside Isaac.

"Maybe we ought to get an early start," he said. "Could be we'll run into a spot a' sunshine and can pull over for a nap."

Isaac yawned and gave a nod.

The rain continued all morning and was still coming down heavy in the late afternoon when they passed the Roanoke River and started across Virginia. With the roads slick and wipers that did little more than spread streaks of dirty water across the windshield, the going was slower than the previous two days. When the thought of using up gasoline to go thirty miles an hour picked at Benjamin's mind, he turned to Isaac and said, "Take a look at that map 'n see if you can figure how many miles to Maryland."

Isaac unfolded the map and started measuring with his thumb. His nose was buried in the map and he didn't see the accident. Benjamin did.

The back tire of a car fifty, maybe sixty, yards in front of them exploded with a loud bang. The car spun sideways and skidded across the road. For a moment it balanced itself on the two right tires, then toppled over and rolled down the embankment. After three bounces it slammed into a stand of pine trees.

Benjamin gasped. "Holy shit!"

Without considering the danger to himself he pulled to the side of the road, jumped out of the truck, and started down the rocky climb.

The car had come to rest on its left side with the front end folded up like an accordion and sparks shooting from the underside of the chassis. Benjamin had seen enough truck fires to know this one was going to go quickly. He had maybe five minutes. If the driver wasn't out by then, he was good as dead.

Catching onto the front wheel then pulling himself up onto the crumpled fender, Benjamin reached for the passenger door. Stuck. It was either jammed or locked.

"Grab the hammer outta my toolbox 'n toss it down," he called up to Isaac.

Isaac climbed into the bed of the truck and pulled the toolbox from beneath a pile of boxes. The flames coming from the underside of the car were now visible.

"Hurry up!" Benjamin yelled, the sound of desperation in his voice. For a split second he thought about climbing down. He had Isaac to think of, and staying there wasn't safe.

Before Benjamin could measure the responsibility of saving a life against staying safe to care for his son, the hammer came flying through the air. It landed atop the rear end of the car. He inched his way back and grabbed onto it. Without changing position, he drew his arm back and hit the window as hard as possible. The blow sent a spider web of cracks across the glass. He swung again and again until there was a hole his arm could fit through. Pushing his arm through the open space, he pulled up the lock button and pried the door open. The driver was unconscious. Benjamin tugged the young man from behind the wheel, hefted him onto his shoulder, and climbed down.

Minutes later the car exploded into flames.

The driver was little more than a boy—seventeen, eighteen at the most—and judging by the way his left arm hung loose it was broken. Benjamin moved the young man to a flat grassy spot sheltered by some trees and called for Isaac to bring down a jar of water from the truck.

"Get a few of those towels too," he added.

"They's wet," Isaac hollered back.

"Don't matter none," Benjamin said. "Bring 'em anyway."

Isaac stood to one side as Benjamin rolled a wet towel and placed it under the boy's head. He was breathing but unconscious. It was a good ten minutes before the boy's eyelids fluttered open, and another twenty before he could gather enough presence of mind to speak his name.

"Paul," he finally said. "Paul Jones."

"From around here?" Benjamin asked.

"Not far," Paul mumbled. "Wyattsville."

"You want to go home or the hospital?"

Paul thought a moment. Given his memories of those terrible days in the hospital, he had no desire to be back there. He didn't remember everything about that day; he remembered walking into the store to apply for a job, remembered lurching into the man with a gun and the sound of shots, but not much after that. He did however remember waking up in the hospital, being handcuffed to the bed and told he was being charged with the robbery.

A shudder shivered down Paul's back and he finally answered, "Home."

"Is there somebody what can care for you?" Benjamin asked.

Paul started to nod, but when he moved his head a sharp pain cut across his shoulder and down his arm.

"Owwww!"

"For sure you got a broken arm," Benjamin said. "And that left leg looks like it might be broke too. Try 'n wiggle your foot."

A look of concentration spread across his face, and Paul finally managed to move his ankle back and forth. He gave a soft moan. "I think it's my knee."

"Could be," Benjamin replied. "It's swelled up for sure."

Father and son sat beside the boy until he said he thought he might be able to stand, and then Benjamin gave him his arm. Paul latched onto the arm, but before he could pull himself to a kneeling position he fell back and groaned.

"I don't think I can do it."

"That's okay," Benjamin replied. "If you ain't got a problem riding with us, I can take you home." He turned to Isaac and said, "Fetch that map out of the truck. Let's see how far this Wyattsville is."

"I'd sure appreciate that," Paul replied wearily. "I'd be glad to pay for your time and trouble, Mister…?"

"Just Benjamin. Benjamin Church, 'n you don't have to pay me nothing."

"Oh, yes, I do." A pained grin came onto Paul's face. "After all you've done for me, my Uncle Sid would have my hide if I didn't."

Benjamin chuckled. "Well, I wouldn't say no to maybe getting a tankful a gasoline."

Getting Paul back up the hill and into the front seat of the truck was easier said than done. Benjamin tied two towels together as a makeshift sling for the boy's arm, but there wasn't much he could do about the leg. In the end he tied four more towels together, anchored Paul to his back like the shell of a turtle, then crawled up the rocky incline on his hands and knees.

By the time they got situated in the truck and pulled back onto the road, it was after seven and already dark but at least it was no longer raining.

On the drive to Wyattsville Benjamin's leg started throbbing. It was the right leg, the one he'd broken in a tractor accident years back. It ached when it rained, but now it was aching twice as much because of the climb up the hill.

Isaac squashed himself close to Benjamin, so he wouldn't press against Paul's arm or leg but there seemed to be no comfortable position for anyone. When the old truck bounced over even the smallest bump, Paul winced.

Benjamin understood the pain the boy felt, so he struck up a conversation to keep him from dwelling on it. When they thumped across the railroad tracks he asked, "How long you lived in this Wyattsville?"

"Almost two years. Me and my kid sister live with an aunt and uncle." Paul wriggled his right arm onto the armrest then said, "We're kind of adopted."

"Kinda ad-opt-ed?" Isaac echoed. "What's that mean?"

Paul gave a painful little laugh. "It means the Klaussners took us in, but they aren't really blood relatives. They're just good people with big hearts."

Benjamin smiled despite his aching leg. "Them is the best kind."

By the time they approached the outskirts of town it was past eight-thirty. In trying to keep the boy from thinking about his pain, Benjamin had gathered bits and pieces about how Paul and his sister had left West Virginia and traveled to Wyattsville.

"Your Aunt Carmella's a mighty big woman to take two strangers in," he said. "Ain't many what would do that."

He pulled up in front of the big house and climbed out of the truck. "Wait here, I'll ask your uncle to lend a hand." He started up the walkway. Instead of stepping onto the front porch, he circled around the pathway and headed for the back door.

Paul saw this and turned to Isaac. "Where's he going?"

"Back door," Isaac answered.

"That's the long way around."

Isaac gave a look of incredulity as if to indicate the boy was asking something he should have known. "We ain't allowed to the front."

"Not allowed to knock on the front door?" Paul asked. "Who told you a dumb thing like that?

"Ain't nobody told me." Isaac shrugged. "It jest is."

Carmella Klaussner had been keeping the remainder of her beef stew warm on the back burner for almost three hours. She'd expected Paul home by five, five-thirty at the latest. It was a Friday night and after a week of rising early for of school Jubilee was ready for an early bedtime, so shortly after the clock sounded six Carmella served dinner. When Paul did arrive home, she reasoned, there'd be plenty of stew still in the pot.

But when six turned into six-thirty and ultimately into seven, Carmella grew increasingly worried. It could happen that Paul would be a little late, but he was never this late. As the clock stuck nine, she felt an icy cold panic grab hold of her heart and at that very moment a knock at the back door sounded. She yanked the door open and gasped. "Please don't tell me!"

"Don't tell you what?" Benjamin asked.

"Don't tell me something's happened to my boy!"

In the short span of little more than a year, Paul had gone from being a lad suspected of shooting Sidney to becoming Carmella's boy.

"If Mister Paul is your boy," Benjamin replied, "then I'm real sorry to say this, but he done had an accident and got busted up."

"Oh, my God!" Carmella wailed.

Not waiting for more of what looked to be the onset of hysterics, Benjamin said, "He's gonna be okay, it's just a broke arm 'n maybe leg."

"Oh, my God!" Carmella wailed again. "Is he in the hospital?"

"No, ma'am. He's out front, sitting in my truck. I got a bum knee, 'n I come to ask if Mister Paul's uncle could lend a hand to carry him in."

"Sid...neeeey!" Carmella screamed. "Get down here right now!"

Hearing the urgency in Carmella's call Sidney dashed down the stairs, taking two and three steps at a time. Red-faced and wheezing, he asked, "What's wrong?"

"It's Paul, he's been hurt!"

"He ain't bad hurt, just a broke arm and maybe leg," Benjamin repeated. "But I'm hoping you can lend a hand carrying him in."

"Of course I will," Sid said. "Where is he?"

"Out front in my truck."

When Benjamin turned and started back down the walkway, Sidney followed. Carmella was right behind them saying back-to-back "Our Fathers" and asking God to please let Paul be okay. When they reached the truck Benjamin pulled the right door open and there sat Paul, his face tight with pain and his arm tucked in a loop of still-damp towels.

"Oh, my God!" Carmella wailed again.

Benjamin

I know bringing Paul home is the Christian thing to do, and I'm not looking for pay for doing it. But I surely hope his uncle comes through with putting gasoline in the truck. The truth is I'm running mighty low, and we ain't got money enough for much more.

If I run out of gas before we get to Maryland, it's gonna be a lot harder to find day work. Judging by all those "No Coloreds" signs I seen Virginia folk ain't gonna take kindly to me knocking at their door and asking for work, no matter how much their trees need trimming.

I can't say nothing out loud, because I don't want Isaac to know how bad off we are. The boy's got heartache enough. I keep trying to make light of the situation, because right now that's all I can do.

It's a daddy's job to take care of his boy and, God willing, I'm gonna figure a way to do it.

THE GUESTS

As they lifted Paul from the truck, Carmella dashed inside and telephoned Doctor Willard.

"Come right away," she said. "Our boy's been hurt in an automobile accident."

Without giving any further details she hung up and turned to telling Sid and Benjamin how they should carry Paul.

"Watch you don't bump his arm going around the corner," she said, "then take him down to my sewing room."

The bedrooms were all upstairs, but the sewing room was just down the hall from the living room. In truth Carmella did little sewing but often slipped away for a nap on the soft, comfy daybed.

Benjamin hoisted Paul with a firm grip beneath his shoulders, and as they moved through the house Sid called out step-by-step directions.

"Another foot," he'd say, "then turn right." Isaac trailed wordlessly behind.

When they reached the sewing room Benjamin lifted Paul onto the daybed, and Paul settled with a soft moan. Benjamin smiled.

"I think you is in real good hands now, Mister Paul," he said, "so we're gonna be moving on."

Carmella reached out and put her hand on Benjamin's arm. "It's late. Have you had supper?"

Before Benjamin could answer, Isaac shook his head. "Unh-unh."

"Then please stay," she urged. "I've got a big pot of beef stew hot and ready to serve."

"Thank you kindly, ma'am," Benjamin said, "but me 'n Isaac got to get back on the road. We're headed to New York."

"New York!" Sid exclaimed. "That's a two or three day drive. Maybe four in that old truck."

Carmella's hand was still locked onto Benjamin's arm, and she was making no move to let go. "After all you've done for Paul I can't possibly let you leave without having a bite to eat."

The thought of a home-cooked meal was certainly appealing, but Benjamin was taken aback. Only once before had he eaten a meal in a white person's house; that was Ella Jean Grayson. After he'd painted her house the full way around, she'd dished up a plate of fried chicken and sat him at the kitchen table. She'd remained in the kitchen but not sat across from him.

"You sure about this?" he asked.

"Of course I'm sure." Carmella turned to Sid. "Stay with Paul while I set out supper for our guests."

Motioning for Isaac and Benjamin to follow her, Carmella led them to a lovely dining room with a polished wood table and high-backed chairs.

Feeling a bit out of place, Benjamin said, "There's no need to fuss; eating in the kitchen is just fine for us."

"Nonsense," Carmella replied. "You're our guests." With that she pulled a white linen cloth from the drawer and spread it over the table. In minutes the table was set with tall glasses of water, a basket of bread, and a large bowl of steaming hot stew. She motioned for them to sit, and then she sat across from Benjamin.

"We ate earlier with Jubilee," she said, "otherwise I'd join you."

After a while, Carmella rose and went to check on Paul. A few minutes later, Sid entered the room and sat where she'd been sitting.

"You've got to excuse Carmella," he said. "She's a worrier. She fusses over those kids like she's raised them up from babies."

"There ain't nothing wrong with that," Benjamin said. "My Delia was the same. Isaac was our only baby, and she surely did make a fuss over him."

Isaac beamed as he heard mention of Delia.

Once back in the sewing room, Carmella plumped a pillow for Paul's head and covered him with a quilt. "You'll catch your death of cold being wet like this."

Paul let go of a deep sigh. "Aunt Carmella, I'd be dead for sure if Benjamin hadn't pulled me out of the car."

Carmella dropped into the chair alongside the bed with a gasp. "Good Lord, I had no idea."

Although not speaking would have been a far easier thing, Paul went on to tell of all that had happened.

"After the tire blew, the car skidded and rolled down the hill," he said. "When it flipped over I felt my head slam against something; then I blacked out." His breathing became shallow as he closed his eyes and hesitated for several minutes.

Carmella knew he was reliving the experience. She sat silently and waited.

"When I came to," he finally said, "the car was a blackened shell. I would have been inside it if not for Benjamin.

Carmella felt an icy shiver slide across her heart. "Thank God he was there."

Paul's head dropped deeper into the pillow, and a tear rolled from his eye.

"I felt so helpless," he said. The words were drawn out, heavy and slow. "Even after I'd regained consciousness, I couldn't haul myself up the hill. Benjamin carried me on his back."

A faraway look came into Paul's eyes. "My God, how can you ever repay a man for doing something like that?"

"Right now I don't know," Carmella replied, "but we'll find a way."

It seemed a long forty-five minutes before Doctor Willard arrived. When he got there he came in, kissed Carmella on the cheek, then spent a half-hour examining Paul. Pulling the chair closer to the bed he waved a penlight back and forth in front of the boy's face, telling him to follow the light. With a skilled touch, he felt up and down both legs and arms. Paul winced when he touched the left arm.

The doctor nodded. "This one's definitely broken, and I think you might've suffered a concussion. Feeling any dizziness? Nausea?"

"No," Paul answered, "but if I try to straighten my leg it's really painful."

The doctor nodded again. "Fractured knee, I suspect."

Hovering over the doctor's shoulder, Carmella asked, "Does that mean surgery?"

"I don't think so," Willard answered. "The arm feels like a clean break and the knee can heal itself, given time and rest. Of course," he added, "you'll have to check on him a few times tonight because of that concussion. I think he's past the danger point, but we can't be too careful."

"Oh, dear God," Carmella murmured.

The doctor stood and put his hand on her shoulder. "It's nothing to fret about, Carmella, I'm just being cautious."

"Will you be back tomorrow?"

"No, but you can bring Paul down to the hospital in the morning. I need an X-ray of that arm and leg." He wrapped Paul's arm with a temporary splint and put it in a sling. "Once I see the X-ray, I can put a cast on the arm."

Doctor Willard gave Paul a shot for the pain, then packed up his bag.

"A light diet tonight, nothing heavy," he warned.

By the time Carmella returned to the dining room, Benjamin and Isaac were just finishing up.

"Good," she said, "I'm glad to see you've eaten." Before she sat, she walked around the table and came up beside Benjamin. She placed her hand on his arm and said, "Thank you for saving my boy. I'm forever indebted."

"You don't owe me nothing," Benjamin answered. "I did what anybody would've done. It's pure luck I happened to be there."

"Oh, it's not luck," Carmella replied. "It's a master plan. God puts people where He wants them to be." She leaned into the words and spoke with an air of confidentiality.

"You see," she said, "He put Paul in the grocery store to save Sidney, and He put you on that road to save Paul. It may not be obvious at first," she smiled, "but we're all linked together in one big master plan."

"Oh, I don't think…" Benjamin was going to explain how he would have actually been closer to Baltimore if not for the rain, slick roads, and an old engine that kept overheating, but he never got the chance.

Sidney raised his hand. "Don't bother," he said in a way that indicated he'd been down this road before. "Once Carmella's made up her mind, there's no sense arguing."

Instead of settling into a chair, she scuttled into the kitchen and came back with a steaming pot of coffee and a plate piled high with cookies.

The fragrance of the coffee reminded Benjamin of Delia, and he tried to hold on to the thought. As Carmella stood beside him to fill his cup, for one split second he could imagine she was Delia. He looked up. With her pink skin and light eyes she was as different from Delia as the rose is from the wildflower, but despite the differences there was a familiar sameness.

"The smell a' that coffee sure brings some sweet memories," he said sadly.

It was near eleven when he finally stood to leave. "Is there a river or creek anywhere near here?" Benjamin asked.

"Creek?" Sidney questioned. "What for?"

"Isaac likes to fish. It's too late tonight, but in the morning he could—"

Carmella frowned. "You're planning to camp outside? A boy his age shouldn't be sleeping on the cold wet ground."

"It ain't like—" Benjamin was going to tell how Isaac slept in the cab of the truck, but Carmella didn't leave much space between saying one thing and another.

"That's downright foolish," she said, "especially since we have a perfectly good bedroom sitting empty upstairs."

This was a situation Benjamin had never before encountered, and it left him at a loss for words. He stumbled through some flimsy excuses for leaving, but when she continued to insist he finally said, "Miss Carmella, it's real kind of you to ask, but us sleeping here wouldn't be proper."

"Proper?" Carmella argued. "Who's to say what's proper?"

"I ain't looking to speak out of turn," Benjamin replied, "and I ain't never met your neighbors, but it could be they won't take kindly to you having colored folks in your house."

"They have no say of what I do in my own house!" Carmella said defiantly. "You didn't stop to look at the color of my boy's skin before you pulled him out of that car; what makes you think I care what color yours is now?"

Benjamin just stood there with a blank expression on his face.

Carmella drained the last of her coffee then said, "It's past time Isaac was in bed. Come on, I'll show you where your room is."

Benjamin and Isaac wordlessly followed along as she started for the staircase. Halfway up she turned back and in a shushed voice said, "Be real quiet, because Jubilee's asleep."

"Jubilee?" Benjamin repeated.

"Paul's sister," she whispered and continued up the stairs.

CARMELLA

I *know I can be a bit hasty and rush to judgment on things, but I'm* *determined not to make the same mistake I did last time. When* *Sidney was shot in that robbery, I right off assumed Paul was the* *one who did it. That poor boy was lying there in the hospital,* *unconscious and unable to defend himself, and without hearing one word* *of his story I labeled him guilty. Not only did I assume he was guilty, but* *I also did everything in my power to see that the full force of the law* *came down on him. I never gave one iota of thought to the fact that* *maybe he was trying to save Sidney, not kill him.*

Once the truth came out, I knew I had a lot to make up for. And *thank God I've been able to do it by providing those kids with a home* *and enough love to last a lifetime.*

Tonight I looked into Benjamin's eyes, and I didn't see one speck of *evil there. Yes, his skin is dark as a Hershey's chocolate, but his heart is* *lily white. Any fool can see that.*

I figure God is giving me a second chance to make up for my *misjudging people, and this time I'm going to be smart enough to take it.*

I put Benjamin and his boy in the fancy guest room because I wanted *them to have the best. Even that is pitiful small recompense for saving my* *boy's life, but it's all I have to give for now. Maybe I can think of some* *other way to repay his kindness. It's something to sleep on, that's for* *sure.*

THE PLAN

I n all his life Benjamin had never seen such a bed. He'd grown used to a mattress stuffed with straw and dry cornhusks, and in the army he'd slept on a wooden plank with a paper-thin canvas pad. This mattress was soft as a cloud, and the blanket covering it was light as a feather. Isaac sat on the side of the bed then bounced back up.

"Is we really allowed to sleep on this?" he asked.

Benjamin shrugged. "I reckon so."

Isaac crawled beneath the cover and was sound asleep in minutes. Not Benjamin. It felt wrong to be here, to be sleeping in a room in a white man's house. Sid had been warm and friendly, yet an uneasiness had settled in Benjamin's stomach. He'd eaten in a white woman's house once before, so that was okay. At dinner he'd sat on a wooden chair, a hard surface that could easy enough be wiped clean. But here in this room, in this poof of soft fabrics, he felt dirty. Too dirty to climb beneath the covers.

Benjamin thought of the pond back in Grinder's Corner, and at that moment he wished he could run to it and jump in. Maybe if he were to scrub hard enough the black of his skin would wash away, and he'd be light enough not to soil the pale-colored sheets.

Carmella had showed him where the bathroom was. Not an outhouse like his, but a bathroom like the houses in Bakerstown. He was not allowed to use those bathrooms, and he'd never once tried to. Yet Carmella said, "Here's your bathroom." She'd invited him to use it with a single admonition.

"Just be quiet," she'd whispered, saying that the girl's bedroom was right next door.

Benjamin sat in the chair for a long while. He remembered Delia's bedroom when she lived with her parents in Twin Pines. It was like this: long curtains at the window, a carpet on the floor. He'd been in that room just once, and he'd not touched the bed. He'd only held the bag while Delia tossed her belongings into it.

He looked around the room. A lamp with a switch turning it on and off; a picture of a woman holding flowers; a wooden dresser so polished it glistened, even in the dim lamplight. This was a room he wished he could have given Delia. It was the type of place where she'd once lived. She'd left it to be with him. Benjamin lowered his head into his hands and cried. It was the muffled sound of regret mixed with heartache.

After a long while he creaked the door open and walked across to the bathroom. He washed his face and hands in the sink, then dried them on sleeve of his shirt. It was not fitting that he should use the embroidered towels hanging on the rack. It was somehow wrong. When he returned to the bedroom, he stretched out on the carpet and tried to sleep.

Isaac and me will leave early tomorrow morning, he told himself. *I'll do whatever I've got to do so we can keep going. Sooner or later, we'll find a place right for us.*

Living in a white man's house is not right, he thought; then he closed his eyes and sleep eventually came.

Paul slept for several hours, but he woke long before dawn. In the dark of the sewing room he searched for the memory of yesterday. He could almost feel the car sliding out of control and the panic clutching at his heart. It happened in seconds, but the recollection of it stretched itself into what seemed like hours. He'd heard a scream when the car went airborne, and he'd somehow thought it came from Jubilee. After that there was nothing until he opened his eyes and saw Benjamin hovering over him.

Thinking back on the conversation they'd had on the ride home, Paul recalled how Benjamin spoke in vague and uncertain terms about where he was headed. New York, Philadelphia, or maybe Baltimore. The more he thought about it, the more he became convinced Benjamin wasn't headed toward anything. He was running away from something. But what?

Paul knew next to nothing about the man who'd saved his life. Benjamin said they were from Alabama, but he'd not said where. He'd asked for nothing, and yet he appeared to be without much of anything: a rocking chair and a bunch of soggy boxes in the back of a truck that was maybe twenty years old.

It was almost two years ago, but Paul could still remember the day he'd walked down the mountain carrying Jubilee on his back. Like Benjamin he'd had only the vaguest idea of where he was going and what he'd find there. He'd left the mountain with just one thought in mind: to find a home for Jubilee. As they'd walked from the bus station into Wyattsville, he'd caught a glimpse of himself in a store window and seen a fear of the future in his eyes. Benjamin had that same look.

Before the first rays of light had creased the sky, Paul came to see Benjamin as a version of himself. When he heard the footsteps on the stair, Paul had already decided what he had to do.

"Benjamin?" he called out. When no answer was forthcoming, he said, "Can I see you for a moment?"

Benjamin hesitated; he'd hoped to slip away before anyone was awake but that wasn't possible now.

"Wait here," he told Isaac and turned toward the sewing room.

"You call me, Mister Paul?"

Paul laughed and motioned to the chair. "Sit down, Benjamin, and for Pete's sake, stop calling me Mister Paul."

"Yes, sir," Benjamin answered.

"Don't call me sir either. My name's Paul. Just plain Paul. You call me Paul, and I'll call you Benjamin, okay?"

Benjamin started to say "yes, sir" but he caught hold of the word before it was out of his mouth and simply nodded.

"Sit down," Paul said. "I've got something I need to talk to you about."

Still uneasy about taking such liberties, Benjamin sat with his back stiff and his hands on his knees.

"I've got a problem," Paul said. "Uncle Sid counts on me for working in the grocery store. Unloading cartons, stocking the shelves, sweeping up, things like that. Now that I've got this broken arm, I'm not gonna be much help."

Paul hesitated a moment looking for the right words. Lean too much one way and it wouldn't sound needy enough; lean too much the other way and it would have the chime of charity.

"Anyway," Paul said, "I know you're on your way to New York, but if you're not in a hurry to get there I could sure use a hand for a few weeks." When Benjamin didn't answer right away, Paul added, "Of course I'd be willing to pay for your time."

Benjamin twitched his mouth to one side and rubbed his hand across the scruff of his beard.

"I could sure use a bit of money," he said, "but I got to find a place for me 'n Isaac to stay."

"Aunt Carmella said you're welcome to stay here."

Benjamin raised an eyebrow and gave a sorry shake of his head. "I ain't looking to argue with you, Mister Paul, but—"

"No mister," Paul cut in.

Benjamin nodded. "Okay. Anyhow, I'm more 'n happy to get work, but me and Isaac staying here ain't a good idea. Colored folk and white folk ain't supposed to live in the same house."

"Who told you that?"

"Nobody told me, it's what I *know*."

"Well, maybe what you know is wrong. You ever consider that?"

Benjamin shook his head. "I know what I see, and I ain't never seen nothing to the contrary."

"Well, I have," Paul said. "When my daddy was in the coal mines he worked alongside a man named Edgar, a man way blacker than you. When Daddy died, Edgar was the only one to come and offer help. He said Jubilee and I could live at his house if we'd a mind to."

"And you didn't do it, huh?" Benjamin nodded knowingly.

"No. But not because Edgar was colored." A look of sadness slid across Paul's face. "It was because of a promise I'd made to Daddy."

"What kinda promise?"

Paul thought back on that night. There were times when it seemed a thousand years ago, and moments like this when it was so close he could still feel the agony of it.

"That I'd never work in the coal mines," he said.

For several moments they sat there saying nothing; then Benjamin spoke. "I know Miss Carmella is every bit as good as your daddy's Mister Edgar, but Isaac and me still got to get our own place."

They finally reached an agreement; Benjamin would work at the store but he'd find his own place to stay.

"Well, you have to at least stay for breakfast," Paul said, "so Uncle Sid can tell you what all needs to be done."

"Okay then," Benjamin replied. The actuality was he didn't know if he'd find a place or not. He figured if worse came to worst, he and Isaac could sleep in the truck until he earned enough money for the rest of their trip. But if it came to that, he certainly wouldn't mention it in front of Carmella.

It seemed to Isaac that his daddy had been in that room forever, so he sat down on the bottom rise of the staircase to wait. He closed his eyes and leaned his head against the wall, thinking how he could have still been lying in that nice soft bed. He was lost in the thought when Jubilee stepped down beside him.

"Who are you?" she asked.

"Isaac," he answered.

"How come you're sitting here?"

"I'm waiting for Daddy." Isaac motioned to the sewing room.

Jubilee walked over to the room and peeked in. "Are you Isaac's daddy?" she asked Benjamin.

"Unh-huh," he nodded. "Is he misbehaving hisself?"

"No, he's just sitting on the step." By then she'd noticed Paul's arm and bombarded him with questions about it. When Paul told of the accident and recounted how Isaac's daddy had saved his life, she crossed the room, gave Benjamin a hug, then disappeared out the door.

Not long afterward, Paul heard Carmella in the kitchen. When she hollered that breakfast was on the table, Benjamin helped Paul hobble to the dining room.

The table was longer than it had been last night, and there were now six chairs where there had been just four. Sid sat at the head of the table; Jubilee and Isaac sat next to each other on one side. Still keeping his leg cocked at that half-bent angle, Paul lowered himself into a side seat and motioned for Benjamin to sit beside him.

There was a bowl of butter and a basket of biscuits on the table, but moments later Carmella came in with a platter full of scrambled eggs, sausages, and ham. Sidney's eyes lit up.

"Well, well," he said. "Isn't this a nice surprise."

With a rather pleased look on her face, Carmella said, "It's Saturday and we've got company, so I thought something special was in order. Don't get used to it," she added. "On Monday, you're back to oatmeal."

While she poured the coffee, Paul told how he and Benjamin had struck a deal.

"Benjamin's going to stay and help out in the store until I'm healed," Paul said. "My right arm's okay, so I'll work the register and he can help out with the heavy stuff."

"That's good to hear," Carmella said. "I worry about Sidney overdoing it. You know a man his age..." She let the rest of her thought trail off.

"Even though we'll have company," she added jokingly, "it's still oatmeal on Monday."

"I like oatmeal too," Isaac said as he stuffed a piece of sausage in his mouth.

Benjamin knew he had to say something. "Miss Carmella," he said apologetically, "we're not gonna be here on Monday. I'm happy to be working in y'all's store, but we got to get our own place."

"Nonsense," Carmella said. "We've got plenty of room."

"That may be," Benjamin replied, "but colored folk and white folk needs their own separate places."

"That's a very bigoted statement," Sidney said. His words had a sharp sound to them.

Benjamin turned. "I don't mean no offense, Mister Sidney, but—"

"That's what all bigots say—I don't mean any offense—but it doesn't end the hate!"

"Stop it, Sidney!" Carmella said angrily. She turned to Benjamin. "Please forgive Sid. He lost two cousins in Germany and—"

"You don't need to make apologies for me," Sidney snapped. "Bigotry is bigotry, whether you're Jewish, black, or white. It's people hating people they don't even know who started that war! Sooner or later somebody's got to say something!"

Sid angrily pushed back from the table and sat there steaming.

The clatter of forks was suddenly gone; there was only a big heavy silence hanging in the air.

Jubilee was the first to speak.

"I don't hate nobody," she said. "Me and Isaac's friends." She stretched out her skinny little arm and wrapped it around Isaac's shoulder.

"I don't hate nobody neither," Isaac added.

The hard set of Carmella's mouth softened. "That's because you're children," she said. "Children only hate when they've got reason."

BENJAMIN

I know Mister Sidney and Miss Carmella are trying to show us a
kindness 'cause of bringing their boy home, but to me it's got the
feel of charity. Sleeping in such a fancy room is like taking
something that don't rightfully belong to me, and it plain out don't sit
well. I'd sooner be sleeping in the back of the truck.

When a man's already down low, he sure don't need anybody feeling
sorry for him. I left Grinder's Corner 'cause I was too ashamed to stay,
and I done made up my mind I ain't never gonna let Isaac see me that
way again.

A boy has got to be proud of his daddy. If he ain't proud of his
daddy, he ain't never gonna be proud of hisself.

That sure ain't what Delia wanted for Isaac.

COMING TO AGREEMENT

When the silence became thick as early morning fog, Carmella tried to poke holes in it with meaningless bits of chatter. She spoke of the biscuits being slightly burnt, the price of apple butter going up two cents, and the weather forecast for rain in the afternoon. No one listened. When the silence stayed, she shooed the children away from the table.

"You've finished eating," she said. "Now go on outside and play before that rain gets here."

Once they were beyond earshot, she turned to Sidney. "You should be ashamed of yourself," she said angrily. "Such talk in front of children!"

"Me?" he replied. "I'm not the one." He looked toward Benjamin. "He's the one who made a big deal about—"

Paul, not usually one to find fault with anybody, cut in. "Uncle Sid, you jumped the gun on this one. You didn't even wait to hear what Benjamin said."

"I heard what he said," Sid replied. "I heard as much as I needed to hear."

"No, you didn't," Paul argued. "Can't you let go of your anger long enough to ask Benjamin why he feels as he does?"

"Okay, you want me to ask, I'll ask." He turned to Benjamin. "So what's your excuse?"

"Sidney!" Carmella snapped. She said nothing else. There was no need for additional words. Sid had seen the look often enough to know exactly what it meant.

He turned back to Benjamin, his voice more condescending than apologetic. "Maybe I was a bit harsh in speaking—"

"A bit harsh?" Carmella grumbled.

"Okay, I was wrong," he corrected. With words that had a more genuine ring to them he said, "Sometimes I'm too quick to judge a person and end up doing the very thing I detest. It's possible I was wrong about your reasoning..." He let the thought hang there, waiting for Benjamin to pick up the thread.

Benjamin sat silently, his eyes fixed on the sausages still on his plate. When he finally spoke his voice was soft, almost like that of a child.

"I ain't never known a man like you, Mister Sidney. You're not big in size, but you is sure big in heart."

Sid, a bit sensitive about his height, started to speak. "I don't know that I'd say—"

Carmella gave a warning glare, and he stopped mid-sentence.

Still looking down at those two cold greasy sausages, Benjamin continued. "Where I come from we learn from the time we come into this world we got to do what the white man says. White people got their place, and we got ours. It ain't something—"

"And where is it you're from?" Sid asked.

"Grinder's Corner, Alabama."

Sidney shook his head, a sorrowful slow movement meant to show a measure of disgust. "Alabama, huh?"

"Yes, sir."

"Harrumph," Sidney grumped. "I guess that's explanation enough."

Carmella let go a sigh of relief. "Well, now that you better understand one another, maybe you gentlemen can come to an agreement." With that she stood and left the table.

For several minutes the three men sat there in silence. Sidney picked up a biscuit and slathered butter on it. Benjamin cut the tip end off a cold sausage and stuffed it in in his mouth. It was a bite so small he could have swallowed it whole, yet he sat there chewing and chewing. Paul pushed a pile of eggs from one side of his plate to the other but didn't bother to eat.

Eating was little more than a cover-up for the silence. Paul's eyes went from Benjamin to Sid, then back again to Benjamin. Both were strong, stubborn men, set in their ways and proud; too proud to bend, too proud to be the one to swallow back their words.

In a situation such as this, someone had to step in. Someone had to offer the olive branch. Plucking a cold biscuit from the basket, Paul asked, "Uncle Sid, can you pass that jam down here?" As he casually spooned the jam onto the biscuit, he said, "It may be that we've come at this the wrong way."

Benjamin and Sid waited.

"We all have our wants and don't wants," Paul said. "But before we can get to what we want, we've got to listen to what the other person doesn't want."

"I'm not opposed to doing that," Sid said.

Benjamin nodded. "Me neither."

Paul looked over at Sid. "Uncle Sid, I think you and I feel much the same. We're grateful to Benjamin for pulling me out of that car and bringing me home, so we're looking for a way to repay his kindness."

"I done said you don't owe me nothing," Benjamin cut in.

Paul turned to Benjamin. "I know, but you're not hearing what we want. Just as you felt a sense of pride in doing a kindness, we want to feel that same pride by repaying it. You can't ask us to accept your kindness if you're not willing to accept ours. That's the same as a smack in the face."

Benjamin's jaw dropped. "I ain't intending no—"

"I know." Paul nodded. "But it's how Uncle Sid sees it." He turned to Sid. "You on the other hand are trying to repay Benjamin by giving him something he doesn't want, something he's uncomfortable taking."

"Uncomfortable?" Sid grumbled. "What's so uncomfortable about living—"

"Uncle Sid, I don't mean to sound disrespectful, but you're not listening to Benjamin any more than he's listening to you."

Sid gave a slight grimace and quietly leaned back in his chair.

"Those things," Paul said, "are what's at the heart of this matter. But the actual problems are that we need somebody to help out in the store until my arm heals, and Benjamin needs to earn some traveling money."

"I ain't looking for a handout," Benjamin said indignantly.

"And I ain't offering one," Sid shot back. "Only thing I offered was a job. You work and I pay you for doing the work."

"I got no problem with that," Benjamin said, "but I ain't gonna move in like family and sleep in that upstairs bedroom. It just ain't proper."

Sidney scooted closer and plunked his elbows on the table. "Well, if that's your only problem, we can fix that."

Benjamin leaned forward, listening.

"We've got a playroom downstairs in the basement. It's clean and dry but not fancy. I was planning to rent it out to a handyman, but I could instead rent it out to you for a dollar a day."

"A dollar a day?" Benjamin repeated. "Ain't that a bit high?"

"Well, I've got to figure in the cost of food for you and the boy," Sid said, making it sound like a business negotiation.

"You got a stove down there?" Benjamin asked.

"No stove, but there's heat and a bathroom."

Benjamin rubbed his whiskers thoughtfully. "No stove, huh?"

Sidney shook his head. "Nope. You and Isaac will have to eat up here with us white folks. I've come halfway. Now it's up to you to come the other half." He struggled to hold the dour look on his face and not smile.

"A dollar a day," Benjamin repeated. "And how much you gonna be paying me?"

"I'll pay you what I paid Paul when he started working at the store: thirty-seven dollars a week. I first take out my seven dollars for room and board, then give you thirty dollars cash at the end of the week."

As Paul listened he held back a grin. The truth was he'd made thirty dollars a week. Sid had tacked on an extra seven dollars to pay for the rent he was charging.

Thirty dollars was considerably more than Benjamin ever made in Bakerstown and he would have been willing to sleep in the truck to make that kind of money, but there would still be the problem of Isaac. Sleeping was one thing, but what would he do with Isaac while he was working?

The whole deal looked sweet to Benjamin—with one exception.

"What kinda neighbors you got around here?" he asked apprehensively.

"Neighbors?" Sidney repeated. "What do the neighbors have to do with—"

"Are they gonna get put out 'cause you got coloreds living in your house?"

"Of course not," Paul answered. "They're good neighbors."

"Any of them good neighbors got coloreds living in their house?" Benjamin asked. "Hired help, maybe?"

"Not that I know of," Sidney said. "But I'm sure they wouldn't—"

"If it don't make no never-mind to you," Benjamin said, "I'd sooner you tell folks I'm hired help instead a' claiming we's company."

A short while later Benjamin got in his truck and followed Sidney to the store. Isaac remained at the house playing with Jubilee as Carmella cleared the table and began readying herself to take Paul for his X-ray.

When Sidney parked in back of the store, Benjamin pulled in alongside of the car and followed him in. Benjamin had insisted on driving "hisself," and weary of arguing over trivial things Sidney had curtly answered, "Fine."

For the first few hours they were like two lovers getting past a spat; they said what had to be said in as few words as possible, then moved on to the next thing. There was no chitchat or pleasantries tucked in between the tasks. Sidney handed Benjamin the broom and told him to start sweeping up. After that he cleaned the front window and loaded bags of potato chips onto a rack. It was near ten when Sid pointed to a carton and showed Benjamin the shelf where the cans were to be stacked.

"Three rows," he said and turned back to the counter.

Benjamin pulled out the first few cans and started stacking, but when he caught sight of the picture of green beans on the label he laughed out loud.

"If that don't beat all," he said, "putting green beans in a can."

"What's wrong with green beans in a can?" Sid asked.

"Ain't nothing wrong with it." Benjamin chuckled. "I just ain't never seen it before."

"You've never seen green beans?"

"Sure I seen green beans, I just never seen 'em in a can. We growed ours."

"What about in the winter?"

Benjamin stopped stacking and stood there with a can of beans in each hand. The sad memory of Delia standing at the stove passed through his mind.

"My Delia used to cook up vegetables from the garden and put them in glass jars to last through winter." The sadness in his face was obvious, even when he turned back to stacking cans.

For a brief moment, the wall between them disappeared. It was only two men connected by a bridge of unspoken sadness and painful memories. Sidney sensed the connection, but it was gone in a flash.

Perhaps if Emma Withers hadn't walked in at that moment he would have asked about Delia, but as it happened Emma was in a mood to talk. Once she stared telling about her niece's wedding, Sidney knew he could do little but listen. As she rattled on, he watched Benjamin finish stacking the cans and move back to the storeroom. Several other customers followed behind Emma, and when the store was once again empty Benjamin was in the back scrubbing out the refrigerator.

Sometimes a single moment came and went in a person's life. It was there and then it wasn't. It was a moment that belonged to the present but stretched far into the future. Such a moment could change everything. Sidney thought back to the day Hurt McAdams walked into the store and pulled out a gun. It happened almost two years ago, but it was still right there in the forefront of his mind.

The morning had started out as ordinary as all those that came before it; then Sid looked up and saw the flash of gun coming from McAdams' pocket. Standing to the side with the "Help Wanted" sign in his hand, Paul had seen it too. He lunged for the gun just as Sidney grabbed his rifle from beneath the counter and fired.

What if Paul had hesitated? What if he'd turned back to look for the baby sister he'd left sitting on the bench across the street? What if he'd ducked down to save himself? He'd done none of those things; instead he'd stretched his arm out and grabbed for the gun. In doing so he saved Sidney's life.

Sometimes life provided opportunities to reach out and make a difference, and when that happened a man worth his salt had to step up to the challenge.

That thought was churning through Sidney's mind when he came up behind Benjamin and said, "When you finish that, let's grab a cup of coffee."

Benjamin turned and smiled.

SIDNEY

*A*ll men have pride. It doesn't matter if you're on the lowest rung of life or at the top of the ladder. Take away a man's pride and he's got nothing. That's why I have to charge Benjamin for staying here.

I tried explaining there's not enough money in the world to pay someone for saving your boy's life, but Benjamin didn't see it that way. He saw it as charity. When a person's needy, he tends to think that way.

From what I can see it doesn't look like they've got a whole lot of possessions, but Benjamin certainly has got a lot of pride.

The funny thing is that while I disagree with his way of thinking, I've got to respect the man. He's looking to make a better life for his son, and that's something you simply can't argue with.

TALK OF BABIES & BOMBERS

I t was early afternoon when Paul hobbled into the store, a leather brace on his leg and a plaster cast on his arm. The rain had already started, and Carmella walked alongside him stretching her arm in the air to hold a small red umbrella over his head. They had the look of a pair of mismatched socks, one stretched out long and skinny, the other shrunk to half its size.

Sid and Benjamin were both behind the counter, laughing like they'd shared some kind of joke. "I never would a' guessed it," Benjamin said and gave another chuckle.

"Guessed what?" Carmella asked.

Sidney gave a guilty grin "I was telling Benjamin about that time we passed through Alabama on our way home from Arthur's bar mitzvah."

"Oh, Sidney," she groaned. "That story's twenty years old. It wasn't funny then, and it still isn't funny."

"Okay, maybe it wasn't funny then," Sidney said, "but looking back it's funny."

They chatted for a few minutes, and then Carmella convinced Sidney to take the afternoon off.

"Benjamin and Paul can handle things," she said, rationalizing that it was a rainy afternoon and the store wasn't going to be that busy. "Besides," she added, "I've got a few things I need you to do at home."

Once Sidney disappeared out the door, Paul lowered himself onto the stool behind the register and Benjamin went back to filling in empty spots on the store shelves. Other than a couple of questions as to what went where and the few chores that needed to be done, there was little conversation.

After everything was unpacked and shelved, Benjamin broke down the cardboard boxes and tied them for the trash collector. By mid-afternoon there wasn't a thing left to do, and that's when he and Paul settled into long stretches of conversation.

"How'd you come to meet Mister Sidney?" Benjamin asked.

Paul gave a sad little laugh. "He shot me."

It was one of those funny but not funny moments. Paul went on to tell of how he'd walked in looking for a job and got caught up in a robbery.

"The shooter got away," he said, "but Uncle Sid and I ended up in the hospital, neither one of us able to tell what happened. The police figured I was in on the robbery, so once I regained consciousness they arrested me."

"Why you didn't say you was innocent?"

"I didn't remember. I didn't even know who I was until the detective brought Jubilee in to see me. He was a friend of Olivia Doyle, the woman caring for Jubilee. She called him and said Jubilee was looking for a brother who'd disappeared the day of the robbery. He put two and two together and got to thinking it might be me."

"Whew," Benjamin said. "You're lucky to find a detective what listened." He hadn't intended to tell Paul or anyone else what happened with Sheriff Haledon, but once they began talking it spilled out like rainwater from a leaky barrel.

Tragedy is a thing to be shared, and as they sat there listening to the rain pinging against the window he told the whole of it: how in the dark of night he'd spied on Luke Garrett and reported his findings to the deputy.

"I figured a man of law had to do what was right," Benjamin said sadly, "but I was wrong as wrong can be."

A hard edge settled across Benjamin's jaw as he told Paul that he was certain the deputy had warned Luke Garrett, and how by the time the sheriff got back from vacation the whitewall tire was missing and Garrett was clean-shaven.

"But the sheriff could investigate it, couldn't he?" Paul asked. "Somebody had to notice the guy had a beard a week earlier."

"Yeah, I'm betting plenty a' bodies noticed, but white folks don't turn on their own."

"What about some of your own people?" Paul asked.

Benjamin gave a sarcastic grunt. "In Alabama, a colored man's word ain't worth speaking. Sheriff Haledon told me what's done is done. He said the best I can do is take care of my boy and that was the end of it."

"All you needed was one friend," Paul said, "one person willing to stand up and say 'I know the truth'."

Benjamin sat there and thought back on the people he'd worked for, white people mostly. Abigail Evans had always treated him fairly; she'd even invited him in for a glass of cold lemonade last summer. When she heard what happened to Delia, she'd held his hand and told him how sorry she was for his loss. And Butch Dudley, he'd shared in the work of painting his house. Benjamin could still see the splatters of yellow paint on both white and black hands. They'd passed the turpentine soaked rag back and forth, wiping away the spots of paint stuck to their skin. Butch was an honorable man, a daddy to two boys, not someone likely to lie for a man like Garrett.

There were others, perhaps some would be willing to swear Benjamin was a man who spoke the truth. But did any of them even know Luke Garrett? Benjamin felt a lead weight drop into his heart. He knew the truth was that he'd not asked one of them. Not one. He'd just sat there and listened when the sheriff said nothing more could be done. He'd not argued or fought for the truth. Isaac had argued for the truth, but Benjamin had not.

The sound of the rain was a heartless reminder of the night Delia was killed. The image of lifting her from the muddy roadside came to mind, and Benjamin's eyes grew teary. He rubbed his shirtsleeve across his face and wiped them away.

He stood and stared down at his feet. He'd told everything there was to tell but said nothing about how Luke Garrett had yelled the word "nigger." That somehow seemed too shameful to tell.

"Maybe there was such a friend," he finally said, "but I was too busy feeling sorry for myself to go looking for them."

"We've all got regrets," Paul said. He moved closer and wrapped his right arm around Benjamin's shoulder. "It's always easier to know what you should have done when it happened yesterday."

On Saturday the store closed at six, but lost in their shared stories and the drumming of rain Benjamin and Paul lost track of time. They were still standing there talking when the telephone rang. Paul lifted the receiver and said, "Klaussner's Grocery."

"Oh, thank God you're there," Carmella gasped. "I was worried sick when you and Benjamin didn't come home."

Paul glanced up at the clock on the wall. Seven-fifteen. "Sorry, Aunt Carmella, we lost track of time."

"Well, for heaven's sake, come on home," she scolded. "I've had dinner waiting for over an hour."

After the lights were out and the store locked, they circled around the building to the back where Benjamin's truck was parked. With his leg stiffened by the brace Paul found it difficult to get into the cab, so he sat sideways as Benjamin lifted his leg and eased it over the edge of the door.

As they sat at the dinner table, Benjamin felt the tension in his stomach melt away; not because of a single word or gesture, but something he couldn't touch his finger to—a sound maybe. He ate slowly and listened.

It was the sound of ordinary, everyday small talk, the sound of a family gathering and sharing. It brought back memories of Delia and the early years of their marriage, a time when Otis was alive and their own table was ringed with the same happy sounds. When Carmella laughed he could almost hear the sound of Delia's laughter threaded through long-forgotten conversations and suddenly it came to him: laughter was the cord that tied a family together. Sadly, he couldn't remember the last time he and Isaac had really laughed together. He knew it had not happened since the night Delia died.

He looked across at Isaac sitting next to Jubilee and watched them share grins of mischief. Isaac was young. Young enough, perhaps, to move on without carrying a sack of fears and regrets on his back. Last night at the dinner table he'd held out his plate for a second helping and gobbled it down with gusto. Afterward he'd plopped down on the puffy bed and slept the sleep of angels.

For a brief moment Benjamin wished his heart could once again be that of a child. Watching them together, it was difficult to distinguish boy from girl or black from white. They were simply two kids enjoying a friendship.

"Benjamin?" Sidney repeated.

"Oh, sorry," Benjamin answered. "I was thinking back."

"Isaac was saying that you lived on a farm in Alabama. What kind of farm?"

"Ten acres, leased. Year-round crop rotation. Watermelon in the spring, corn in the summer. Winter, mostly turnips and chicories."

"Don't forget those green beans," Sidney said, laughing. "I know you grew green beans that didn't come from a can." He chuckled again and told the story of that morning.

Everyone laughed and oddly enough, even Benjamin found himself smiling.

"Nothing tastes as good as vegetables from the garden," Carmella said. "When I was a little girl Mama used to go outside, pull a zucchini from the vine, and fry it up fresh that very evening. I've never tasted a canned vegetable good as that."

The conversation had already moved on to another topic when she added, "Next summer I think I'll plant a vegetable garden right here in the backyard."

Since supper had gotten off to a late start Jubilee stayed up way past her bedtime, and it was almost ten o'clock when the kids tired of playing and Sidney led Benjamin and Isaac to the rented playroom. They clomped down the wooden stairs into a basement that stretched out longer than it was wide. The floor was covered in squares of green linoleum, and bookshelves lined the back wall. On one side sat a grouping of two easy chairs and a cluster of small tables; on the other side a double bed that looked to be as big and plump as the one Isaac slept in last night. The only difference was this bed was covered in a dark green wooly blanket.

"Plenty of stuff here to read." Sid steered Benjamin back to where the bookshelves lined the wall. "And games, if you like that sort of thing."

The shelves were crowded with books, toys, and games, but

Benjamin reached out and picked up a World War II Bomber model airplane. "Who made this?"

"Me." Sid grinned. "I made all of them."

"This looks like the B-17 Flying Fortress," Benjamin said. "I worked on these when I was stationed at Maxwell."

"You were at Maxwell?" Sid sounded impressed. "Ever do any flying?"

Benjamin shook his head. "Just worked on repairs, servicing mostly, bringing in replacement parts."

"I always wanted to fly one of those babies. I was close to forty when the war broke out, too old for the draft." He hesitated a moment then added, "After Pearl Harbor I was ready to enlist, but Carmella wouldn't hear of it. She was going through a rough time then, and I couldn't leave her."

"I didn't meet Delia 'til I was out," Benjamin volunteered. "Good thing 'cause we had Isaac not long after we was married."

"Count your blessings," Sidney replied. "We lost three babies, the last one full term, but he came stillborn. That was in December of thirty-nine."

A wrinkle of regret pulled at Sid's face then turned to a grimace. "Losing that baby tore Carmella's heart out, especially after Doctor Elgin told her she wasn't ever going to have another one."

As Sidney and Benjamin stood there talking, Isaac climbed into bed and snuggled under the covers. He had one last thought before he drifted off to sleep: he was sleeping in the same soft bed as last night, only this one had a wooly blanket covering it.

After Sid left, Benjamin dropped down in one of the worn chairs and sat there for a long time. He knew he was as different from Sid as night was from day, yet the more he tried to count up the differences the fewer there seemed to be. The rain had stopped and the moon was high in the sky when he finally climbed into bed alongside Isaac and closed his eyes.

SIDNEY

*T*hinking back on the years after Carmella lost those babies
brings back a lot of sad memories. The first two were girls, the
last one a boy. Peter, that's what we named him. It was
Carmella's daddy's name. That baby died two, maybe three days before
he came into this world, according to Doctor Elgin. The umbilical cord
wrapped around his tiny little throat. On the day of the funeral, Carmella
was so weak she could barely stand. I told her she was too sick to come,
but she insisted on being there.

That time was the worst. When Carmella went past her seventh
month with no trouble, we were convinced this baby would make it. We
started getting ready, and after I painted the bedroom an ivory color
Carmella stenciled the wall with a row of yellow ducks splashing
through puddles. Every evening she'd meet me at the door, bursting at
the seams to show what else she'd gotten for the baby. Those were good
days. Those were days when her eyes sparkled like a diamond reflecting
happiness.

Then when we came home from the hospital with no baby, it was like
misery moved in and took charge of everything. We were both hurting,
and there was nothing anybody could say or do to make it better.

I closed the door to that ivory-colored room and neither one of us
opened it for nearly a year. Then one evening when Carmella was out at
her Ladies Auxiliary meeting, I got rid of the crib and everything else.
The Mallorys were having their first baby, and I told Steve he could have
it all, the whole kit and caboodle. Only thing he had to do was come and

get it. A few weeks later I wallpapered the room and tried to cover over thoughts of our not having a baby.

Of course it didn't work. Trying to cover up something that painful is like trying to ignore your clothes being on fire. You can't pretend it's not there, because the inside of you is turning to ashes.

No matter how much I itched to be a pilot I couldn't leave Carmella, so I started building model airplanes. It was hard not being part of something that meant so much to our country, but looking back I know I did the right thing.

SUNDAY

Klaussner's Grocery Store was not open on Sunday. It never had been and according to Sid Klaussner, it never would be. He claimed God rested on that day, and he was entitled to do the same.

Benjamin, however, was a man who had worked seven days a week for as long as he could remember. More often than not he started to work before the light of day was in the sky, and just as often he trudged home on the edge of darkness. Rising early was a thing he'd gotten used to doing, and it wasn't a habit easily broken. A day of idleness was a day wasted, in his mind. If there was no work to be done, a man could take his boy fishing or hunting—except in this case that wasn't an option because Isaac was off playing with Jubilee. Benjamin thought of calling the boy and going in search of a stream where they could sit and fish, maybe bring home catch enough for dinner, but the sound of the boy's laughter dissuaded him. He hadn't heard Isaac laugh like that since that night, that terrible night.

Benjamin sat in the chair and started flipping through the pages of a *Time* magazine that was nearly a year old. He didn't stop on any given page long enough to read even a line or two; he just gave the pictures a quick glance and moved on. Sitting still made Benjamin feel itchy all over. It was like wearing wool underwear in the hot summertime.

He set the magazine down and scanned the shelf of books, but not one jumped out at him. There was a when time he'd loved to read. Back at Maxwell Air Force Base, he'd read handbook after handbook on engines, motors, mechanics, almost anything he could get his hands on. With each new thing he learned he felt he was coming closer to one day being a master mechanic; but after he got the letter saying his mama died, he lost all interest in reading. With Otis there on the farm alone, Benjamin knew what he had to be: a farmer.

Death changes people; it changed Benjamin. With each tragedy, his heart became heavier. In places where there had once been the lightheartedness of hope, a hard rock of responsibilities moved in. When his mama died he took on the responsibility of Otis, and when Otis died he tried to shoulder the burden of Delia's grief to save her from her sorrow. But when Delia died, the rock became a boulder. A boulder so large that he would be unable to stand if he allowed himself to think about it.

Benjamin stood and began pacing across the playroom floor. Each stride covered three of the eight inch linoleum squares. He'd go ten paces, then turn around and go back to where he started. Over and over he did this, all the while thinking. Random thoughts came and went like flashes of light. One moment he could see the future Delia had spoken of, and the next minute he could see nothing but a dark and ominous cloud of trouble.

After countless trips back and forth across the green linoleum, he muttered, "I've got to get out of here," and walked through the basement door into the backyard.

Out here there was air. Out here he could breathe. Benjamin looked around; it was a nice yard, bigger than he'd thought it would be. Three large oaks that needed trimming; bushes being strangled by weeds. From force of habit, he bent and pulled a long twist of crabgrass from the edge of the lawn. In just a few minutes, he'd gathered a handful of chickweed and dandelion. He walked around to the side of the house, found a garbage can, and pulled it into the backyard.

Somehow the weight of his heart seemed lighter when he was working. Working left less time for thinking, and thinking meant coming face to face with what he'd left behind as well as what lay ahead. Work was better; far better.

Once he'd pruned the vines that were within reach, Benjamin dug through his toolbox and pulled out a handsaw. He was climbing through the branches of the oak when Prudence Wentworth opened her window.

"Excuse me!" she yelled down. "What are you doing in there?" Her voice had a commanding, answer-demanding ring to it.

At first Benjamin was startled. He hadn't seen anyone when he walked outside and the bushes, surrounding the yard, gave a good measure of privacy. But then he hadn't looked at the upstairs window where Prudence had her nose sticking through the curtain.

Although he'd taken it on his own to start trimming trees, he answered, "Mister Sidney hired me to clean up the yard."

"On a Sunday?" she said skeptically.

"Yes, ma'am."

Prudence slammed the window down without saying another word.

Less than a minute later, the Klaussners' telephone started ringing. Carmella answered it.

"Do you know there's a colored man tearing up your backyard?" Prudence asked, her voice high-pitched and shrill.

Unaware that Benjamin was even out there, Carmella left her bowl of carrot salad sitting on the counter and stretched the telephone wire to where she could peek into the backyard. Seeing Benjamin drop from the low branch of the oak, she laughed. "Oh, that's Benjamin."

"Benjamin who?"

"Church, I believe is his last name. He's the young man who brought Paul home after the accident."

"Oh." Prudence gave a sigh of relief. "So you gave him a job working as your yard man. For a minute I was worried—"

Carmella chuckled. "Benjamin's not our gardener. I think he's just doing that to be nice, or maybe because he's bored."

"Bored?"

"Probably. You know how quiet it is around here on Sunday. Paul's studying, Sidney's napping, and I think the kids are playing checkers."

"What kids?"

"Jubilee and Isaac; he's Benjamin's son."

"You allow him to bring his son to work?" Prudence gasped.

With her voice growing a bit testier, Carmella said, "He's not working today. During the week he works at the grocery store, not as a gardener. And he didn't bring his son anywhere, they're staying with us."

"Carmella Klaussner!" Prudence snapped. "Please tell me you do not have a Negro man living in that house!"

It was a long few moments before Carmella answered, and when she did the words were icy enough to cause frostbite.

"If you are referring to Benjamin, yes, he and his son are staying with us."

"Lord God!" There was a long silence before Prudence spoke again. "You do know it was a Negro man who killed Martha Pillard's son, don't you?"

Carmella gave an exasperated sigh. "That was over twenty years ago. In happened in a bar fight. In Norfolk, not Wyattsville. And," she added, "truth be known, Tommy Pillard was a brawler from way back. When he was ten years old—"

"Don't make light of this, Carmella! You don't know a thing about this man—"

"Yes, I do," Carmella cut in. "I know he was kind enough to risk his own life to save Paul. In my mind anybody who would do a thing like that is a good man, and I don't give a damn if his skin is green with orange polka dots." With that she slammed the receiver down so hard it left a ringing in Prudence's ear.

"How dare you speak to me like that," Prudence stammered, but by then the dial tone had come back on.

"Just you wait," she grumbled. "I don't think Martha is going to take kindly to this."

AND THUS IT BEGAN

P rudence Wentworth was a founding member of the Wyattsville chapter of the Daughters of the American Revolution, and she had a brass plaque attesting to it displayed prominently on the mantle in her living room. To her way of thinking anyone who couldn't trace their heritage back to serving in what she called the 'Great War' was an outsider and of no benefit to the community. Two seconds after her conversation with Carmella ended, Prudence picked up the receiver and started dialing Martha Pillard's number. The telephone rang seventeen times, and although it seemed obvious Martha was not at home Prudence was too angry to give up.

"First she had to take in those two street urchins from West Virginia," she grumbled. "Now this." She continued to listen to the ring for a good fifteen minutes, and then her anger swelled to the point where she could no longer hold back.

Grabbing a pair of gardening gloves, Prudence stomped out the door into her front yard. It had been years since she'd plucked even a dead rose from the bush, but now she needed an ear and whose ear didn't matter. She remained out there in the hot sun pulling buds from still flowering plants, until John Thompson happened along.

It took little more than a nod for her to let go of what had been racing through her mind.

"Have you heard the news?" she asked John.

"What news?"

"We've got a Negro family living in the neighborhood."

With an anger that was obvious, she yanked a newly-planted yellow mum from the ground, tossed it into the pail, and looked square into John's face. "You know what that means, don't you?"

John, who was not much of a talker, just stood there looking at her quizzically.

"Once one moves in, there's more coming."

John tried to think of where anybody could have moved in; as far as he knew there wasn't an empty house on this block or the next.

"The place will be overrun with coloreds hanging out windows and playing in the streets." Prudence gave a troubled sigh and added, "You can just guess what's going to happen to property values, right?"

"Moved in where?" he asked.

"With the Klaussners."

Still looking a bit puzzled John repeated, "With the Klaussners?"

"Yes, indeed." Prudence gave an affirmative nod. "I wouldn't have believed it if I hadn't seen it with my own eyes."

She went on to describe Benjamin as the biggest, blackest Negro she'd ever laid eyes on.

"There he was," she said, "walking around the backyard like he owned the place."

"Maybe he's working for them."

"Unh-unh." She narrowed her eyes and raised her brows. "I came right out and asked Carmella about it and she told me he's a friend of Paul, that boy they took in."

Prudence leaned over the fence and in a hushed voice said, "Those two kids are from West Virginia, and you know how those mountain communities are. They think it's just fine to live side by side with coloreds."

At a loss for words, John tugged at his ear then turned to leave.

In one last desperate attempt to pull him over to her way of thinking, Prudence hollered, "It may not seem like much now, but how do you think Mary Beth is gonna feel when you've got a colored boy chasing after your daughter?"

John stopped and turned back. "Chasing after Elizabeth? At twelve years old? She's not even—"

"Not right now maybe, but just you wait! Once they get a foothold in the neighborhood, the next step up is marrying a white girl."

"Hogwash!" he said and walked off.

Although John knew Prudence Wentworth was a busybody who went about stirring up trouble where there was little or no cause, her last comment got stuck in his head. Elizabeth was a beautiful blue-eyed blonde, a gentle soul with a sweet disposition. The kind of girl any man would want. He'd always figured she'd marry well; a doctor or lawyer maybe. Now, according to Prudence, there was an ominous threat living just three doors down. That thought picked at his brain until late in the evening when he asked Mary Beth if she'd heard anything about such a rumor.

"You know Prudence," she laughed. "She's always looking for something to complain about."

"Maybe so," John answered, "but do you think there's any truth to the rumor?"

Having already started up the stairs with a stack of folded sheets she'd brought in from the line, Mary Beth didn't answer.

When the Klaussners sat down to supper on Sunday evening, Carmella thanked Benjamin for the work he'd done in the yard but never mentioned Prudence Wentworth's telephone call. It was simply an unpleasantry better forgotten.

On Monday the Klaussner household went back to its normal routine: hot oatmeal with brown sugar and canned peaches was served for breakfast. Before the table was cleared everyone began wandering off to start their day. Sid and Benjamin were first to leave. They started for the store at seven-thirty; a short while later Paul headed for an accounting class, and Jubilee tromped out to wait for the school bus. She'd asked to take Isaac along, but the answer was no. Carmella knew she could do what she wanted in her own house, but the Virginia schools were segregated and there was no way of getting around it.

"How come I ain't got school?" Isaac asked.

"You've got to be a permanent resident before you can register," Carmella answered. It was a lie of convenience, because she knew there was no colored school in Wyattsville. The closest was two towns over and twenty miles away.

Isaac looked up. "What's a permanent resid—"

"Someone who's lived in the town for a long time," Carmella said lightly.

"How long?" he asked hopefully.

Carmella squatted down and looked into the boy's face. How could she possibly tell an innocent child the truth?

"I don't know exactly how long," she said, "but for now you can study your lessons right here at home." She pulled Isaac to her bosom and held him there for almost a minute. When she finally let go, she began telling him how at one time she'd been a teacher.

"Of course, that was a long time ago," she said. "Before Sidney and I started thinking about having a family."

They sat at the kitchen table, and Carmella handed Isaac a notepad and pencil. "Let's start with spelling."

In the Grinder's Corner School there was never a time when a teacher gave a student such one-on-one attention, and Isaac wallowed in the specialness of it.

"When you didn't be a teacher no more, was that 'cause Mister Paul got born?" he asked.

"No," Carmella laughed. "Paul and Jubilee came to live with us two years ago"

"They ain't your real babies?"

"I'm not their birth mother," Carmella said, "but they're my babies. God gave them to me as a present."

"You figuring God's gonna give you any more babies?" Isaac asked.

Carmella chuckled. "You ask way too many questions. Now stop stalling and let's get to that spelling."

By mid-morning Benjamin had already swept the store and the sidewalk in front of it. He'd also restocked the shelves, cleaned the front window, and polished the brass handle on the front door.

"There's not much else to do right now," Sidney said. "Take a break; grab a cup of coffee if you want."

As far as Benjamin was concerned, unless a river of sweat was rolling down your back and your legs were too weary to be walking taking a break was the same as sitting idle.

"How about I clean up that other refrigerator instead," he suggested.

"Don't bother," Sidney replied. "It's broken. I think the motor's gone."

Benjamin's face lit up. "Might be I can fix it."

Sidney gave a pessimistic shrug. "Try if you want, but I think it's shot."

Once Benjamin disappeared into the back storeroom, Sidney went on about the business of waiting on customers. Other than a bit of banging around back there, he didn't hear from Benjamin again until almost three-thirty.

When he finally came from the back of the store, Benjamin's overalls were spotted with oil and a large clump of gray dust clung to the side pocket. Beaming with pride, he said, "I got her going."

Sid looked up with astonishment. "You fixed the refrigerator?"

Keeping that same prideful grin, Benjamin nodded.

"Well, if that's don't beat all," Sid laughed. "I figured that thing was ready for the junkyard."

Still proud of his achievement, Benjamin went step by step explaining how he'd gone about fixing it, and although Sid listened he didn't understand most of what was said. When Benjamin finished, Sid said an achievement such as that called for an ice cold Coca-Cola. He pulled two from the refrigerator case, opened the bottles, and handed one to Benjamin.

As they stood there talking, Sidney asked Benjamin if he'd ever had a civilian job as a mechanic. "Appliance repairman, garage mechanic, or working on airplanes maybe?"

"No, sir," Benjamin laughed. "Just in the army."

"Shame," Sid said thoughtfully, "because you sure are good at it."

They finished up the Coca-Colas and talked for another twenty minutes, but Sid never once mentioned the thought that had come to mind.

CARMELLA

*P*rudence Wentworth is a trouble-making busybody. I know it's not right to say such things about a neighbor, but she is someone who truly deserves it. I have never heard that woman say a kind thing about one single person.

Why, she even complained when little Nancy Kellerton came knocking on her door to sell a few boxes of Girl Scout cookies.

I know she's lonely and unhappy being by herself all the time, but maybe if she'd be a bit nicer people would be more inclined to stop by for a visit.

She's never even laid eyes on little Isaac, but she's up in arms about him being here. Well, as far as I'm concerned she can just kiss my butt. I don't care what color that little boy's skin is, he's a damn sight more pleasant to be with than Prudence Wentworth.

I haven't mentioned this to Sidney or anyone else, and I don't intend to.

The truth is I like having Isaac here, and I like teaching him. The way he wriggles around and tries to get past answers he doesn't know makes me laugh. If I ask him to spell a word he doesn't know, he'll say he's got to go to the bathroom or ask for a cookie. It's a game we play; I give him the cookie, then ask him the same word all over again. He starts giggling; then I start giggling too.

I can tell you this. The moon would turn blue before Prudence Wentworth said anything worth so much as a snicker.

A Simmering Situation

On Sunday evening Prudence Wentworth stood at her front
window watching for Martha Pillard's return until well after
midnight. She tried telephoning several times, but still there
was no answer.

It made no sense. Martha was retired and did little more than putter
around the kitchen. Once a week she went grocery shopping and there
was the occasional Tuesday night bingo game at the church, but
Prudence could not remember a time when Martha was gone for more
than a few hours. Monday morning she returned and rang the doorbell
again but this time when there was no answer, she circled around to the
back and peered through the kitchen window. There was little to see. A
yellow dishtowel folded across the rim of the sink, everything neatly in
place, but no Martha.

Prudence began to worry. She and Martha were both widows.
Widows were easy prey. Any stranger in the neighborhood would have
been cause for concern, but a Negro stranger was doubly so. Anything
could have happened. She walked around to the side of the house and
stood with her foot in the flowerbed to peer into the bedroom. No signs
of a struggle. Prudence returned to the front, tried the doorbell one last
time, then decided to call the police. She was starting back across the
street when Darlene's car pulled up and Martha stepped out.

"Where in God's name have you been?" Prudence shrieked.

"Visiting Darlene and the kids," Martha replied.

With a begonia petal still stuck to her shoe, Prudence exclaimed,

"I've been calling since yesterday, and when you didn't answer I assumed the worst!"

"What worst?"

Grabbing hold of Martha's arm and leaning in, she whispered, "There's a big black Negro living next door to me, and he looks a lot like the one who stabbed poor Tommy."

Martha's face turned white as a sheet, and her expression was just as flat. "That's not one bit funny," she said. "You know that man was sent to prison."

"For twenty years," Prudence replied. "It's been almost twenty-five."

Martha let out a huge whoosh of air and clutched her hand to her heart. For a moment she swayed like a woman about to faint, but Darlene got there in time and grabbed her mama's arm. She turned to Prudence with an angry glare in her eye.

"What have you done to Mama?" she shouted.

"I told her the truth," Prudence answered. Then she explained about the Negro who had moved in with the Klaussners. "They have no idea who he is or where he came from," she said, "and from what I've seen of the man he could easily as not be the same one who stabbed your brother."

Hearing it for a second time made Martha feel woozier than ever. "I've got to go inside and sit down," she said.

As Darlene helped her mama through the door, Prudence followed.

"I don't like upsetting people," she said, "but people have a right to know what's happening to our neighborhood. If we're not careful…"

Martha listened to the words trailing off and thought back to the night Tommy was killed. He was barely eighteen and as far as she knew not much of a drinker, yet they'd said it happened in a bar fight. Five Negros and a white bartender all claimed Tommy was drunk and fairly belligerent when the fight started, but she'd doubted the validity of that story. Tommy wasn't the type. Despite the testimony of all six witnesses, Martha believed then and still believed her boy was simply a victim. A white boy killed for the money in his pocket.

After the trial Martha spent weeks, months, and years bemoaning the fact that Tommy's assailant had gotten off with just twenty years when he should have been put to death. Over time she stopped talking about it, but she never forgot. The hatred she felt was still there, just under her skin, and it throbbed like the pounding of a kettle drum.

"Carmella Klaussner never had a boy stabbed by a nigger," she said angrily. "What right does she have to bring one into our neighborhood?"

"It's not just him," Prudence said. "He's got a kid with him, and that surely means trouble. Next thing you know we're gonna have colored schools and a neighborhood so thick with them we'll be afraid to step out at night."

"That couldn't happen here in Wyattsville," Darlene said.

"Oh, couldn't it?" Prudence replied. She swore there was an area of Portsmouth that five years ago was a nice neighborhood and had now turned all black. "Once they get a foothold in a neighborhood, they take over," she warned.

Darlene had been an impressionable fourteen-year-old when Tommy was killed, and through the years she'd heard only her mama's version of the story.

"I don't want a nigger living next door to Mama," she said. "We've got to do something."

For seven months prior to the arrival of her first-born, Darlene worked as a typist in a downtown law office; this, she felt, gave her the necessary expertise for drafting a petition demanding the Klaussners move.

Prudence hadn't expected anything quite so drastic.

"Maybe we ought to just say not have any colored people living in their house," she suggested.

But by then it was too late; Darlene had already pulled out her daddy's old typewriter and started clacking out the letter.

"We'll ask everybody on the street to sign it," she said. "That way they'll have no comeback."

When Darlene finished the letter she handed it to Prudence. "This ought to get rid of the problem," she said pompously.

Prudence stood there and read it. "Blight on our neighborhood? Legal action? Forced eviction? Don't you think this is a bit too strong?"

"Not one bit," Darlene answered.

Martha of course agreed with Darlene. But after a good bit of discussion and three more revisions, they ended up with a letter requesting the Klaussners remove their house guests to avoid the necessity for legal action. Prudence wanted to remove the threat of legal action, but Martha and Darlene stood firm on that.

Darlene was a lot like Martha, and once she set her mind to hating a thing there was no stopping her. On Tuesday morning she arrived at her mama's house with the twins in tow and a clipboard tucked under her arm. Arm in arm she and Martha walked up and down the street knocking on doors and asking folks to sign a petition to keep coloreds out of the neighborhood.

Their first stop was at Rodney Edwards' house. "Hell, yeah," he said and signed his name without bothering to read what was written on the petition.

Once that happened Darlene's confidence grew, and she regretted softening up the language of the petition.

"We should've insisted they move," she told her mama.

Martha gave a barely perceptible nod. The truth was she'd spent a sleepless night tossing and turning. Hour after hour she thought of Tommy and could almost feel the knife being thrust into his chest. The problem was her memory of it got muddied when thoughts of Carmella Klaussner crept in.

They'd been friends for thirty years. After Tommy died, Carmella was the one who came with baskets of fresh-baked muffins and sat alongside her during those long and lonely days. And then four years ago when Tommy's daddy keeled over with a heart attack, Sid Klaussner handled everything. They'd always been good neighbors, friends even, but now there was this.

When Martha's heart began to go soft she considered giving up the angry petition, but then she called to mind thoughts of Tommy and the fire of hatred flared again.

At the Burkes' house there was no answer so they moved on to the Lamberts'. Sylvia and Dale Lambert were younger than many of other homeowners. Before they'd moved to Wyattsville, Sylvia had spent seven years as a social worker in the city of Philadelphia. The moment the door opened, Darlene thrust out the clipboard and asked Sylvia to sign the petition.

"It's to keep our neighborhood safe," she said.

Instead of signing Sylvia read every word, then started asking questions.

"This man in question," she said, "is he a convicted felon?"

Darlene shrugged. "Possibly."

"Possibly?" Sylvia repeated. She went on to ask a dozen different questions, none of which Darlene could answer affirmatively.

"You've got nothing against this man," Sylvia finally said. "There's no way I'm going to—"

"My son was stabbed to death by a nigger," Martha offered up feebly.

"But it wasn't this man," Sylvia replied. Without further ado, she closed the door.

At the end of the day Darlene had four signatures on her petition, six houses where there had been no answer, and five homeowners who'd flat out said no. Alexia Franklin had looked Martha square in the eye and said she ought to be ashamed of herself, turning on a friend in such a nasty way.

As they walked home Martha's shoulders were slumped and her head bent. Darlene put her arm around her mama's shoulders and gave a soft squeeze.

"Don't worry, Mama," she said. "We'll get the rest of them tomorrow."

UGLY ANGER

I t took nearly two weeks for Darlene to get to every house on Bloom Street and present her petition. She knocked on the Millers' door nine times before she finally caught them at home on a Sunday morning. After a week of working night shifts at the hospital Pamela Miller was in no mood for conversation when the doorbell rang at seven o'clock that morning. She listened to the first half of Darlene's speech about saving the neighborhood then told her to stick that petition where the sun don't shine and slammed the door so quickly it hit the tip of Darlene's nose.

For a moment Darlene stood there too stunned to move; eventually she grumbled, "There's no need to get snippy." But by then Pamela was back under the blanket.

For the first week Martha trudged along arm-in-arm with Darlene, but when it began to seem that half the people she counted as friends weren't willing to sign such a petition she lost her enthusiasm for the project and said she didn't think she could continue. Wearily lowering herself into a chair, Martha gave a sorrowful sigh.

"They just don't understand how different Negros are," she said, "I guess you've got to come face to face with their meanness before you understand it."

"That's why you've got to come with me, Mama," Darlene begged. "You can make them understand. You can tell them about Tommy, about how awful—"

"You do it, Darlene," Martha replied. "It's too much for a woman my age."

Knocking on the doors by herself, Darlene got a much cooler reception. On the day that it poured rain, she went to five houses and didn't come back with a single signature. Alfred Spence said he wasn't in favor of colored folks moving into the neighborhood, but since Darlene didn't actually live on the block he wasn't signing anything.

"Send your mama back," he said. "If she asks, I might be willing to sign it."

As the days passed, a strange hush settled over Bloom Street. Just weeks earlier there were residents coming and going, placing pumpkins on their doorsteps, sweeping leaves from the walkway. Now there seemed to be no one. Neighbors passed one another with little more than a nod. Those who'd signed Darlene's petition spoke to the others who had, but those whose names were missing from the petition were tagged "Bleeding Heart Liberals" and avoided. That single sheet of paper created a divide in the community as palpable as a string of burning crosses stretched across the lawns. On a drizzly morning when Martha stepped outside to fetch the newspaper, Sidney saw her and waved but she ducked her head and scurried back inside as if she hadn't seen him.

Things began falling apart that second week. One night the Klaussners' garbage can was overturned and the trash strewn across the side lawn. That Carmella blamed on a raccoon.

"They're just foraging for food," she said and suggested maybe Sidney bring home one of those heavyweight galvanized cans with a tight fitting lid.

Two days later they were sitting down to supper when they heard something hit the front of the house. When Sidney went to investigate, he found a splatter of raw egg running down the door. At that point he had his suspicions, but it was simply that: suspicions.

Carmella insisted it was teenage boys pulling some leftover Halloween pranks.

"Remember last year," she said, laughing. "They had toilet paper hanging from all the oak trees."

Sidney pretended to chuckle at the thought, but the truth was he'd seen the look in Benjamin's eyes.

The following evening Archie Dodd knocked on the door with the pretense of needing to borrow a screwdriver. Before he had both feet inside the door he mentioned that he smelled coffee and wouldn't mind having a cup. He followed Sid into the kitchen and plopped down in a chair. Carmella filled two mugs, then set a dish of chocolate chip cookies in the center of the table.

For a long while the two men sat there chatting about everything and nothing: the weather, business, the football season.

"Unitas looks good," Archie said.

Sid nodded. "If his arm hold out the Colts could go to the championship."

It was bits and spurts of conversation, things that were of no consequence and offered little to talk about. When Carmella finished wiping the counter and left the room, Archie leaned in and spoke in a hushed voice.

"There's something you should know," he said and began to tell of how Darlene was going from house to house with her petition.

Sid listened intently but remained silent.

"You've got a lot of friends here," Archie said. "Friends who aren't willing to sign that thing, but the truth is they're all running scared."

"Scared of Benjamin?" Sid asked. "How can they be scared of someone they don't even know?"

Archie shrugged. "Maybe they're not scared of Benjamin; maybe they're just scared of change."

As Archie continued to speak of the violence rearing its ugly head in cities across the country and how it had affected people's way of looking at things, Sid sat there and thought. He'd known something was afoot but had not realized it had gone this far. Tomorrow he would have to call Martin. He'd sent a letter a week earlier, but the mail could be slow. A letter could even get lost.

"People can accept you having him work in the store," Archie said, "but the bottom line is they don't want coloreds living in their neighborhood."

"Well, I guess they'll do what they have to do," Sid replied. "But

I'm not going to ask Benjamin to leave. He's had enough hardships and—"

"He's in for more if he stays," Archie cut in. "The anger Darlene is stirring up is ugly. Yesterday she was bringing around the newspaper clipping that shows Tommy with a knife sticking out of his chest."

"Is that true?"

Archie nodded. "It isn't like you can't fix this," he suggested. "I know for a fact Willie Schumann has a furnished room over the garage and needs a man for the night shift. If Benjamin's handy as you've been telling me, I bet Willie would let him stay there just for helping out a few hours in the evening."

"That garage is on the far side of town, right next to the highway."

"Yeah." Archie nodded. "That's why nobody's gonna object to him living there."

"Benjamin's got a son, an eleven-year-old boy. There's no place to play, no school—"

Archie gave another shrug. "He could go to Claremont."

"That school's over twenty miles away!"

"But Willie's place is safer than here."

"We've got sixteen houses on Bloom Street," Sid said. "How much danger can there be from a handful of working people and a few widows?"

"Maybe not much from these people, but anger spreads. Sometimes people get mad at life, and they start looking for something to take their mad out on."

The mugs of coffee sat there and grew cold as they continued to talk in that same hushed voice. It was near eleven when Archie stood to leave.

"Whatever you decide," he said, "I'll be there to back you up; the decision is yours."

Archie, a bear of a man with a bald head and round belly, reached out and wrapped his arms around Sid. "Call if you need me," he said and walked out.

There was no mention of the screwdriver he'd come to borrow.

Long after everyone else had gone to bed, Sidney sat in the darkened living room wondering what to do, wondering whether this was this how it started. He thought back on the last time he'd seen his cousin, Ezra Klaussner. It was in 1920, almost forty years ago. Ezra, his mama, papa, and a baby sister they called Tootie crossed the Atlantic in a steamship to come for a month-long visit. Ezra was fourteen at the time, two years younger than Sidney. They'd played together, tossed a football back and forth, swam in the river, and eyed the pretty girls down on Main Street.

At the end of their month-long stay Ezra and his family returned to Germany, but for nearly twenty years they had remained in touch. Just a letter now and then; an announcement of Ezra's marriage to Margot, and then the birth of their daughters along with black and white snapshots showing the happy family.

Now they were all dead. Or supposedly dead. No one ever knew exactly what became of all those people. They were whooshed away in the dark of night and never heard from again. Ezra's letters stopped coming in 1941.

Sidney thought about that last letter he'd received. It was in the early years of Hitler's regime. "A bit of ugliness, certain to pass," Ezra wrote. "Nothing to be concerned over. The people of this town are our friends; no harm can come to us here. I am certain it is safe to stay."

He closed his eyes and could still see the slant of Ezra's handwriting. Had he not seen the danger when he wrote those words?

Sidney's eyes filled with tears. Did each man have to make his own decision, or were we in fact our brother's keeper? *Perhaps,* Sidney thought, *it's a bit of both.*

It was nearing dawn when he crawled into bed and snuggled close to Carmella, feeling the warmth of her body and breathing in the sweetness of her scent.

In the coming days he would warn Benjamin, but first he had to talk to Martin.

SIDNEY

*Y*ou *think you know people; you think these are your friends, they can't possibly turn against you. And then something like this happens.*

I can't help believing this is how it was with Ezra. I know for a fact he felt safe in Fulda. He knew of the hatred but didn't see the danger. If he had he would have taken his family and fled. Any man would. What good are possessions if you lose those you love?

The shittiest part of all this is that I truly like Benjamin. He's a man I'd be proud to have as a neighbor. But the bottom line is that this isn't about what I want, it's about what's best for Benjamin and Isaac. Like it or not, I've got to consider their safety. People you might normally think sane do crazy things when they get riled up.

Personally I don't give a rat's ass what these neighbors think, and I'm certainly not going to ask Benjamin to leave. I couldn't do it. He deserves better.

What I want to do is help him find a better life somewhere else. Hopefully a place where a bunch of opinionated idiots don't have a ramrod stuck up their butt. I'm counting on Marty to make it happen.

After hearing what Archie said, it honestly makes me wonder if I want my own family to live here on Bloom Street.

This kind of hatred is a terrible thing. It corrupts people from the inside out. Boils on the skin are better than bigotry. At least you can lance a boil and get the poison out. With bigotry there's nothing you can do.

THE PETITIONERS

The next morning Sidney pulled an old address book from the drawer in his nightstand and dialed Martin Hinckley's telephone number. It had been two, maybe three years since they'd spoken, but in some ways it seemed like yesterday. He placed the first call before they left for the store. When there was no answer, he slid the address book in his pocket with plans to call later.

For three days he carried that address book in his pocket. Sometimes he called in the morning, sometimes in the afternoon, and twice after supper in the evening. It was nine o'clock Wednesday evening when Elsie Hinckley finally answered the telephone.

"I've been calling for days," Sidney said. "Is everything okay?"

"No." She sniffed. "It's terrible. Marty had a heart attack. Sunday night I was sitting there laughing at the Jack Benny show and all the while I thought Marty was asleep but when I went to wake him—"

"Is he okay?" Sid asked anxiously.

"He's in the hospital." Elsie gave a long sad sigh. "I told him. A thousand times I told him, 'Marty, you work too hard'."

"He's always been that way," Sid said.

"He's not getting any younger you know. He's fifty-eight next June."

Once Sid learned that Marty was on the mend and due to be released later in the week, he asked if there was anything he could do, any way to help.

"You could stay in touch," Elsie said fondly. "And you can tell

Marty not to be working so hard. He might listen to you," she added. "He never listens to me."

Sid replaced the receiver and smiled. *Same old Marty*, he thought.

Exactly one week after he'd spoken with Elsie, all hell broke loose. It started on Wednesday evening at seven-thirty. Sid knew the precise time because with the clock chiming for the half hour, he'd not heard the doorbell the first time. It was only after a fist started pounding on the door that he came to answer it. When he snapped on the porch light and opened the door, he came face to face with a crowd of people. Darlene stood smack in the middle of the pack.

She waved a copy of the signed petition in the air. "Mama don't want niggers living next door," she yelled. "Nobody else does neither!"

There was a low grumble going through the crowd, but it was the sound of Darlene's voice that brought Carmella scurrying to the door. She came up behind Sid and spotted Martha standing next to her daughter.

"Martha," she exclaimed, "what in the world is going—"

"You don't need to be talking to my mama," Darlene snarled. "She's not one bit interested in anything you have to say!"

"Martha?" Carmella looked toward the woman she'd known for so many years, but Martha lowered her face and took a step back into the crowd.

Sid looked at the crowd and called out the names of his neighbors as he scanned the faces. "Tom, is this what you want to do? And Henry, you too?"

"It ain't what we want to do," somebody in the back yelled. "It's what we've got to do!"

In a booming voice weighted with anger and resentment, Sid said, "Well, then, where are your hoods? Where's the burning cross? Isn't that the way this is supposed to be done?"

"It ain't like that," Henry Jacobs answered. "We're just trying to keep the neighborhood safe for our families."

"And you think I'm a threat?" Sid asked.

"Not you but that colored fella—"

"That colored fella," Sid echoed cynically, "saved Paul's life. He didn't stop to check if he was black or white, he just pulled him out of a burning car and brought him home."

"Bullshit," a gruff voice yelled. "I heard they was friends from a bar."

"Yeah," a woman added, "I figure the nigger gave him that broken arm in a fight!"

A guffaw came from the back, but before anything more could be said Paul pushed past Sid and stepped out onto the porch, forcing some of the crowd to back down a step or two. In the glow of the porch light the white plaster cast looked yellowish and considerably larger.

"Benjamin is not a nigger," Paul said angrily. "He's a Negro man who's a daddy just like most of you. He didn't ask to come here, and he didn't ask to stay here. He's here because I asked him to help us out in the store."

"Bullshit," the gruff voice repeated.

Sid stepped out onto the porch and stood beside Paul. He recognized the voice and nodded in the direction it came from. "Bob, I didn't hear you yelling 'bullshit' when you had that broken leg and Paul mowed your grass all summer."

"I said I'd pay him."

"You never did and he never asked you for a dime, did he?"

In a considerably smaller voice, Bob Paley answered, "No, but—"

"But nothing," Sid cut in. "That's what decent people do, help each other, lend a hand when it's needed." He took a step sideways and peered around Darlene so that he was looking straight at Martha.

"What about you, Martha?" he said. "Did you forget all those nights Carmella sat with you after Tommy's death?"

"I didn't forget," Martha answered flatly. "But don't you forget it was a nigger who killed him!"

"Shame on you; shame on you all!" Sid said.

Nobody answered, and Henry Jacobs moved down a step.

Darlene turned back to the crowd. "Ain't nobody gonna say what we got to say?"

When no one answered, she thumped her hands on her hips and stuck her snooty little nose in Sid's face. "Get him out of here by Friday, or we're getting a lawyer!"

Sid didn't blink an eye or move a muscle. "Do what you have to do," he said without backing off an inch.

Paul, who for the whole of his life had been taught to respect a woman's delicacy, did something he'd never before done. He swung his left arm out and gave Darlene a shove that sent her tumbling into Henry Jacobs.

When Sid turned and went back inside the house, Paul followed him.

As the door closed they heard Darlene yell, "Just you wait, this fight ain't over!"

Benjamin heard it too.

PAUL

*I*f Mama was looking down and saw what I did tonight, she'd cringe for sure. Once when I smacked Jubilee for scribbling on my school paper, Mama gave me a talking to I'm not ever gonna forget. 'I don't care what a girl does to you,' *she said,* 'there's no excuse for raising your hand. If it's something you can't deal with just walk away.'

I've been taught to treat ladies with respect, but tonight I just couldn't help myself. Seeing Darlene push that pointy nose of hers into Uncle Sid's face was more than I could take. A man can walk away if somebody's hurting him, but if it's somebody he loves that's a different story. When somebody attacks someone you love, you've got to stand up for them. Woman or man.

Sid Klaussner's one of the kindest men I've ever known. I've never heard him say a bad word about anybody, and he sure don't deserve to be talked to the way she did.

I'm sorry Darlene lost her brother, but that don't give her cause for hating everybody else.

If Darlene took time to get to know Benjamin, she'd see he's a lot like us. He's a man with a heart full of hurts on the inside; the only difference is he's got black skin on the outside.

If you ask me, having black skin ain't nearly as bad as having a black heart like Darlene.

VOICES IN THE NIGHT

When the doorbell first rang, Paul and Benjamin were downstairs playing checkers. Seconds after Paul laughingly said he was playing at a disadvantage because of the cast on his arm, he heard the shriek of Darlene's voice.

"I'll be right back," he'd said and stood up from the table. He hurried up the stairs as fast as he could go and Benjamin followed along, but when Paul pushed his way out onto the porch Benjamin hung back. When he caught sight of the crowd, he stood behind the side wall in a spot where he could hear but not be seen.

Listening to the anger in Darlene's voice, Benjamin knew the thing he feared had come to pass.

In moments of anger heated words fly quickly and there's little time for taking stock of your surroundings, so Sidney didn't realize Benjamin was there until after he'd slammed the door. As he stomped back through the room, he saw the dark figure and turned.

"Dear God, Benjamin," he said, "I'm sorry you had to hear that."

"You got nothing to be sorry about," Benjamin replied. "Things is what they is."

"That's not true," Sidney argued. "That was just a bunch of loudmouth—"

Nervously shifting his weight from one foot to the other, Benjamin said, "Isaac 'n me been trouble enough for you. It's time for us to get going."

"No," Paul said emphatically. "If you leave that means they win."

215

Benjamin gave a cynical little chuckle. "They's gonna win anyway."

Hearing such a thing made Sidney madder than he already was. Normally a soft-spoken man with a jovial tone to his voice he launched a tirade, saying that he planned to fight fire with fire.

"It's not just you, Benjamin," he said. "It's the principles of human decency."

Benjamin was going to say human decency wasn't the same for colored folks as it was for white, but before he had the chance Carmella came in and shushed them all.

"This is not a conversation I want the children to hear," she said firmly. "If you have a need to talk of such things, then go out in the backyard and do it."

Sidney gave a nod and headed toward the basement stairs. Paul followed with Benjamin right behind him. Benjamin was the only one who'd noticed the tearful look in Carmella's eyes. When he passed by he leaned over and in a soft whisper said, "That woman what lost her son ain't mad at you, Miz Carmella, she's just mad at the meanness of life."

"Thank you, Benjamin." Carmella fondly touched her hand to his arm. It was a fleeting thing, a moment, maybe two at the most, but it was a gesture that would remain in Benjamin's heart for a good long time.

One by one they tromped down the basement stairs, across the playroom, and out the door into the backyard. With the chill of winter already in the air the cushioned wicker furniture was gone, stored for the winter. There was one green metal chair, cold to the touch, but better than the ground; Sidney lowered himself into it. Benjamin sat on the low wall of a planting bed, and Paul leaned his back against a support post.

Sidney was the first to speak. "For God's sake, have these people gone mad?"

It was a long time before anyone answered Sidney's question, and the silence settled in like a heavy fog.

"They ain't gone mad," Benjamin finally said. "They're just feeling what a whole lot of other folks feel."

"And what's that?" Paul said sharply. "A hatred of anybody who's different?"

"That's exactly what it is!" Sidney snapped. "And this is how it starts." He went on to tell the story of his cousin, Ezra.

"This past week I've been thinking about Ezra a lot. I think about him and that beautiful family he had. Gone. All of them gone." Sidney lifted his hands to his face and rubbed his eyes. There were no tears to be brushed away, just a sharp pain poking at the back of his eyelids.

"How do we fight evils such as this?" he asked sorrowfully.

"For some leaving is the only way to fight," Benjamin said. "If Ezra left Germany, he might a' saved his family."

Paul hesitated, torn between wanting Benjamin to stay and wondering what was best.

"To stay or leave isn't always an easy decision," he finally said. "If not for that promise to Daddy, I might not have left West Virginia." He told of the day he'd carried Jubilee down the mountain on his back.

"I was more scared than I let on," he said. "We had no home, nobody to turn to, very little money, and I didn't even know whether or not I'd find work."

Benjamin gave an understanding nod. "There's times when you see a place bleeding the soul right out of your body, and still you stay. Not 'cause you wanna be there, just 'cause you're scared of leaving."

Sidney turned to Benjamin and asked, "What finally made you decide to leave Alabama?"

"Isaac," he answered. "I want him to grow up being proud of hisself. Delia used to say there's no hope in Grinder's Corner."

As Benjamin sat there talking, her words came back as clearly as if she was whispering them in his ear. "Grinder's Corner is a place where colored people don't do nothing but live and die, that's what she'd say."

With a melancholy look tugging at the edge of his mouth, he finished the thought. "I wish I'd seen the truth of them words sooner."

As they sat and talked, a gray squirrel jumped from the oak tree and scampered off in a swirl of dry leaves. The evening grew colder, but no one left. Benjamin spoke of things he'd never before given voice to. He told of the night Delia died and how he'd searched for hours before finding her and Isaac lying alongside the road.

"They was lying in the rain for hours 'fore I found 'em," he said. He lowered his head into his hands and sobbed. It was a cry that could barely be heard, but Martha Pillard heard it.

It was eight-thirty when Martha first discovered Sissy missing.

"Darlene," she said, "have you seen Sissy?"

Busy making a list of lawyers she'd be contacting, Darlene answered, "No, Mama, I ain't seen the damn cat, and I got other things to be thinking about."

"There's no need to get snippy," Martha answered.

Going from room to room, she bent down to check beneath the furniture and in closets. Once she'd looked in every imaginable place downstairs, she climbed the steps and started searching the bedrooms. She lifted the bed skirts and looked in every cubby, but Sissy was nowhere to be found.

"Darlene," she hollered down. "Did one of the twins let Sissy out?"

"Nobody let Sissy out. Check under the bed."

With a worried look stretched across her face, Martha hobbled down the stairs calling Sissy's name. She looked in the kitchen and under the sofa, then turned back to Darlene. "You sure the kids didn't let her out?"

Paying no attention to the concern in Martha's voice, Darlene said, "Mama, I'm trying to get some work done here. The kids don't give a damn about that cat. If she got out, she got out on her own." She angrily scratched a line through the name she'd just written and started over again.

Martha opened the front door just far enough to stick her head out and called for the cat, but there was nothing. It wasn't like Sissy to disappear that way. She was declawed, a house cat. She didn't belong outside. Martha turned back, shrugged on a black wool sweater, and stepped onto the porch. Leaning heavily on her cane, she maneuvered her way down the three steps and began poking at the bushes.

Once when she heard the rustle of dry leaves she stopped to check, but there was nothing.

"Maybe a chipmunk," she reasoned and began working her way around to the side yard. It was darker there, more difficult to get a firm footing. Martha, who was edgy to begin with, moved slowly and quietly. From time to time she whispered the cat's name, but when there was no response she moved on.

Certain it had been one of the twins who'd let Sissy out, Martha grumbled that Darlene should have been the one to go in search of the cat. She knew it was an unrealistic expectation. Darlene would have given a single call, then come back and said Sissy was gone.

Martha seldom left the house at night. Her bones ached in the damp chill, and darkness was her enemy. With just one good eye, she couldn't see well and had to poke at the ground to feel where she was stepping. Last year when Louise Green went out to drop a bag of trash in the garbage can, she'd stepped in a gopher hole and spent three months hobbling around with a cast on her leg. Martha thought of that when she moved into the backyard.

Edging her way toward the far end where the tool shed stood, she heard voices. They were low and barely distinguishable. She stopped and listened. The first voice was unfamiliar; a man telling of a rainstorm and a woman hit by a car. At first Martha could catch just a few words here and there, but the sorrow of his voice drew her in. She inched her way closer to the tall hedge that separated one yard from another.

"It's because of Isaac," the voice said. "How can a boy grow up happy when he knows his mama's killer's walking around free?"

Free? Martha thought. *At least Tommy's killer went to jail.* She continued to listen, inching closer and closer until she was standing in the thicket of the hedge.

The next speaker was Paul; Martha recognized his voice right away. It was strong and sharp, still carrying that twang of West Virginia.

"All this hatred," he said. "It's so wrong. How can it be fair that some men are born black and some white?"

Sidney spoke, and his was a voice almost as familiar as Martha's own. "It's not just black and white," he said. "Look what happened to Ezra."

Someone mumbled an answer Martha couldn't hear, so she pushed back the branch blocking her way and edged further into the brush.

"Folks start to fear somebody or something, then it grows into hate. I know it's hard to believe now, but Carmella was that way with Paul." Sidney gave a weary sigh and continued. "She's one of the kindest women on earth, but when she thought Paul was responsible for the shooting she hated him with a vengeance. She did everything possible to see he was punished and never once stopped to consider whether or not it was fair."

"Hard to believe that of Miz Carmella," the stranger said.

Martha stood there listening until a squirrel leapt from an overhanging branch and landed on her shoulder. She let out a piercing shriek and fell forward into the thicket of the hedge.

All three men jumped up and came to investigate. Martha's cane lay under her chest, and she couldn't get to it.

"Martha?" Sid said, then bent to see if she was okay. "Are you hurt?"

"I'm okay," she mumbled. "Just can't get up."

With Paul on one side and Sidney on the other, they lifted her from the brush and set her back on her feet. Benjamin picked up the cane and handed it to her.

"What were you doing in there?" Sid asked.

"Sissy got out. I've been trying to find her."

"She an orange-y looking cat?" Benjamin asked.

Martha nodded.

"I seen her going up the tree." He pointed to the oak in the Klaussners' backyard.

Benjamin and Paul started toward the tree and, hanging onto Sid's arm, Martha hobbled along behind.

Sure enough, the cat was up there, two limbs down from the top.

"Sissy baby, come to Mama," Martha called, but the cat didn't budge. She repeated it several times, promising treats, holding up her arms and wiggling her fingers. The cat huddled close to the tree trunk and mewed.

"She's scared to jump," Benjamin said. "I can fetch her if you want."

"Oh, yes, please," Martha pleaded.

There were few things in life Martha valued as much as she did Sissy. In the long and lonely evenings, the cat came and sat next to her on the sofa. Stroking her fur and listening to her low purr as it rumbled through the small body reminded Martha she was still alive. In time she had begun conversing with the cat in much the same way she'd spoken to Big Tom.

"Let's watch the Ed Sullivan Show tonight," she'd say as if she were talking with her dead husband. The truth was Martha found Sissy a lot more loyal than Darlene and definitely easier to like.

Benjamin was used to climbing trees; he'd trimmed half the oaks in Bakerstown. He was up and down in almost no time, and when he handed Martha the cat she looked up into his face and smiled.

"Thank you," she said, and a touch of sincerity floated up through the words.

Afterward, Sid helped Martha back to her front door. Halfway through the door, she stopped and turned back. For a moment it seemed as though she was about to say something, but the moment passed and she stepped inside with nothing more than a good night nod.

Darlene was still sitting at the desk. Hearing Martha's footsteps, she turned and triumphantly leaned back in the chair.

"Well, Mama," she said, "it's done! I got six lawyers willing to work for us. We're gonna get that nigger out—"

"Shut up, Darlene," Martha snapped.

"Mama! I thought you'd be happy—"

"I'd be a whole lot happier if you'd go home where you belong." She set Sissy down on the floor and turned toward the staircase.

"Well! Of all the ungrateful—"

Martha glanced back over her shoulder. "Go home. I've had enough of you for one night." She continued up the stairs, and the cat padded along. As Darlene stormed out, Martha heard the front door slam like a hurricane had blown through.

A Sleepless Night

F ew people on Bloom Street slept that night. Most went to bed at their usual time, then tossed and turned with worrisome thoughts churning through their minds. Archie Dodd slept soundly, knowing he'd been a true friend and done the right thing. Henry Jacobs suffered a severe case of angina and didn't once close his eyes. He blamed it on Mildred's potato leek soup and swore he'd never again touch the stuff.

"We've had that same soup every Wednesday for the past twenty years," Mildred reasoned. "It never bothered you before."

Ignoring the thought Henry climbed out of bed, went downstairs, and fixed himself a Bromo-Seltzer. When it seemed the acid indigestion had eased up a bit he returned to bed but still could not sleep. At first he fumed, remembering how Sidney had singled him out in front of everyone. It was like a big fat finger pointing to him as the culprit. He wasn't the one who started this. He'd simply gone along with what the others wanted. Why should the burden of guilt be dropped on his shoulders?

When Henry began to run low on things to be angry about, he started remembering the pain in Sidney's eyes. By dawn he'd come to the conclusion that it would have been better if he'd not signed Darlene's petition. The girl had always been a troublemaker, and he was a jerk for letting himself get suckered in.

Bob Paley didn't fare much better. After the confrontation at the Klaussner house, he came home and plopped down in the chair in front of the television. He sat there for nearly an hour before he snapped the television on, and then it was only because Barbara demanded to see the news.

At five-thirty the next morning she came downstairs and found Bob still sitting in that same chair, his eyes wide open and a test pattern buzzing across the television screen. She took one sniff and caught the stink of vomit on him.

"Haven't you gone to bed?" she asked, but when she spotted the half-empty bottle of Irish whiskey sitting on the side table it was answer enough.

Adding a thoroughly disgusted tone to her words, Barbara said he'd better get his ass out of the chair and start getting ready for work.

"Maybe I would be getting ready for work," he said, "if you hadn't stuck your nose in other people's business."

"What's that supposed to mean?" she said indignantly.

Bob, mad at himself and mad at Barbara for convincing him to sign the petition, said, "You know exactly what I mean. You cost me a good friend 'cause of some colored guy I've never even seen!" He looked up with the meanest imaginable look tugging at his face. "I got a feeling you ain't never seen him either, have you?"

"Well, I haven't actually," Barbara stammered. "But Prudence did."

"Prudence Wentworth!" Bob screamed. "You had me go up against a friend 'cause of what some girl who don't even live here and *Prudence Wentworth* said?"

"It's not just what they said—" Barbara began to argue, but by then their words had grown so loud they could be heard two streets over.

Maybe it was because in the morning the people on Bloom Street rose and had to face themselves in the mirror, or maybe it was simply the lack of sleep, but the same argument was repeated in six different homes that morning.

Martha Pillard was the lone exception. Now that she'd sent Darlene and the twins home, she had no one to argue with. She had only herself and the memory of the voices she'd listened to last night. Before she'd come face to face with Benjamin, based on the sound of his voice she'd pictured him as a man with pale skin and light hair, perhaps graying at the temples. She'd also felt the brokenness of his soul when he spoke of his dead wife, and she knew he was someone who suffered a loss as great as hers.

She could still see Benjamin lifting the cane from the ground and passing it to her. His skin was dark as the night, but the expression on his face had been one of concern and reverence, not anger. Turning to the cat, she said, "Sissy baby, you could have been stuck in that tree for God knows how long if it wasn't for that Negro man."

The cat gave a long luxurious stretch then snuggled its head into the curve of her neck.

"You know, Sissy," Martha said, "I think we might have misjudged that colored fella."

The cat purred, which for Martha was proof enough.

Sidney rose early that morning. He'd planned to wait another week or two before calling Marty again, but he had to do something now or Benjamin was going to leave. He hadn't said so, but Sidney saw it in his eyes.

Last night after going to bed he'd lain awake for endless hours, his thoughts jumping back and forth from Ezra to Benjamin. When the first rays of daylight broke through, Sidney went to the window and checked. The blue truck was still parked in the driveway. Benjamin was still there, but Sidney knew the truck would be gone tomorrow. He woke Carmella, explained what he was going to do, then said, "Go downstairs and make sure Benjamin doesn't leave before I get there."

Carmella always dressed before she came down to start breakfast, but on this particular morning she stood at the stove wearing a faded blue chenille bathrobe. When Benjamin walked into the kitchen, she was layering strips of bacon across the griddle.

"Miz Carmella," he said, "I got something to—"

"Can it wait until after breakfast?" she asked. "I'm a bit busy right now."

"Well, I reckon."

"Good." She answered in an easy way, one that gave no indication something else was in the wind. Without turning away from the stove she said if Benjamin was looking for something to do in the meantime, he could carry the dishes and silverware to the table.

"Yes, ma'am," he said. As he lifted the stack of dishes from the side counter Benjamin sniffed the bacon. He suspected the Klaussners already knew what he was going to say and this was their way of doing a special goodbye. Bacon didn't happen on a Thursday for no reason; Thursday was an oatmeal day.

Like many of the residents of Bloom Street, Benjamin had spent a sleepless night. Not because of the decision he'd had to make; that was inevitable and he'd known it from the start. It was the sadness in his heart that held sleep at bay, the sadness of leaving people who felt like family.

It was an odd sort of family—Sidney, Jewish; Carmella, Catholic; Paul and Jubilee, orphaned children of a West Virginia coal miner; Benjamin with skin dark as night and Isaac a light coffee color that was somewhere between him and Delia. No two of them the same, yet they fit together like different pieces of fabric in a quilt. A quilt that, despite the mix of colors, felt cozy and warm.

When the pink of morning began to show along the edge of the horizon, Benjamin was still awake. Alabama, even with all its anger and prejudices, had been home and it had not been easy leaving. Now, less than a month later, he was leaving another place that in a strange way felt like home.

You and Isaac have a place here for as long as you want to stay, Sidney had said. And he'd meant it; but Benjamin couldn't forget the angry words that came from outside. Bakerstown was more than a thousand miles away and yet here it was, pushing its way onto the Klaussners' doorstep. How far north, Benjamin wondered, did a man have to travel to reach a place where people were colorblind?

Breakfast was nearly a half-hour later than usual, and when Sidney took his place at the head of the table he was smiling. Before Benjamin had a chance to speak his mind, Sidney said he'd just finished talking with his old friend, Marty Hinckley. He glanced at Carmella and smiled. "You remember Marty, don't you?"

Carmella nodded and returned the smile.

"Marty and I go way back," Sid said nostalgically. "We went to school together in New York."

"You lived in New York?" The surprise in Benjamin's voice was obvious. He'd never pictured Sidney anywhere but right here in this house.

"I sure did," Sid answered, "Brooklyn. Marty and I started riding the subway when we were just teenagers." In words that were warmed by memories, he told stories of the fun they'd had going to shows in Manhattan and visiting the concession stands at Coney Island. He gave a raucous laugh. "You wouldn't believe the bathing suits ladies wore back then."

Although to others at the table it may have appeared Benjamin was hanging on every word, he was actually thinking through an idea that had come to mind. Would it be too much, he wondered, to ask for one last favor? With Marty being a Northerner, maybe he'd be willing to suggest a place where they could settle, a place where he could find work.

As Benjamin considered the best way of phrasing such a request, Sidney gave a nostalgic sigh and said, "Then I moved down here to Virginia, and Marty moved to Pittsburgh."

Benjamin felt a whoosh of disappointment slide across his heart.

Sidney noticed.

"Marty loves it in Pittsburgh," he added. "He's got a real nice business and was doing great until he had that heart attack last month." Despite the way Sidney allowed the words to sound a bit remorseful, a strange sad-but-happy look remained on his face.

Carmella wore that same crooked smile when she said, "Come on, Sidney, get to the point."

Sidney nodded then looked at Benjamin. "I'm going to ask a favor," he said. "You don't owe me and you can say no if you want to, but I owe Marty so I've got to ask."

Benjamin set the strip of bacon back on his plate and leaned in.

Unfolding the story word by word, Sidney explained how Marty owned a small airport on the edge of Pittsburgh and needed a man with a good understanding of motors and engines.

"I'm not gonna lie," he said. "It can be long days, but the job comes with a piece of farmland and a nice little house right there next to the airport."

"You figure he'd be willing to hire a colored man?" Benjamin asked.

Sidney stretched his arm across the table and placed his hand on top of Benjamin's. "When I told him how you'd fixed that old refrigerator, he said you were exactly what he was hoping for."

Benjamin gave a grin that stretched the full way across his face. "That sounds real good, Mister Sidney. Real good."

MARTHA

I went over and told Carmella how sorry I was for causing her all that trouble. I half expected her to toss me out on my ear, but she didn't. Instead she put her arms around me and gave me a hug that was a lot sweeter than I deserved. Her doing that made me feel more ashamed than I already was.

When I got back home I started thinking about all this mad I've been carrying around inside of me. No mama deserves to see her boy die, 'specially not in such an ugly way. When it happened to my Tommy, it was a whole lot easier to blame colored folks than believe my boy could have been up to no good himself.

I ain't making excuses for myself; I'm just saying how it was.

After listening to how that poor Benjamin lost his wife, I can tell he's hurting bad as me. Maybe worse. At least I got justice for what was done to Tommy; he didn't even get that. In my mind that's a bitter pill to swallow.

Seeing things in the light of day, I guess I'd be okay with him staying. Of course it's too late for that now.

I tore up Darlene's petition. Ripped it into tiny little pieces that couldn't ever be pasted back together. That's what it deserves, but it ain't much in the way of making amends. The only other thing I can do now is hope that poor man finds a good life for him and his boy. That ain't much either, but it's all I got to give.

THE GOODBYE

G iven the excitement that followed such an announcement, that morning's breakfast lasted until almost ten-thirty. Sidney continued telling stories of Marty, and Benjamin asked question after question. Even after the last piece of bacon disappeared from the table, they continued to sit and sip coffee. Three times Carmella refilled the cups, and after all the biscuits were gone she brought out a basket of fresh-baked corn muffins.

"I was kind of rushed," she admitted sheepishly, "so these are from a mix."

Sidney told all he could think of to tell about Marty Hinckley, his wife, Elsie, and the small airport. When nothing else came to mind, he tugged Benjamin into the den and placed a call to Pittsburgh.

"I thought you fellows might like to talk to one another," he said and handed the receiver to Benjamin.

Martin Hinckley's voice was husky and jovial. When he gave out a roll of laughter, Benjamin knew it was something that came from deep down inside.

"I'm mighty glad to have this job," Benjamin said.

Echoing Benjamin's words, Marty replied, "Well, I'm mighty glad to have you." From another person it might have had the sound of mockery, but Marty's way of saying it made the words feel as comforting as a thick warm stew.

Klaussner's Grocery Store never opened that day. It was after eleven when Paul and Sidney went down and taped a note to the front door. *Klaussner's closed for the day,* it read. *Sorry for any inconvenience this may cause.*

They spent close to two hours in the store, but neither of them swept the floor or wiped the counters. Instead they pulled cans and boxes from the shelves and stacked them one on top of the other.

"Should I include syrup and pancake mix?" Paul asked.

Sid nodded. "Don't forget a dozen cans of green beans, some Spam, and a box of Velveeta."

By the time two o'clock rolled around the trunk of Sid's car was filled with enough food to last a month, maybe more. Tucked in among the foodstuffs were several candy bars, a box of cleanser, and three bars of soap.

Jubilee, who'd cried at the thought of Isaac leaving, was allowed to skip school that day. She went with them when Carmella took Benjamin and Isaac to the Saint Vincent DePaul thrift shop.

"Pittsburgh gets cold," Carmella said, and she'd insisted on seeing they had the proper type of clothing.

Margaret Thumper ran the shop and was a close friend of Carmella. She was happy to help. Once she heard what they were looking for, she disappeared into the back room and returned with armful after armful of jackets, coats, and sweaters. Although sorting through all those clothes took nearly three hours, Isaac came away with eight wool sweaters, three pairs of corduroy pants, two pairs of jeans, an assortment of shirts, boots, mittens, and a parka that was toasty enough to bake muffins.

Benjamin settled for a single sweater, a heavy jacket, and three long-sleeve shirts. Although he now had more than one hundred dollars, he knew the money would be needed for traveling and getting settled. When it came time to pay he pulled the bills from his pocket and asked how much.

Margaret Thumper laughed. "Nothing," she said. "This is an exchange shop. People bring in the things they don't need, and others come and take what they do need."

Looking a bit bewildered, Benjamin asked, "For free?"

"Unh-huh." Margaret nodded.

Carmella gave a sly wink and smiled.

The remainder of the afternoon was spent loading Benjamin's truck. Although he'd arrived with a toolbox, a rocking chair, and few boxes of next to nothing, the flatbed of the truck was now packed tight with food, clothes, boxes of cookware, dishes, and towels, all things Carmella claimed she no longer needed. Once everything was in place, they anchored a heavy black tarpaulin to cover it all.

It was close to four o'clock when Benjamin and Isaac said goodbye to the Klaussners, and every eye was a bit tearful.

"Drive carefully," Sid advised. "It's about four hundred and fifty miles, and Marty isn't expecting you until late Friday or sometime Saturday, so you've got plenty of time for stops."

Carmella hugged Benjamin to her chest and pressed a twenty-dollar bill into the palm of his hand. "It's too cold for that boy to be camping outside, so promise me you'll stay the night in a proper motel."

Benjamin didn't see the need for such a thing, but he nonetheless promised. There was no way he could not promise a woman like Carmella. He and Isaac climbed into the truck, and as he pulled away from the curb he turned back for one last look.

Sidney, Carmella, Paul, and Jubilee stood on the edge of the front porch, their arms raised in one final goodbye, tears glistening in their eyes, and a look of sadness tugging at their faces. It was a picture that would stay with Benjamin for the rest of his life. When Isaac became a grown man and grandchildren nested on Benjamin's knee, he would still be telling the story of their stay at the Klaussners'.

That afternoon Henry Jacobs stopped by the store. He'd left work mid-afternoon claiming a headache, which wasn't far from the truth. It would be easier, he figured, to casually wander in on the pretext of needing cigarettes or a packet of Bromo-Seltzer than to go, hat in hand, knocking on Sidney Klaussner's door. He was knee-deep in shame over the way he'd been fool enough to go along with the petition, but coming out with a full-fledged apology pinched like tight underwear. Doing it this way he could start up a conversation, ignoring the events of last night, then work his way around to saying he'd changed his mind about the petition and was withdrawing his name.

When he saw the sign taped to the door of the store, he began to worry.

First he rattled the door, but there was no answer and the inside of the store remained dark, so he walked down the street and telephoned the Klaussners' house.

With everyone outside packing things into Benjamin's truck, the telephone rang and rang with no answer. For an hour-and-a-half Henry drove around wondering what to do, and when he could come up with no solution he decided to return home. Passing the Klaussner house he slowed to little more than a crawl, thinking he might catch Sid in the front yard. There was no one outside, and the blue truck was gone.

After another sleepless night, Henry knocked on the Klaussners' front door at seven o'clock the next morning. He was alone.

Sid opened the door, expecting more of what happened two days ago.

Without looking directly into his friend's face, Henry said, "I'm truly ashamed for taking part in that ugliness."

Sid pulled the door back and asked him in.

During the last forty-eight hours Henry had done a fair bit of soul-searching, and he'd come to the conclusion that a full-fledged apology was warranted.

"If you was to toss me out, I'd understand," he said. "I ain't expecting forgiveness. But I wanted you to know I'm ashamed of what I did."

He blamed it on his own stupidity and Mildred's advice. After he'd stumbled through several minutes of up and down apologies, he said if the Klaussners wanted the colored man living in their house he was gonna stand with them.

"For all the bullshit that's gone on," he said, "the bottom line is it's your house and you can do what you will with it."

Sidney waited as Henry sputtered and stammered through a litany of excuses, then he said, "Benjamin's already gone."

"Gone?"

Sid nodded. "He left yesterday afternoon."

"Because of what happened?"

"No. That was his plan all along. He only stayed to help us in the store."

"Then why didn't you say something?" Henry asked. "Why didn't you tell those crazies—"

"I didn't think I had to," Sid replied. "Those people were our friends. I thought they'd understand and accept my belief in a man as truth."

They stood and talked for a long while. It wasn't a warmhearted conversation; it was simply the groundwork that would eventually lead back to friendship. When there was nothing more to say, they shook hands and turned back to the door. Sid opened the door, and as Henry passed by Sid reached out and clapped a hand on his shoulder.

"Don't worry," he said, "we'll get through this in time."

SIDNEY

*S*tanding on the porch and watching Benjamin drive away left an empty feeling inside of me. It wasn't just me; I could see it on Carmella and Paul's faces also. Little Jubilee was flat out crying. That's the good thing about being a kid; you're not ashamed to let your emotions stick out in the open.

I know leaving is what was best for them, and I think Benjamin's going to be thrilled when he finds out what Marty has in store for him. Sometimes what we want and what's best for somebody we care about just isn't the same thing. It's that age-old saying about if you love something you've got to set it free.

But I can tell you this. If Benjamin had decided to stay, I would have fought tooth and nail to keep him and Isaac safe. I'm not a man given to flowery words and statements, but so help me God, I will never forget what he did for our Paul. Neither will Carmella.

ROAD TRIP

When they left Wyattsville, Benjamin and Isaac rode in silence for a long while. Isaac still wore the catcher's mitt Paul gave him on his left hand. He kept tossing the baseball from one hand to the other, back and forth, back and forth.

"You think they got a baseball team in Pittsburgh?" he asked.

Benjamin nodded. "Pittsburgh Pirates. They're pretty good, according to Marty."

"You figure we can go see a game?"

"In the spring, maybe. They don't play in the wintertime."

"What's kids in Pittsburgh do in the winter?"

Benjamin shrugged. "Build snowmen maybe."

On that first day they traveled almost two hundred miles. They went north through Virginia then crossed over the eastern edge of West Virginia and stopped before they got to Morgantown. Benjamin had anticipated he'd be further down the road, but with no sleep the night before and a day crammed full of shopping, doing, and packing, his eyelids were too heavy to continue.

Thinking back on his promise to Carmella, he pulled off the road and into the parking lot of the Mountain Way Motel. The sign blinked "Vacancy", but there was no other sign indicating whether colored people were welcome.

"Wait here," Benjamin told Isaac as he climbed out of the truck. He walked around the building looking for a back door or a sign; there was nothing. He returned to the front of the building, pushed open the door, and peeked in. Behind the desk was an elderly woman with a topknot of cotton white hair. Her skin was the pale color of Delia's.

"You looking for a room?" she asked.

"Yes, ma'am," Benjamin answered.

"Eight dollars 'n you get free breakfast."

Benjamin smiled. "I got my boy with me, that okay?"

"The room just got one bed," she answered. "But it's a big one."

Perhaps it was force of habit. Perhaps the cautionary fear of overstepping the boundaries he'd known all the years of his life. It's impossible to say what prompted him to do it, but Benjamin suddenly blurted out, "I'm colored."

The desk clerk chuckled. "I'm old, but I ain't blind. Now if you want that room, get over here and sign the register."

Benjamin moved to the desk and signed his name. The old woman fished a key from the cubby behind her and handed it to him. "Cabin six."

As he walked out the front door, he felt a strange new sense of pride. It was a first in this new life.

That night Benjamin slept soundly. There were no more decisions to be made. He had a job and a home for Isaac. As long as he had Isaac, he'd have a piece of Delia.

When sleep descended on him Delia was there. She was no longer the broken woman he lifted from the muddy roadside and carried into the hospital. She was young again, as she'd been in the early years of their marriage. She laughed that same lighthearted laugh he remembered from the day of the barbeque. In the sweetest moment of the dream she leaned close and pressed her cheek to his. *This is good,* she whispered, but when he turned to answer she was gone and he felt himself coming awake. For several minutes he remained there in the bed, trying to sleep, trying to reach back and catch Delia one more time, but it was no longer possible.

During the night the temperature plummeted to a chilly forty-two degrees, so Isaac pulled on one of his wool sweaters from the Saint

Vincent DePaul shop. It was bright red with a sprinkling of snowflakes decorating the front.

"Ain't it a bit early for that?" Benjamin asked.

Isaac stepped back from looking at himself in the mirror and shook his head. "I's getting in the mood for snowman building."

Benjamin laughed. "Snowman building, huh? Well, first we'd better go get that free breakfast."

Breakfast was served in a small room next to where Benjamin had signed the register. Bunched fairly close together were eight small tables, and at the far end he saw a kitchen counter. The woman he'd spoken with last night stood behind the counter.

"Whatcha in the mood for?" she asked.

When Benjamin hesitated she added, "We got eggs, bacon, sausage, grits 'n pancakes."

Isaac gave a grin and said he'd have pancakes, bacon, and sausage. Benjamin ordered eggs. Eggs were something he had a fondness for. On the farm they'd always had eggs, even when there was little else. Still clinging to the memory of his dream, he wanted to once again breathe in the sweetness of eggs sizzling in a pan.

When the woman handed the two platters across the counter Benjamin eyed the room searching for a table set apart from the others, a colored section perhaps. When he saw none, he learned over the counter and asked, "Are we supposed to sit in here?"

"Ain't no place else to go," the woman answered.

He took the plates and carried them to a table near the back of the room. At the next table a bearded white man flipped through the pages of a newspaper. Seemingly unaware of anyone else, the man sipped his coffee and read. After several minutes he folded the paper and set it aside.

"Where you headed?" he asked.

It was something Benjamin hadn't expected, and it took a moment before he answered, "Pittsburgh."

The man looked at Isaac. "Looks like you're ready for some snow," he laughed. He drained the last of his coffee and stood to leave. "Have a good trip," he said then started out.

Benjamin hesitated a second and called after him, "You too."

On the second day they had a little more than a hundred miles to travel. It would be a short day. They'd arrive well before dinnertime, and Benjamin would have time to unload the truck and get settled in. Monday he would start work.

A million thoughts rolled through Benjamin's head. He tried to picture the house, Marty's face, the kind of work he'd be doing, but right now everything was a foggy shade of gray, too far ahead to see clearly and without a past to look back on.

He eased back on the gas pedal and slowed the truck. There was no need to rush. For too many years he'd rushed from one job to the next, never taking time to enjoy the moment. Never taking enough time to enjoy Delia and Isaac. This time it would be different. This time he would be both daddy and mama to Isaac. He'd make time to listen when the boy had a story to tell. He'd get to know Isaac as Delia had known him.

Now crawling along at thirty miles an hour, he turned to Isaac and asked, "How you feel about moving to Pittsburgh?"

Isaac smacked the baseball from his right hand into the catcher's mitt and back again.

"I guess it's okay," he said. "I like having new clothes 'n stuff, but I miss playing with Jubilee 'n having Miz Carmella teach me lessons."

"I miss them too," Benjamin replied sadly. "They surely are good people."

"I miss that nice playroom what had toys 'n games," Isaac added. "When Miz Carmella finished lessons, she give me cookies."

"Now I got a good-paying job, maybe we can see to some after-school cookies."

Isaac looked across and rolled his eyes, "They ain't gonna be good as Miz Carmella's."

Benjamin laughed. "Probably not."

Isaac said nothing more; he just sat and stared out the window. They passed by a few billboards saying it was only fifty and then forty miles to Pittsburgh; the images were of brick buildings and steam belching steel mills. Isaac looked at them with childlike disappointment. After a long while he asked, "You think there's kids what's gonna play with me in Pittsburgh?"

"Pittsburgh's a city, just like Bakerstown was a city," Benjamin replied. "We ain't gonna live in Pittsburgh. We're gonna live a ways out in the country, where there's plenty a' things for a boy to do." He gave Isaac a grin and added, "It's a place where you can see real airplanes coming and going."

Isaac turned with an expression that seemed to question whether such a thing could be true. "Even if I sees airplanes, it ain't gonna be good as playing with Jubilee and living in that nice playroom."

He gave a low mournful sigh, one that made him sound decades older than his years. "I wish we could a' stayed there," he said. "That place was perfect."

Benjamin was relieved that neither Isaac nor Jubilee had heard the ruckus on Wednesday evening. When Paul started up the stairs, he'd turned up the volume on the television and both kids sat there mesmerized by *Wagon Train*.

Stretching his arm across the seat, Benjamin pulled Isaac a bit closer. "Perfect ain't a place," he said. "It's a time when everything's good and we're happy. Folks don't live in perfect, they just get to pass through every so often."

"You ever passed through perfect 'fore, Daddy?"

Benjamin nodded. "I sure have," he said and began telling of the night he first met Delia.

"Your mama was the prettiest lady I'd ever laid eyes on..."

As Time Passed

Back on Bloom Street it took many months for the wounds to heal. During the next few weeks several of the neighbors stopped by to apologize. Barbara Paley brought Carmella a potted plant. Prudence trotted over with two dozen homemade chocolate chip cookies.

"Being a widow makes me overly frightened of strangers," she said.

It wasn't much of an apology, but Carmella could see little value in carrying a grudge so she brewed a pot of tea and invited Prudence to sit.

Not all of those involved came to apologize. Some neighbors held on to the belief that they'd been right. They scurried in and out of their houses without ever glancing to the right or left.

But in time such anger wearies a person. It weighs on them like a heavy coat, worn threadbare and without warmth. After a while the wearing of it becomes a burden, so it gets pushed to the back of the closet and forgotten. That's pretty much what happened with the last few holdouts on Bloom Street.

When winter turned to spring, crocuses broke through the earth and people started once again setting out pots of daffodils and spring lilies. By then the memories of that night had faded to nothingness. Although no one spoke of it and few cared to remember, the truth was that the residents of Bloom Street were never quite the same.

In the wake of such bitterness a new understanding was born. A greater tolerance, you might say. On Saturday afternoons when Sid returned from the store, he'd often find his lawn mowed. When Paul returned to college, Bab Paley's son volunteered to work in the grocery store after school. And that first Christmas a basket chock full of homemade cookies, cakes, and candies was left on the Klaussners' front porch. No name; just a card saying, "Merry Christmas from your friends."

In early January, Sid Klaussner received a letter postmarked Pittsburgh, Pennsylvania.

Dear Mister Sidney,

I hope you, Miss Carmella, Paul, and Jubilee is all doing well. We surely did enjoy that box of Christmas presents you sent. Isaac said he ain't never tasted a cookie good as the ones Miss Carmella makes. He loves his new school and has made lots of friends but still misses Jubilee and talks about her often.

Settling in has been real easy. Mister Marty had a house ready and waiting for us. It's not big as yours, but it's got plumbing and electricity inside. We been here less than two months, but already it feels like home.

I'm real happy working for Mister Marty. He lets me manage the place by myself. Once or twice a week he stops by to check on things but don't stay long. His missus makes sure of that. She says he's still recuperating, but he says he ain't never felt so good.

The real exciting news is that soon as the snow melts, Mister Marty is gonna start teaching me to fly. He figures six months maybe, then I can get a license and do the crop dusting.

Life's funny, ain't it? I joined the army air force thinking I'd learn to fly and never got to so much as sit in the pilot's seat. Now here I am. Pittsburgh's a long way from Grinder's Corner and it's a whole different world, that's for sure.

The letter continued for three pages. Benjamin talked of the town, of how they'd had Christmas dinner at the Hinckleys', and how Marty had given Isaac a train set he'd had as a boy.

As Sidney sat there and read, he could feel the joy in every word.

That evening when they sat down to dinner, he read the letter aloud for the family. Despite the fact that Carmella had made a double chocolate fudge cake for dessert, there was no clattering of forks. Everyone sat still and listened.

When Sidney finished reading, he looked up and his eyes glistened with a few teardrops not yet spilled.

"Sidney Klaussner," Carmella said, "are you crying?"

"No, I am not," he replied gruffly. "I'm just glad things worked out for Benjamin. He's a good man."

"He sure is," Paul added.

"Can Isaac and his daddy come visit us?" Jubilee asked.

Carmella smiled. "I doubt they want to come back to Wyattsville," she said sadly.

"Maybe not," Sidney replied. "But I think a visit to see my old pal Marty is long overdue…and who knows, we might even pay a call on Benjamin and Isaac."

The future is always an unknown, but this much I can tell you: Sidney and Benjamin remained friends for the rest of their lives. Isaac went off to college just as Delia had wanted, but he became neither a doctor nor pastor. He studied engineering, and when he returned to Pittsburgh he became the manager and co-owner of the airport Benjamin eventually inherited from Marty.

Benjamin never again married, but in the years to come he dated a number of charming ladies. Although they enjoyed many wonderful evenings together, his heart forever remained with Delia.

ALSO BY BETTE LEE CROSBY

The Wyattsville Series:

Spare Change, Book One

Jubilee's Journey, Book Two

Passing Through Perfect, Book Three

The Serendipity Series:

The Twelfth Child, Book One

Previously Loved Treasures, Book Two

Wishing for Wonderful, Book Three

Cracks in the Sidewalk

What Matters Most

Blueberry Hill, A Sister's Story

Life in the Land of Is, *the amazing story of*
Lani Deauville, the woman hailed as the World's
Longest Living Quadriplegic

A NOTE FROM THE AUTHOR

Then will the eyes of the blind be opened
and the ears of the deaf unstopped
NIV Isaiah 35:5

Writing a novel is never easy; writing a novel that explores the good and bad in people offers an even greater challenge and I could not have done it alone. Every day I thank Our Heavenly Father for blessing me with the ability to tell stories and giving me the courage to tell them as they should be told. Cruelty, profanity, and bigotry are an ugly but very real part of this world we live in. It is only by seeing this bitter side of truth that we can appreciate the goodness, generosity and love that surround us.

My inspiration for this story came from many sources, not the least of which was my Southern heritage. I have seen a South not unlike the one portrayed in this book. At the time black people were subjected to humiliating circumstances and held down under the weighty thumb of Southern traditionalists who did not consider their actions cruel. Separate but equal, they said. Yet the truth is that although it was separate, it was far from equal and to survive the black man had to live a life of acceptance.

Even poverty was not colorblind. In the first half of the twentieth century there were many areas of the South where poverty-stricken whites lived alongside blacks. There were no race riots, no boycotts, no huge outcry; there was only poverty. Although both families struggled to put food on the table and children all too often went to bed hungry, the white man held his head just a little bit higher because he was white.

They say that Divine Providence often steers our footsteps, and I believe this is true. As I was working on this novel, I came across President Jimmy Carter's memoir *An Hour Before Daylight,* and it provided a great source of inspiration. Reading this memoir reminded me of the tales my mother once told. Not tales of good or bad, simply tales of what was.

I hope you enjoy this story of a time gone by. Some will call it the "good old days," and others, like me, will disagree. I trust that as you read you will see beyond the evils men do and find the goodness of God's grace.

ABOUT THE AUTHOR

Award-winning novelist Bette Lee Crosby brings the wit and wisdom of her Southern Mama to works of fiction—the result is a delightful blend of humor, mystery and romance.

"Storytelling is in my blood," Crosby laughingly admits, "My mom was not a writer, but she was a captivating storyteller, so I find myself using bits and pieces of her voice in most everything I write."

Crosby's work was first recognized in 2006 when she received The National League of American Pen Women Award for a then unpublished manuscript. Since then, she has gone on to win numerous other awards, including The Reviewer's Choice Award, FPA President's Book Award Gold Medal and The Royal Palm Literary Award.

To learn more about Bette Lee Crosby, explore her other work, or read a sample from any of her books, visit her blog at:

http://betteleecrosby.com